DO NOT REMOVE
CARDS FROM POCKET

THE
SUN
MAIDEN

THE
SUN
MAIDEN

Erika Taylor

ATHENEUM • NEW YORK • 1991

MAXWELL MACMILLAN CANADA • TORONTO

MAXWELL MACMILLAN INTERNATIONAL
NEW YORK • OXFORD • SINGAPORE • SYDNEY

This is a work of fiction. Names, characters, places, and incidents either are the product of the author's imagination or are used fictitiously. Any resemblance to events or persons, living or dead, is entirely coincidental.

Copyright © 1991 by Erika Taylor

A portion of *The Sun Maiden* appeared in the *Santa Monica Review*.

Atheneum
Macmillan Publishing Company
866 Third Avenue, New York, NY 10022

Maxwell Macmillan Canada, Inc.
1200 Eglinton Avenue East, Suite 200
Don Mills, Ontario M3C 3N1

Macmillan Publishing Company is part of the Maxwell Communication Group of Companies.

Library of Congress Cataloging-in-Publication Data
Taylor, Erika.
    The sun maiden / Erika Taylor.
        p.   cm.
    ISBN 0-689-12130-X
    I. Title.
PS3570.A9254S86   1990
813'.54—dc20   90-25445   CIP

10   9   8   7   6   5   4   3   2   1

Printed in the United States of America

For SYBIL and SCOTT
. . . *'cause I know how much it pleases.*

And for JIM KRUSOE

I have been incredibly lucky to know really supportive, great people, all of whom I can't name because it would take up too much space. Here are some of them:

Love and gratitude to Patrick McCord for all the hours of line-by-line discussion that was immensely helpful and *right*. Big thanks also to: Ann Hood, Sheila La Farge, Nancy Krusoe, Jack Lechner, Sam Maser, Charles Zucker, Ellen Levine, Kathleen Alice Wilhoite, and Leland Zaitz, who has brought more joy to my life than I ever thought possible.

In addition the author wishes to thank her weekly writer's workshop for their kindness and criticism during time spent on this book.

Part One

JUNE

In the Restaurant

Chapter 1

I pulled much too quickly into the parking lot because I was going to be late again. Also my hat and bow weren't ironed. Again. Out of my car, running, I tried to see through the windows if they were busy yet. Couldn't tell. After getting inside I forced myself to slown down, and just move as calmly as possible toward the locker room like no big deal.

"It is now 5:20." Rafi's body blocked the door to get upstairs. "Please start taking this work more seriously, you have too much lateness. That's it. Do you see what's being said here?"

"Yes. I'm sorry."

"I'm sorry also, you are nice girl, J.O." He moved to one side letting me through. "Now go get changed."

The women's dressing room had a cement floor and rows and rows of lockers that gave the whole place a swimming-pool feeling. I spun my combination lock too nervously, so it took three tries before I could open the door and yank the white uniform off its hanger.

"Rafi wants you to take the counter tonight," Lily said coming into the room behind me. "Have fun, we're still short a busboy."

Lily was a big, black woman who'd been working here about fifteen years, and I could tell she didn't like me very much. Thought I wasn't trying. Lily treated me the way year-round people treat the summer people in some small resort town, distant and slightly condescending.

"Okay," I said, "I'll be ready in a minute." The counter meant all coffee and $3.99 dinner specials.

Lily crossed big-woman arms and leaned in the doorway. I

wished she'd leave. I was trying to get my hat to stay in place with only two bobby pins because the others were holding together my broken watch strap. I glanced over at Lily, the only two-hundred-pound person I'd ever seen who was really sexy—though not bikini sexy, this was something else. A ten-foot mahogany table polished gleaming so it caught the light just so, Lily was sexy like that. I'd heard she used to hang out with Little Richard in the sixties, "My Other Life," she called it smoking with Rafi after we closed. Rafi and Lily were friends; he always talked about how great she was. I didn't think she was so great.

"Give me your hat and bobby pins," she said, voice flat, face expressionless.

I thought about how nice it would be to just lie down on the cool floor and refuse to move. "Here."

"Only two?" Her hand was still extended, gravel calloused.

Wordlessly I took the other bobby pins from my watch strap and put the watch in my pocket.

"I don't know what your problem is, hon." She ran hot water in the sink and waved my wrinkled hat over the steam. "I really don't know."

In five seconds Lily had it neatly pinned to my hair, but when I thanked her there was no answer.

Running downstairs I thought of the only thing I really loved about The Sun Maiden—it wasn't fake. Los Angeles was filled with fake diners where people put slits in their uniforms and blasted fifties music, places where nobody said "hon" unless they were kidding. At The Sun Maiden everyone said "hon" even if they didn't like you.

"J.O., can you come here for a moment?" Rafi asked as soon as I was back on the floor. I walked over to where he stood, the manager's spot by the register.

Rafi was in his early thirties and balding. Strangely. At the very top of his forehead was one small tuft of black hair surrounded by baldness, which made me wonder why that last piece was still there and if it made him feel better or worse to have it. He spoke with a heavy accent, though his vocabulary was pretty good. Rafi loved learning new words and once in the middle of the dinner rush stopped me with a baked potato stuck on a fork. "What's this?" he had asked.

"A baked potato stuck on a fork?"

"It's impaled." He drew the word out long and smiled, saying it again. "Impaled."

Rafi's eyes were a dreamy blue. He didn't wear glasses but squinted and held things close to his face so often that once Lily told him to go see a doctor.

"I know." He had paused meaningfully. "I'm myopic."

Now, his eyes were closed, the bridge of his bony nose held between first finger and thumb. "J.O." He opened his eyes and leaned toward me. "This is good business."

I nodded.

"Look at Lily, why are you thinking the customers like her so much?"

I nodded again. It took a second before I realized he wanted an answer. I thought customers probably liked Lily because they knew she'd kill them otherwise, but I didn't say that. I said, "Lily's a great waitress."

"Bam." Rafi snapped his fingers and I nodded once more. "Lily works her section very brilliantly; she takes an order, Bam it's on the table. Turn over, Bam in and out. Whatever they want, they want the Moby Dick, done specially, you know, no tartar or something, Bam, she's there in and out."

Rafi had snapped his fingers every time he said "Bam," and I had nodded my head. I hoped no one was watching.

"All right, today the hat is looking improved, but you've got to get better with the other things. I know you can. It's not difficult really." He touched my shoulder. "Now go on."

Before walking away I glanced at Rafi's square jaw which I secretly liked, especially the part just under his ears where it came together at almost a right angle. Something about that was sort of tough and personal at the same time.

By seven o'clock a million food orders sat on the pickup counter. All mine. All getting cold. I had no idea where any of them belonged. "Order up, J.O., pick up," the cooks yelled ringing that obnoxious little bell. Milkshake was all over the front of my uniform, customers screaming, "Waitress, waitress," but I couldn't answer them. I felt disappeared, as if somewhere a giant needle had skipped on a giant record and I was stuck forever in the tiny place with the lost notes. There was a crunching underfoot. Oh, please no, I thought and fished around inside my empty pocket. Yes, it was my watch.

"J.O., do you want help?" Rafi loomed suddenly next to me; "Here, you need soda water," he pointed at the milkshake stain. "Never mind, later. I'll do fresh coffee and to-go orders. You serve food and get new customers, okay?" Quick fingers reached forward to straighten my collar.

"Okay," I said trying not to cry.

At about eight o'clock Smeg came in with a pink fur top hat, eye makeup, and a smallish lump coming out of his left shoulder. He had started hanging around The Sun Maiden about a week ago and for some reason thought we were friends, "Hi, J.O., I'm home." Smeg sat at the only empty stool, the wobbly one people avoided.

Customers ate and were gone. I finally got caught up and Rafi went back to stand near the cash register, his profile hard hooked and distant like the Indian on an Indian head nickel.

"Ready to order?" I asked Smeg, hoping he'd realize I didn't want a conversation.

While waiting he had peeled the labels off two ketchup bottles, surrounding himself with little pieces of ripped-up paper. Smeg seemed even thinner today. "One sec, did you talk to your boss?"

"About what?" I asked even though I knew. He wanted to work here.

"Come on, you promised you'd find out if The Sun Maiden was hiring, I really, really have to get a job."

"Oh yeah. I'm sorry, the manager said nothing was open." That was a lie. We needed a busboy but no way, not Smeg.

For a second his face got kind of wincey with disappointment, which made me feel bad till I reminded myself I was just barely holding my own job, and he would make things much worse.

"How's the meatloaf, J.O.?"

"Good."

"I'll have it then, rice, no vegetables, coffee to drink. 'It's a beggar's life' said the Queen of Spain."

"But don't tell that to a poor man," I answered him back almost against my will. Very obscure Steely Dan song, but a good one, and I was surprised Smeg had quoted it. Sometimes my roommate, Samantha, called me "The Period Piece," and I'd tell her it wasn't my fault most great music was over fifteen years old.

"Hey," he was staring at me enthusiastically, "we're on the same track, paths crossed at the third rail." Smeg's eyes, nose, and mouth were unusually big for his skinny head so that every expression looked exaggerated. Too much face.

As soon as I brought food, the lump on Smeg's shoulder began to move, and then a white rat crawled from the neck hole of his T-shirt. It had very pink eyes.

"Ummm. You can't bring animals in here."

Smeg paid no attention as the rat jogged down his arm and onto the counter.

"Listen," I glanced toward Rafi trying not to panic, "you've got to get rid of that, please, please, I'm already in trouble."

"Fear." He kissed the top of the rat's squirmy head and put it back inside his shirt. "Her name's Fear and she's perfectly nice unless you're a roach, Hee-Hee." The famous Smeg laugh high and fake. "Don't worry, I'll keep her very hidden if you give me some Sweet N Low."

I pulled two packets from my orange bow. All of us had to wear these ruffled bows pinned to our shoulders, and when tied right they held Sweet 'N Low in a pocket in the middle. My Sweet 'N Low was always falling out. Rafi had said he knew when I was working because there would be a trail of little pink squares all through the restaurant.

"Flavor," Smeg told me grinning huge as he poured Sweet N Low over his meatloaf. Unbelievable. His mouth was like an overpopulated jail barely able to contain grayish crooked teeth.

Rafi's unexpected hand on my shoulder made me twitch. I hadn't realized he was so close. "How's it going?"

"Fine."

"Good. J.O, tonight you do extra side work again since we

haven't hired a busboy yet; I'm sorry, mentally this is making me crazy."

I could feel Smeg start to listen, feel him get very still.

"We're missing a busboy?" I tried to sound surprised.

"Of course we're missing a busboy. We've been missing a busboy for a week," Rafi said looking at me incredulously. "Yesterday we talked specific about this, how can you not remember?"

"Well." My voice came out sounding nasal, a nervous thing which always made me feel about four years old. "I just got confused."

"I don't understand you sometimes, J.O., I really don't."

"Order up," the cook's little bell hit my spine like a poison dart. "J.O., it's getting cold."

Smeg threw a crumpled five on the counter and left wordlessly. He had taps on the bottom of his sneakers so I heard him all the way out the door.

The rest of the night was slow so Rafi, Lily, and I closed a little early. First Rafi put on an Edith Piaf tape, then Lily made fun of Edith's voice, and got ragged on for having no taste. I married the ketchups. Rafi asked Lily for a back rub, she said no, he begged, and it was always the same. The two of them.

As soon as she touched his shoulders, Rafi let out a moan, slumping fake comatose against the counter. "I love you, Lily," he said as his body relaxed, head rocking slightly on folded arms. "Forget Edith, you're my woman now."

I said, "What should I do to become a better waitress?" My own question caught me completely unawares like when you're talking and spit by accident, that startled half beat of silence.

They both stared. Lily's face had the flat endless look I'd seen in pictures of third world children. "Carry plates," she said and continued the back rub, her arm muscles bulging as she dug into his shoulders.

"It's more than that." Rafi leaned forward and squinted at me. "I've always felt a contention you could be a great waitress if you learned priorities." Absently pushing Lily's hands away he jumped off the counter stool. Getting into it. "There's let's say ten people, and four have food up, two want water, one wants to order, three want checks. What do you do?" While talking he counted each person on his fingers so they ended up extended with his palms facing me.

"I don't know," I said too tight, nasal.

"Well, it doesn't matter as long as you are making choices, J.O., I see you run, I see you sweat, but you choose nothing. Food, checks, new order, water." He pulled the fingers down one by one. "That's it."

"Rafi, I have a friend waiting at home, can you cash me out?" Lily got a roll of mint Life Savers from her pocket and popped one in her mouth.

"Ooohhhhh," he turned toward her. "Look who's scoring heavily this evening. Who is it? The musician? May I have Life Saver, please?"

She jerked away laughing at Rafi who tried to bite one out of the package.

As I watched them fool around I could picture Lily perfectly. She walks into her apartment lit TV blue, and says, "Hey there," to the man stretched out on the couch. Some kind of shiny instrument is propped across his legs, a sax. "Heeey," he answers, reaching for her sleepy and sweet, "You're home."

Before leaving Lily handed Rafi a Life Saver and told him to be good. I wished she'd offered me one.

Rafi looked out the window while I finished up, one hand restlessly stroking his own chin and the other at his side. He had delicate spider fingers that clashed with the rest of his body which was short and bunched. The kind of body meant for sports close to the ground. At that second the empty restaurant, Rafi, the window, all made me want things, badly, that I couldn't quite put together words for.

"Cash me out?" I was glad when he began sorting through my checks since that was the one place without mistakes. Numbers. All of them were columned straight and clean with tax multiplied in my head even the half percent. I *saw* numbers. Each one had a feeling, a personality so distinct there was no way to get them confused. Eight: furry and safe. An old woman feeding bread to her toothless dog, that was eight. Seven though seemed glittery, he had made millions in import-export, but never gave a dime to eight, his grandmother. Nine was a gymnast and loved seven so much it almost hurt to look at her.

What did I want? I reached in my pockets, broken watch, two quarters, a matchbook.

Rafi moved his mouth around, and right then I knew a little bit. "I really wanted a Life Saver," I told him.

"Oh? Why didn't you ask Lily from before?"

"I don't know." I thought about Lily, who always made me feel as if I were my own twin, not really me, but a replica. I took a deep breath. "Would you give me yours?"

"My Life Saver? It's almost finished." Rafi took the wet candy out of his mouth and held it between forefinger and thumb. "You want this?"

"Yes."

"Okay." He smiled. "Open your mouth, there, now we are saliva relatives."

"Thanks." The Life Saver crept minty sweet along my tongue.

"You're welcome. Be here at five o'clock tomorrow, deal?"

"Deal."

Rafi smiled again, this time really big, and I smiled back looking at the straight cut of his jaw against the air. In my mouth the Life Saver slivered and broke.

After saying good night I went out to the deserted parking lot, and almost turned back again because Smeg was there, cross-legged on the hood of a car.

"You lied," he said, jumping awkwardly to the ground. "There was a busboy job open the whole time and you knew it." Smeg came toward me across the small parking lot, pink fur top hat in his hands.

"How long have you been here?" I asked, a little frightened. But then I saw him up close. Everything about Smeg seemed completely worn out, even his skin which had gone bluish, as if he weren't getting enough blood.

"Awhile," he told me, "why did you lie?"

I didn't know how to answer that, so I lit a cigarette slow as possible to avoid talking.

"Well, Mrs. Frozen Tundra, I won't be in your army, I'm not putting on a snowsuit." Smeg's voice sounded crackly. "Listen, will you give me a ride home?"

Is he for real? I thought.

"Please? It's the least you can do after lying to me, I only live in Hollywood."

That was about three miles. "I don't know."

"Come on, help me out here, don't be mean. I've had too much mean."

I pictured him walking all the way to Hollywood where people would yell stuff at him from their car windows, and he'd probably get mugged. One ride won't take that long, I thought, still feeling lousy about the busboy job. I couldn't live in my skin if someone were mad at me. "All right."

"Thank you, thank you, this is great."

Usually I made sure to be alone before crawling through the passenger side into my car. Broken driver's door. It felt pretty stupid to climb across bucket seats with the emergency brake scraping against my leg. The car was an old Gremlin, spit-in-your-face green, and I was relieved he didn't make a comment.

"I think you're an unusual person." Propping both feet on the dashboard, Smeg hung his entire arm out the window. "The kind of person who doesn't show off their assets. For instance you might be able to do amazing things with wicker, but not mention it."

Traffic was heavy so I drove on side streets where the characters of different houses flashed by as we passed. Huge white, Spanish, dog barking, overgrown yard. What would my dream house be? I wondered.

"Why are you so quiet?" In one sweeping move he placed his pink top hat on my head. "Is a member of your family crazy?"

"No."

"Take the next left." A pause. "Someone in my family's crazy." Smeg restlessly flipped my sun visor back and forth. "J.O. Warren, huh?"

11

I remembered the registration was clipped there, and it bothered me a tiny bit to have this crazy guy with his crazy family see my last name.

"Where does your family live?" he asked.

"My mom in New York, and my dad lives out here."

"Are you close?" Fear, the white rat, crawled out from Smeg's T-shirt, sitting kind of cute on his bony arm. She washed her face.

"Close to what?"

"Hee-Hee, your father."

"Oh. No, not really." I didn't mention that I had never even met my father, knew almost nothing about him except where he lived. "After you were born," my mom would say, "he stuck around just long enough to sign the birth certificate." My dad didn't like cameras so there was only a single photo of him from the whole two years with my mother. A crowded street in New Orleans.

They stood next to each other, my dad handsome in a fineboned way with 60s hair Indian-straight and almost to his waist. He looked happy, but I couldn't be sure. Just before the camera snapped, my mother had reached up to brush back his hair so that her palm covered his forehead and one eye. Still, enough of him showed to tell our faces weren't alike. As a kid I half believed my mother had made me herself, used the mind power she always talked about.

Then last summer while rummaging through a drawer, the New Orleans photo appeared in the corner of my eye. And I saw something. Maybe it was because I was nineteen, the same age as him in the picture, but I recognized weird stuff about us that was almost exactly the same. The way his left hand rested very low on one hip, cowboyish almost, against the top of his leg. A habit I knew from my own hand. The way he stood with all the weight back on his heels so I also knew without seeing it that the soles of his shoes wore out in funny patterns. I come from this person, I had thought.

Five months ago I moved out here. A change, I told people,

the sun. Gutless. I carried his phone number everywhere in my wallet, but never called. Absolutely gutless. A lot of the time though in public places, I checked around half expecting to see him which was pretty crazy since we probably wouldn't even recognize each other.

"Listen," Smeg said abruptly. "I'm going to apply for that busboy job tomorrow, all right? I really need it."

I glanced over at him, the runny makeup, the colorless hair flattened sweaty from wearing a hat. "Sure." No way is Rafi going to hire this guy, I thought.

"Tomorrow night then, are you working?"

"Yeah." The thing about Smeg was he acted like he wanted something from me, something huge I couldn't possibly give. He was the type who might become involved with a creepy religious cult, and then I'd have to get him to a deprogrammer. Not me, I thought. I'd probably get sucked in too, and then we'd both end up half starved with shaved heads.

We were in the so-so part of Hollywood now, the kind of neighborhood where houses and cars are still nice, but the cats only have one eye.

"Another left here, what are you good at?"

"Good at?" I couldn't figure out if he was gay or hitting on me or what.

"You know, your assets."

"I don't have any assets."

"Come on, everyone has assets, even small ones. Can you make a fire with a pair of glasses?"

I shrugged.

"Well, this is it. I live here."

The building he pointed to was not a nice place. Graffiti, beer cans, the kind of place where stuff happens that people will never admit having seen no matter what.

"Thanks for the ride." Smeg opened the door, and I looked at his face in the interior light. A homeless face. It was as if he didn't really live here, just gave the address so I could drive away. I remembered how beaten he seemed in the parking lot.

"Smeg, wait a sec."

"Yeah?" The homeless face disappeared as he closed the door again.

I said, "It's no big deal, but I'm pretty good at a game with dollar bills. Liar's Poker?" What is this, I wondered. I don't even like him.

Smeg dug through his pockets, legs stretched flat. "You mean the game where you bet on serial numbers? Yeah, yeah, let's play."

"Oh, I don't know."

"Why not?" he asked, one hand flapping a bill around, then quickly covering it as if I'd try to read the tiny print. "You can't just make a festive statement that way and leave."

He was right. Also, I really did miss playing since no one I had met in Los Angeles so far seemed into it. "Okay." I got a dollar from my purse. "Ready? Letter on the left."

"What?"

"Smeg, I'm really tired, have you played this before?"

He began picking at the foam rubber that showed through a rip in my passenger seat. "A long time ago, just brush it up for me. Tell the rules in a few sentences, please?"

"Then I can leave?"

"Yeah, no problem."

"Well, it's like regular poker except you're not just betting on *your* numbers, you're betting on *mine* too. For instance, if you say 'five sixes,' and really only have a pair, you're betting that I'm holding three to make up for it. Or that I won't challenge you. Also, you're allowed to pass, make no bet, but then you lose a chance to challenge."

Smeg nodded, kneeling high on the seat with his body scrunched up next to the watery light.

"Now, what's the letter on the left of your numbers?" I asked. "*P*."

"Mine's *L*, so I go first. Two twos."

Smeg pushed his thumb up against the bridge of his nose shoving glasses that weren't there. "Oh, yeah? Three twos."

"Four threes." Kind of a dumb bet because my dollar only had one, but I knew to trust it. A lot more threes were in Smeg's bill anyway, I could almost smell them.

"Hmmm," he said. "Four sevens."

Definitely possible since I had a pair. So how many did he have? Seven, seven, I waited for the little flex to happen in my head, and when it did I felt the seven personality not strong enough around us. No way were four sevens in this car. "Show them."

Sure enough Smeg only had one, and his dollar went into my pocket.

"Let's play again," he said.

"No. Come on, you don't even have a job." I laughed, embarrassed. "Liar's Poker is what I do, Smeg, it's my asset."

He lost four more dollars before quitting. I felt a little bad taking the money but kept it anyway because of two private rules; always warn the person I will win and never give the dollars back.

He leaned close almost whispering, "How do you do that?"

"Oh, stop, it's just a thing like being double-jointed. A party trick."

"Nope, J.O., you're wrong." Smeg stared at me. He had round brown eyes that bulged out a little as if they wanted to leap from the sockets. "Have you gambled in Vegas? What about larger bills?"

I looked out at his building gleaming nasty in the streetlights. "Nope, only dollars. When the stakes are too high, when I'm afraid to lose, I always do."

Chapter 2

I had met my roommate Samantha the third day I was in Los Angeles. Very lucky. No job, no apartment, I had been driving down the street feeling unassembled when I saw a red-haired woman pounding on the hood of a parked car.

"I'm cutting my heart out," she screamed. "Are you happy?"

Boxes were piled everywhere, and a fierce-looking couch sat in her driveway. It was huge and patterned too strong with leaves and vines, the kind of couch that would make jungle noises when you turned your back.

Another scream: "My head is in the oven."

I stopped the car and rolled down my window. "Are you okay?"

"NO." She smacked the roof.

Just drive on, I told myself, imagining her committing suicide right in front of me and the hours of questioning by stumpy-looking policemen. "What exactly did you *say* to her?"

The woman faced me. She was wearing a cut-off T-shirt that showed Tarzan and Jane swinging on a vine—jungle people, I thought, glancing at the couch.

"I'm great," she said, "I'm just fuckin' great. Fifteen parking tickets in fifteen days, isn't that stupid? Look at this red zone. There's no reason for a red zone to be here." She slammed her fist into the hood again, this time actually making a dent.

It shocked me to see a person dent their own car, a good car, some kind of Nissan, just because they got a parking ticket.

"Wait a minute." I tried not to sound needy. It had been three days since my last real conversation with anyone, but I didn't want that to show. Too pathetic. "Maybe you could buy gray spray paint and just paint over the red zone."

The jungle woman smiled. "Are you serious? Would that really work? I love it, I love it." She reached into the back pocket of her jeans and pulled out a twenty. "I'm going right now, is this enough? How much is spray paint?"

"I'm sure that's fine." What kind of person dents their own Nissan and thinks spray paint costs more than twenty dollars, I wondered.

The woman kicked lightly at the piled boxes which blocked her car. "This is all my ex-roommate's stuff," she said, "Maureen's actually moving in with her boyfriend. Moving in! Meanwhile I get bored with everybody after two and a half dates, pretty bad, huh?"

"Your roommate left?" I thought about getting out of my car, but the only thing more embarrassing than a Gremlin was a Gremlin where you couldn't use the driver's door.

"Yeah, and I'm not touching her boxes," the woman said. "I'm not lifting one finger to help Maureen live with The Bone Man. Mr. B.M." She giggled and turned away from me, yelling toward the building. "Zig-gie, can you please move this stuff? It's blocking my car so I can't leave."

Ziggy, who must've been the boyfriend, came out and stood on the driveway. He was about twenty-two and shirtless with scrap-metal body parts flailing out in all directions. Bones. Poking unexpectedly from his mouth was a nasty brown pipe carved in the shape of a horse's head. "Samantha." The pipe jiggled as he spoke. "Maureen's not here to move the boxes. She went to buy more tape." Ziggy's sweatpants rode low around his hips, edgy hips, they stuck out like giant buckteeth.

Samantha smiled reminding me of the brave guy in movies who smiles defiantly as horrible people torture him. "Will you just move them yourself, please?"

Instead of answering Ziggy sat on the couch and lit his pipe making a cloud of thick bluish smoke that I could smell even from my car. If you filled your closet with dirty laundry, bad hamburger, and a sheepdog, then hosed the whole thing down, it wouldn't have smelled half as bad as Ziggy's pipe.

Samantha stared silently at him, and I could see the different possibilities being tried on in her head.

"Ummm, if you want I'll give you a ride to the store."

"You will? Great." She quickly got in my car, and I hoped she wouldn't notice it was disintegrating around her. "Have you ever once in your life met a bigger asshole?" Samantha asked. "Tell me the truth."

"Never. So, do you have a new roommate yet?"

"No. Wow, this car is incredible. Remember A.B.C. gum from when you were a kid? Already Been Chewed. Well, this is an A.B.C. car, it's so cool."

Is she kidding? I thought.

Samantha started to fool with the duct tape wrapped around the rearview and the whole mirror fell right into her lap. She laughed. I instantly loved the sound, red wine rich and full. That day we painted her curb, but it didn't matter anyhow because when I moved in Mr. Saul, the landlord, said we could park in his driveway. February.

Now it was June, and I drove home hoping Samantha would still be awake when I got there. For once I had a good story, Smeg and Fear. Usually Samantha had the good stories.

After a few blocks I checked the music on the car radio. Superstitious. I did that a lot trying to find insights or omens. Tonight was The Beatles, "Here comes the Sun King," they sang, and I thought if that meant Smeg, we were all in for a terrible life.

Driving through late-night streets the green signals shone ahead of me forever. Traffic jewelry. "Sun King" ended and went into the rest of the medley, great, they were finishing the second side of *Abbey Road*. The streets eased by, Los Angeles city songs, Citrus, Sycamore, Orange, La Brea. All their different personalities offered themselves to me as I passed, Formosa, Martel, Vista, Sierra Bonita. A left on Genesee, singing, "She came in through the bathroom window." Romaine, a quick right. By myself I never got nervous because it didn't matter what was said. The opposite of lonely.

I thought about my dream house again deciding it wouldn't be a house at all, but a rock song. I'd love to actually live inside a rock song, one of the old ones where you can really feel the stretch. "Layla."

The Gremlin's power steering hissed like food in a fryer as I aimed it into our driveway. Then I stopped. My parking space had been taken by a car I'd never seen, a huge white Buick, or maybe Cadillac—hard to tell in the dark. Whoever it was had jammed up really close to Samantha's car. I backed out onto the street again thinking she must have a friend over since the only other person in our building was Mr. Saul. He never had visitors.

When I was about ten feet from the Buick, its brights came on and the car peeled out of our driveway practically sideswiping me as it ripped down the block. Must be the wrong place, I decided staring shaky after them. No friend of Samantha's would have done that.

I parked, got out of the car, and headed toward our house, a single building made into two apartments. Semidetached they called it. Recently Mr. Saul had installed iron security gates across his door and windows which I still wasn't used to. Light from inside seeped through the black mesh making spooky little dots on the ground. I opened our door, plain wood, it seemed naked next to Mr. Saul's, and went into the dark apartment.

On my way down the hall I counted four pennies and a dime from Samantha, who liked to throw change around the house. She was asleep. Quieter than quiet I slipped into her bedroom to watch for a few minutes. Samantha asleep was just like Samantha awake, a thrasher and a groaner. About two times out of five I could get her to talk which tested my secret theory that sleeptalkers spoke in tongues. They were tapped into a Godforce not available during daily life. Maybe.

"Hello? What are you thinking?"

Samantha opened her eyes, and I came closer. "My son Walter was as tough as nails," she said, "and he didn't get it from his father, neither."

"Hey," I whispered. "That doesn't count, it's from a movie we saw. Say something else."

But she just closed her eyes again, finished. Movie dialogue, I turned to leave the room disappointed, and then noticed she'd kicked her blanket to the floor. Samantha lay still as I put it back over her.

In bed I watched the news, there was an aging frat boy reporter out of place on gangland streets. "Under the influence of PCP," he said, "twenty-year-old Jay Olson burrowed a hole into the ground and suffocated." A quick pan to the sheet-covered boy, sobbing mother, police. The reporter continued, "This young man believed he was a gopher, and according to family members would often live in his burrows for weeks at a time. Actual holes in the ground."

I watched the rest of the report hoping they'd show the "actual holes." They didn't. Were the holes like trenches? Or maybe he had a system, a complicated tunnel network. I wondered if he felt happy being underground, blind worms and roots and the sound of his family muffled above him.

Turning off the TV I heard Samantha thump the wall in the other room. Even asleep she never seemed tired, her life was a series of incredible events. Intravenous jolts of pure energy. This month alone she found someone's engagement ring on the street and won a CD player from a radio station. I didn't think that was quite fair since she could've bought ten CD players and not even felt it. Samantha played Officer Beattie, a semiregular on "You're Busted," a sitcom cop show.

In my heart I hoped if I hung around long enough some of her life might bleed to mine the way red bleeds to white in the laundry. Men loved Samantha, though she usually got bored. I felt pretty retarded being almost twenty-one, the same age as her, and having only slept with Foxtrot my whole life.

I met Foxtrot last winter while working for a junkyard in Queens. When people's cars got trashed, I took their information to give to the dispatcher. Foxtrot drove a tow truck and was married. His name wasn't really Foxtrot, but that's what everyone called him since he drove the "F" truck. Alpha, Bravo, Charlie, Delta, the company had trucks all the way to "M." After work we'd park in a vacant lot and have sex, the green vinyl of the front seat sticking to my ass and legs. It made a sweaty ripping sound when I got up.

Foxtrot was short, about five foot four, and his marriage was bad. "Mia don't care what I do. You know I can't remember the last time she let me make love to her," he'd say.

We met twice a week for seven months. On those days I'd shave my legs, and put on Coppertone suntan lotion because he liked the smell. That was nice. In the truck he'd throw a wad of bills on my lap, "Do me a favor, J.O., and count this for me." Foxtrot always carried huge amounts of cash with him.

"Sure." I'd sort through the money as he turned the radio up over the sound of freezing wind and rattling windows. "You have two thousand, four hundred sixty-three dollars." It was always close to the same number, and once out of curiosity I tore off the corner of a hundred-dollar bill. Our affair lasted five months after that, and the same bill was always there.

Sometimes he brought me presents, stuffed animals, barrettes, a gold chain for my birthday. "I love you, babe," he'd say stroking the inside of my thigh. For some reason that was always better than the actual sex, and I'd say, "I love you too," though it wasn't what he thought. I definitely loved him, but it felt like being homesick for a country that didn't exist. Foxtrot was a good person. I missed him sometimes.

Chapter 3

"J.O., are you awake?" Samantha was standing at the foot of my bed as I snapped open my eyes sure that something critical had happened.

"Will you come to Melrose with me?" she asked. "I have to buy a really interesting dress for my date tonight."

I sat up and rubbed my face. "What?"

"A dress that says, 'Maybe I want you, maybe I don't,' know what I mean?"

Samantha's voice always put a skin of importance on every word, like an evangelist. No, that wasn't right. She never sounded completely serious, her voice was more like someone making fun, pretending to be an evangelist.

"I'll take you to breakfast if we go in twenty minutes. I'm starving."

She left the room and I lay back down again wondering if there was enough time to take a shower. Twenty minutes. The best thing about Samantha was also the worst thing—she always, always got what she wanted.

As I got dressed I could hear Mr. Saul in the backyard begin sawing. Very loud. It was the electric kind with a high-pitched screech that traveled under furniture and inside closets.

I went to my window. Mr. Saul stood about ten feet away sawing passionately, hunched so low I was afraid for his face. Not a pleasant saw. It shrieked, jarring his whole body as if instead of sawing pieces of metal it wanted to break free into the sky chopping clouds and decapitating friendly birds.

When I first moved here Mr. Saul was this nice, smart old

man from somewhere else, maybe Russia. He did it right, all the nice old man things. "Such an attractive girl, why don't you have boyfriends?" House slippers, the TV too loud. "Why do you insist on going to The Mayfair Market? Those people they love to steal your money, I only shop at The Lucky Store. It's quite a bit cheaper." But ever since he began inventing The Car Of The Future, Mr. Saul made me extremely uncomfortable.

I watched him lay the saw on the ground, straighten up inch by inch, and carefully take a handkerchief from his back pocket. He wiped his face.

"Let's get out of here before the noise starts again," Samantha yelled from the other room.

Mr. Saul had on corduroys and a new black sweatshirt which said STP in a big red oval across the front. Seeing that shirt on him, definitely not a nice old man shirt, gave me the creeps. It was wrong, like naming a child Spot.

The Car Of The Future used to be a small fun hobby for Mr. Saul, occasional drawings on newspaper margins. Then it started. Huge worktable, diagrams, the balsa wood model he had proudly showed me. The model was bright yellow with narrow diamond-shaped windows, and a Tupperware bowl for its roof. Its hood started out okay, but then gradually thinned to a needle beak point in front so the whole thing looked like the head of some nasty bird. A giant woodpecker. Mr. Saul had told me the pointy hood "made less surface area to do damage in an accident," which I guess was true if you didn't count impaling people as damage. Anyway, not for a minute did I believe he could actually build a car in the backyard. Mr. Saul was a very smart guy, but you needed a team. Hydraulics.

He bent to pick up the saw again, and even from far away I could see his hands were trembly. Samantha thought it was some kind of a breakdown. I turned away and left the room.

We went to breakfast and afterward shopped on Melrose. I'd heard that years ago Melrose used to be underground hip, a 2KOOL4U kind of place, and there were still traces of that, but now it was mostly clothing stores and expensive restaurants. Walking around there always made me feel a little messy.

23

The black dress Samantha chose was the only one I'd ever seen that actually frightened me, snaking thickly around her with a live will of its own. A heartbeat. This dress doesn't need a person to get around, I thought. It can roam the streets by itself at night leaving no witnesses.

Samantha posed in front of me. "What do you think?"

"You have so many freckles," I said.

She adjusted the dress, dipping it lower in back while tightening a long tail of fabric around her hips. The dress obeyed. "Yeah? You should see my dad."

Words that made me stare because she could toss off facts about her father and control evil clothing without a problem. It comes from knowing who you are, I thought. And right at that moment I promised myself to call him when we got home. No matter what.

While Samantha paid for her dress, I waited next to three girls who were flipping through a spinner display thing filled with earrings. They were sixteen maybe, and all had sunglasses shaped like Mickey Mouse's head. I could hear their tweety whispers, "Do you think that's really her? It must certainly be. Should we approach her?"

Samantha loved signing checks with fancy loops and swirls, she did it slower than anyone else I knew, and I thought, come on, come on, wanting to leave before the girls got up their nerve. I hated when Samantha was recognized.

"Let's get out of here, Pancho." She took a step toward the door. Too late.

"Aren't you Officer Beattie from 'You're Busted'?" The girls surrounded her. "You're sooo good, we watch the show in England. We love it."

I hadn't heard their accents before, English accents put me completely off balance since I didn't know the code. With a New York person I could just about tell what high school they went to by the sound of their voice.

Samantha smiled, showing off the new bonding on her top four teeth. They looked beautiful, white, white almost ironed into place. "I'm glad you like the show."

"And who's this?" One of the girls pointed a pale finger at me.

"This is my roommate J.O." Samantha draped her arm over my shoulders. "She puts up with all my bad behavior, J.O., you want a pair of earrings? Pick out the ones you like."

"I don't want earrings." I started to take a cigarette from my purse, but then remembered you can't smoke in clothing stores.

"What do you mean you don't want earrings? Yesterday you were telling me you didn't have any."

The girls watched us from behind their glasses, completely fascinated.

Reaching for the earring display I grabbed the first pair my fingers touched, and Samantha paid for them, chatting with the girls. Don't wear these, I told myself. You're not her PR man, you're not Pancho. But I put them on anyway, heavy silver hoops that clunked against my neck.

Back home I paced around my room trying to psych myself to call my dad. I wished my mom were here even though that would make it completely impossible because of the way she was about him. But I missed her. On my desk was a small calligraphy drawing she sent me of Fifty-nine, a joke that we kept up for years. The idea was to surprise each other with scraps of paper that had random numbers written on them, Eighty-three pouring out with cereal, Twelve folded in the laundry. Part of the joke was never to mention it.

My mouth was very dry, and I listened to Samantha moving around in the other room as she got ready for her date. I tried to lean against the sound.

When I was a kid I used to love the games in *Highlights Magazine*. There'd be a picture of something nice and normal like a family barbecue and the caption would say, "Find the key, find the Indian, the eyeglasses." So I'd look till I caught a secret key disguised in the sun rays, or the head of an Indian in a woman's skirt. In the pictures of my life (me at work, with Samantha, driving) my father was hidden everywhere and nowhere. His job could be any of the jobs my customers did. His favorite color, the kind of car he drove, even his mannerisms were all around at any given moment. He might be totally nuts, or worse, a guy who's left hundreds of women like my mom across the country, broke and with a newborn baby. What would I do then? Nothing. There weren't a lot of choices.

The thick, slow air in my bedroom had an underwater feeling and I forced my hand through it to pick up the phone. He won't know me, he's not going to remember, I thought sitting on my bed next to the one stuffed animal I had since birth. Heather Peeps Haber. You wouldn't know it was supposed to be a horse anymore because as a kid I'd rubbed off most of the face and fur. What's the worst that can happen? Imagine the worst. I held the receiver cool against my fingers. How could anyone not remember having a kid.

I dialed the phone in panic time, bad dream slowness. He answered.

"Hello?" My father's voice was friendly, a normal voice ready for a conversation.

I looked at the horse blob on the bed.

"Hello?" he said again, and at that second my Call Waiting beeped, unbelievable since I got maybe four phone calls a year.

What do I do, who is it, what if it's my mother? I thought.

"Hello?" a little edgy now, he was ready to hang up, and I told myself talk, talk, you lightweight coward. The other line beeped again and my tongue felt all wrong in my mouth like a tumor, shaky hands, Samantha was humming. I couldn't hold on one thing.

Click. As he hung up I tried to see him sitting there, but all I saw was my mother's face when I used to ask questions about him. She'd usually say something fuzzy—"Oh, well, Miles just loved to have a good time." Meanwhile though her face would nail down hard on me, as if she were the one asking instead of the other way around. As if somehow I knew.

My hands were moving I hadn't realized, they touched the phone, my cheeks, hair, rubbing together like a crazy person. I clenched my fists. I slowly took off both earrings and put them back on again. Hoops, they were the kind where it's hard to get the sliver of metal back into the hollow tube. I closed my eyes, concentrating. Little things like that can pull it all together sometimes.

From the other room Samantha yelled, "J.O.?"

"Yes?" The word came out splintered, snapped in half. "What do you need?"

"The ironing board is in here if you want to use it. Come keep me company."

Yes. Company was a good idea.

Samantha's room was the same size as mine, but seemed a lot smaller because of the mess. She believed in the mess, believed in the power of inside-out clothes covering the floor, the bed, and leaking from her dresser. There were half-empty soda cans, TV scripts, a large backgammon set. Also the pens. Samantha would buy a dozen Pilot Razor Points and fling them everywhere telling me, "It's good to always have a pen nearby."

I started to move aside a pile of clothes still in dry-cleaner bags and realized I was holding my stuffed horse. Pretty scary. I set up the ironing board and began on my hat and bow while Samantha fixed her hair, standing naked in front of the mirror. She liked to hang around naked whenever possible, probably an actress thing.

"It's our fourth date, J.O., do you think I should rouge my nipples for later, or is that too slutty?" She smeared a handful of pinkish gel on her head.

I shrugged. "You're sleeping with this guy?"

"Not yet, but I might." The gel made her hair bristle tall and shiny like some kind of underwater plant life. "What's that on the ironing board?"

"A horse." Please don't ask, I thought. Please. I had never explained to anyone about my father because of how it sounded. "The man didn't contact you for twenty years?" I imagined people saying. Yeah, well.

"Listen this has been on my mind." Samantha paused. "I want to tell you something important, okay? You're young, pretty, and nice, it's time for you to make a move in your life, don't you agree?"

"A move." I carefully sat on her bed avoiding the dress like spilled oil next to me.

Samantha continued, "Men. You've just got to go out with this friend of the guy I'm dating. Jeremiah. He's a screenwriter and very artsy but in a good way, and he's got these two beautiful birds."

"No," I said, "I'll tell you right now, no artsy birds." I knew about these birds. Their names would be Agony and Ecstasy, and they'd shit on my head.

"What are you going to do then? You haven't gone on a date since I met you." She picked up the dress and gracefully slipped it over her naked body. "Not a single date."

"It's no big deal." On Samantha's night table was one of those phones that's supposed to look like a piano, and I lightly touched the keys pretending to dial. "It's no big deal," I said again, softly.

"It is a big deal. Do I have lipstick on my teeth?" Leaning close she made a face so I could see them.

"No."

"Good. Anyway, Jeremiah's really different, he's writing a thriller about mail fraud, isn't that different?" She untangled a pair of stockings from a pile next to the closet door. "What do you think, hose or bare leg?" The stockings dangled sheer like spiderwebs from her hand.

"Mail fraud?" I asked. "You mean like when you send away for something, but never get it?"

"I don't know." She threw the stockings back in the pile. "But go out with him, I'm telling you."

I took a deep breath. "I can't. There's someone I like." Why am I saying this, I wondered. There's no one I like.

"Who?"

I shrugged. "Someone I work with, that's all."

"Well, who is he?"

On the floor crumpled in front of my feet was a navy blue antique sweater that lay there humiliated somehow with all the careful beadwork in a messy pile. "Rafi, he's Israeli."

"Israeli, huh? That's hot, camels and spies. Are you going to go out with him?"

I pictured Rafi's face in front of me, the tough angles, the almost-curly hair still thick around his ears. Did I like him? Well, maybe just a little. Only a little. Maybe. "I don't know." I paused. "You look good."

"You think? I'm not sure, it needs something." She stared in the mirror suddenly intense. "A center. It needs a power center to draw you in yet put you off like a bloody handprint on a white wall. Yeah, that's disgusting, but get the idea? A jolt of color to hit you like the scene of a crime, get what I'm saying? A fashion crime."

"Crime," I repeated.

"*Yes*." She whirled facing me. "Your bow, it would be perfect."

I stared at the bright orange cotton still on the ironing board. "That bow? But I need it for work."

"Let me just take a look." Before I could say anything she had it pinned below her right shoulder, the same place I wore it. "This is great, can I use it?"

I stared at the balled-up sweater on the floor which seemed to have been there awhile half covered by a pair of jeans. "Come on, that belongs with my uniform. I'll get in trouble." Someone hand made that sweater, I thought, sewing all those beads on there one by one.

"Please? I've got to wear it, it's this perfect bullet of color. Crime." She smiled. "It sits on my dress like an orange crime."

I got into her bed pulling the blankets around my shoulders. "It's a hankie, Samantha, a hankie for Sweet N Low."

"It's not a 'hankie' at all, it's nothing like a 'hankie.' It's a *bow*. Borrow one from someone else, please? Just for tonight?"

Looking up at her wearing my work bow, my Sun Maiden work bow pinned to her dress as a fashion crime was incredibly depressing. I pulled the blankets over my face. If I had only spoken to him on the phone it wouldn't be like this now, I thought, even though that probably wasn't true.

"What do you want? Tell me what you want and we'll make a deal," Samantha said.

One of her pens was digging into my neck so I shoved it under a pillow.

"You know this is important to me, and I have to look absolutely right. What's the problem? You'll have it back tomorrow."

The problem was I had almost been fired yesterday. Fired. The Sun maiden had no contracts, no residual checks.

"J.O., how often have I asked to borrow something? Never. I help you, I try to get you dates, I take you out to eat, I buy you things. This is unfair, really unfair." I heard her greasing up the anger, Samantha could talk herself into a complete rage in less than thirty seconds.

Maybe it would be better to just loan it to her, I thought, she's a good friend, how many friends did I have at work anyway?

"I can't believe you won't do this one favor for me, J.O., I can't believe it. Here I am offering you anything of mine to keep. Anything you want."

"Okay," I said. Maybe Rafi wouldn't notice, or even better, maybe there were millions of extra bows in the office.

"Great, I love you. What do you want?"

"I don't know." I pictured a factory in the 1940s with rows of women painfully sewing bead after bead, they laughed, they talked about their boyfriends. "The antique sweater," I said poking my head out of the blankets. "This one." I reached down and touched it, fragile in my hand.

"All right, but you have to take better care of it than I do."

I stood up and held the sweater against me, knowing it wasn't my style. Too delicate, a worry sweater. Samantha gave me a funny look as I wrapped it around Heather Peeps Haber and left the room.

I didn't notice the huge man in the huge white convertible till I had backed mostly out of our driveway. He was across the street. I stopped and, trying to seem offhand, watched him for a minute in my rearview. The man sat lengthwise, feet up on the dash and back leaning against the passenger door so he faced our house. Relaxed, but definitely *there*. Could Samantha have some guy obsessed with her? I wondered, remembering the car that had peeled out of our driveway last night. But this guy didn't look obsessed. He looked mean and bored. I drove away sticking his features hard into my mind, bright blond ponytail, fleshy cheeks, muscle-bound. He was probably just waiting for someone, a girl-friend maybe. But still.

The drive from my house to The Sun Maiden was filled with tiny omens that I checked every day. A woman walked her dalmation down Fountain Avenue at exactly five o'clock, bad news, since seeing her meant I'd be late for work. About a mile further though was a class, an acting class. People waited outside the studio with their scripts, actor-casual, super-hyped casual like just standing there was something they'd all been practicing. For me the actors were good news. That meant the class hadn't started yet, and I would be on time.

At La Cienega was a steep hill with a traffic light at the top, and getting all the way up there to Sunset before the light turned red was very lucky. Today I didn't make it. Whenever the Gremlin was stopped on a hill its brakes made a loud whiny noise like a test of the Emergency Broadcast System. I looked out the window trying to pretend I had nothing to do with this car. Right next to me was a woman in a cream-colored Volvo, who made the thumbs-up sign, smiling encouragement. I felt my face go red from her sympathy.

Driving along Sunset I thought about how dumb it was to have lent Samantha my bow. Maybe she's changed her mind. I thought, and the bow will be waiting there when I get to work. Completely irrational. It was the same kind of irrational hope as watching the Academy Awards and hoping for a split second they'll announce your name even though you've never done a movie in your life. Sometimes I imagined my father would be the one to contact me, that he'd always known exactly who and where I was, but hadn't called because of some evil spell or government test.

On this part of Sunset the sleek hotels and restaurants were mixed with heavy-metal clubs so everything felt sort of discon-nected. Rootless. It was like you could just pick up all the build-ings and put them down again in a different order. Right across from the Hyatt Hotel was a tattoo parlor that seemed to be open all the time. Kind of pathetic, I thought. Anyone getting tattooed at four in the morning should probably wait till the next day. Make absolutely sure.

Up ahead I could see The Sun Maiden logo against the sky. The woman in the logo was holding a tray with "The Sun Maiden" written in fancy script where the plates would be. I tried to check if she were wearing a bow, but it was too far away to tell.

"Hi, hon, I'm so glad you're here," Ann, one of the day waitresses said as soon as I came in. She had lots of gray hair pulled back in fancy combs. "Can you take over for me?" Ann was wearing very large greenish earrings that looked like dried Play-Doh, the kind of earrings you had to mention.

"Those are pretty," I told her and pointed.

"Really? You think so? My granddaughter made them in kindergarten, they are so advanced in school now." She started talking about the granddaughter's class while I stared at her bow.

"Ann, could I borrow your bow tonight?"

"Oh, I'd love to, but I'm working a double it's crazy, I shouldn't. Anyway, next they're doing bracelets, and my tiny granddaughter promised to make one to match, isn't that sweet? She calls me Moo-Moo. I don't know why, but it sure is cute. So anytime you're ready to get changed that would help. I need a little break."

"What about Joyce or Irene? Are they still around?" Stay calm, I told myself, it's only an orange piece of cloth, nothing to get hysterical about.

"No, hon, just us chickens. Lily's upstairs."

Lily. Lily would love this, I could already see her giving me that tight woven look. I began walking slowly up the stairs. Lily's bow was probably part of her by now, actually blended with the muscle tissue in her shoulder.

Back on the floor at exactly 5:00, I took over the counter for Ann who had left the syrups empty. Again. Ann was retiring next year so everyone ignored the fact that she never did any side work. There was a Sun Maiden pension plan and everything.

Please, please, I thought, don't let me get The Sun Maiden pension plan.

As usual I didn't notice Rafi till he was right next to me. He had a way of coming up behind you guerrilla quiet, his long fingers sudden on your shoulder. Camels and spies.

"Hi, Rafi." We both watched me pour syrup from the gallon jug into the dispensers, too silent, but I couldn't think of a conversation. "So, how long have you been working here?" I asked finally.

"Eleven months, where is your bow?"

I continued pouring like no big deal. "It's gone."

"Ah." He nodded, sarcastic patience. "Gone. Tell me, gone where?"

I stared at the syrup realizing it was regular maple going into the blueberry containers, did he notice? I wasn't sure. "Someone stole it from my car." The most obvious desperate lie ever in the history of lies ever in the world. Shaky handed now, I put the syrup down.

"I see." Rafi smiled quick and dry, a snakebite smile. "J.O., come to the office with me. We need some talking."

"Are you sure, it's getting busy and—"

"Now."

The Sun Maiden office was so tiny that I always half expected Rafi to say, "You thought this was the office? Oh no, the real office is downstairs. This is the ventilator shaft."

A huge filing cabinet took up most of one wall. "J.O." Rafi sat down at the desk cluttered with stuff, inventory sheets, a half-eaten fruit plate, two light bulbs. "I'm sure you have awareness of what I'm going to say." He suddenly stood again and stretched tight arms over his head, fingertips brushing the fluorescent tubes above us. "I've always thought you could be a great waitress. I've given you many chances, mentally closed my eyes many times." His shirt had become untucked a little so I saw the bottom part that was wrinkled from being inside pants. Gray pants, clean creased.

"It isn't the bow, one bow missing all right. I like you, J.O. I've always liked you, but this is business."

His accent put little stones in the words. I took off my hat. I begged myself not to cry.

"Ever since you started you come late, you can't handle busy floor, and you make mistakes. Always you are making mistakes."

Rafi's tie clip was gold, a crossed knife and fork.

"Like before I saw you put regular syrup in the blueberry things. Why? What is in your head?"

Is it actual gold, or just gold-plated I wondered.

"Perhaps you'll do better in another restaurant." Rafi took a step to the door and I finally lost it, bawling completely out of control. I pressed the hat against my face and just stood there. Finished. Nothing but my own spooky sobs in my ears.

"J.O., come on, don't cry." His hand rested awkward on the back of my head. "It's okay."

My nose was running, no tissue, and I felt like even more of an asshole crying into a hat.

"Come on, please stop. You want some gum?" He nervously poked my arm with a piece of Bazooka.

"I lied."

"What?"

"I lied." Nothing mattered anymore, not even whether he liked me, because it was finished. "My roommate's wearing the bow on a date tonight," I said. From below us came distant kitchen sounds, a Spanish accent yelling "Eighty-six on creamed corn."

"Why?"

"She thought it looked cool." I blew my nose in the hat and stuffed it in my pocket.

"But why did you give this to her?"

There was no rational answer, and I knew that trying to explain was a bad idea, it would make me start crying all over again.

Rafi stared at my face for a long time. His eyes were cozy blue, the color of a cup you might give a child, except for one thing at the bottom of his left iris. A black speck I'd never seen. It reminded me of a freckle, or a single drop of paint spilled against the blue.

Nodding slightly he said, "All right, all right, J.O., we'll make bargain, you finish your shift, and then afterward we go to the beach where I have a contention I can help you. There is something I want you to see."

What's on the beach at night, I wondered, picturing secret, bizarre rituals.

"Have you ever shot a gun before?" His tone was casual, but there was nothing casual about his face, a hardball face, too much for the tiny office.

"No."

"Good. We go tonight, and this will help. You'll see."

Guns on the beach, it had a dangerous feel to it, a wide-open feel. Anyway what did I have to lose. I was finished.

After leaving the office I hung around in the empty locker room for a few minutes to try to fix my blotchy face. Useless. Back downstairs again I stood quietly in the doorway wanting to enjoy that moment before anyone sees you.

Lily and Ann were at the pickup counter, hit extra hard from the dinner rush since we were still short a busboy. You couldn't tell from watching Lily though. No move wasted, every move necessary as she yelled orders while piling seven dinner specials up and down muscled arms. Her face was alive with a deep groove concentration I'd seen on athletes and rock stars. It's the same thing, I thought.

Ann, though, was in lousy shape, screeching at the kitchen. "Please, I'm trailing a hot turkey sandwich, Roberto, please I need it." Roberto ignored her. The double shift had been too much, one swollen foot held fragile off the ground, she was missing a granddaughter earring. For a second I felt so bad I wanted to stop the restaurant, not let anyone move till that earring was found. Instead I walked quickly toward her, ready to take over the counter again.

"J.O." Cold fingers wrapped around my wrist, Smeg's fingers. "I'm here about the busboy job, will you introduce me to the manager as a close personal friend? I really need a job." He tightened his grip. "Do you think I'll be hired?"

Smeg looked completely different. Plain T-shirt, neat hair, khaki pants ironed, it was more than that though. Smeg seemed as if he'd detailed his whole body cleaner than clean, even fixing his eyeballs somehow to make them whiter. I checked his shoulder to be sure he'd left the rat at home. No rat.

"J.O., what's wrong? You've been crying, what happened?" The vampire vise on my wrist immediately became something else much kinder.

"I just got fired. This is my last night."

"Unbelievable." He pulled his hand away and flailed it through the air. "That's awful. It's obscene, J.O., we live in an obscene world."

I took a step away from him. "Could you keep your voice down?"

"Absolutely. Yeah, well, I'm sorry, and if there's anything I can do let me know." He paused. "Here, you can have this."

Reaching into his pocket Smeg pulled out a small printed card which he handed over like some tribal secret. It was a frozen yogurt coupon, Buy Ten Get One Free. "Only two more to go," Smeg said pointing at the numbered squares on the bottom, suddenly shy.

I knew about these coupons, how it took forever to buy all the yogurts so the free flavor slowly got bigger and bigger in your head. "Thank you." As I put it in my pocket something inside me went loose. He had won. I didn't know about having Smeg as a "close personal friend," but he was definitely a good guy, a buddy.

Rafi whizzed by us seating two more parties in Ann's section. "J.O., take the counter, please."

"I've got to help out here," I told Smeg. "Come in later."

"Yeah, okay, and you'll explain exactly how I should be, right? Pump me full of steroids and teach me to bench press, Hee-Hee. See you."

As he walked out the door I noticed spurs on the back of his sneakers, but decided to let it go since Rafi might like them. Spurs went with guns.

By some miracle I kept it together that night, only mixing up one food order, and the guy even said fine, he'd eat it anyway. An average guy except for his suntan. This tan made me nervous.

It looked fierce, ready to spill off his body and down the countertop tanning all the coffee cups and menus in its way.

"So, you want to know about roofing, I'll tell you about roofing," the guy said, aggressive with his chicken pot pie. "It's all in the foundation. You gotta lay the goddamn foundation right, I tried to tell the architect, but he wouldn't listen. Asshole. Can I get a beer from you?"

"Sorry, there's no liquor here." I paused. "But you're really tan."

The guy looked at his arms completely disgusted. "Fuckin' roofing."

Watching him eat chicken pot pie alone at the counter made me feel guilty and depressed. The guy had trouble at work, and all he wanted was to relax with a Beefy Burger, but even that wasn't happening because I had put the order in wrong. I probably would've fired me too. Busing his dishes I wondered if Lily and Ann knew this was my last night. I hoped Rafi hadn't mentioned it otherwise closing with them would feel incredibly awkward.

Smeg came back in a couple of hours. It was slow now, that lag time between early and late, and he immediately flopped on a counter stool and began to spin. "I'm ready for big action."

"No." I leaned forward and grabbed his arm to stop the spinning. "When you talk with Rafi the idea is to be calm, do you know what I mean? Can you be calmer?"

"Sure." Nodding jackhammer quick. "You want me to act like Don Corleone? I can act like Don Corleone."

"No, please."

"Who then? It has to be from *The Godfather*, I just saw it on TV."

He didn't understand. There were no busboy types in *The Godfather*, it was not a busboy movie. "Act like one of the waiters from Connie's wedding," I told him. "The idea is to be calm and invisible."

"Oh." He looked disappointed. "Calm and invisible at Connie's wedding. All right."

Smeg shouldn't have to be a busboy, I thought, he should be a personality that made money. I imagined him in a medfly suit explaining about pesticides. It would start as a public service message, but soon there'd be a cult following with medfly T-shirts, a spot on Johnny Carson.

"So, is that the manager over there?" he asked pointing to the cash register where Rafi stood eating a Danish.

"Yeah. But listen, you can't say your name is Smeg."

"Why not?"

A million reasons rushed into my mind, but I didn't want to hurt his feelings so I said, "It's not a name, that's all." I began to make fresh coffee, standing on my toes to reach the top of the urn. What's the point, I thought. It doesn't matter anymore, I should just crash the whole urn to the ground and then leave. No, that was wrong, it always mattered. Anyway I still had the beach after work.

Smeg said, "J.O.'s not a name either, what's your real one?"

I thought about my father filling in my birth certificate with the name he gave me right before he left. The name had nothing to do with who I was, just an unrelated piece of paper, and in my head I didn't even pronounce those words. Didn't even think them. "I'm J.O. What's on my birth certificate isn't important."

Smeg rolled his clean eyes. "Yes it is, Hee-Hee, I can tell."

Angry little pokes went through me like walking barefoot on gravel, and I leaned across the counter toward him. "Is fart a name? Is snot a name? No, and neither is smeg. You must have another one, don't tell me you're actually named that."

Silence.

"Come on, it can't be so awful."

He mumbled a word sounding like "Annie," and I wished I hadn't pushed it because if Smeg's parents named him Annie no wonder he didn't want people to know. "What?" I asked softly.

"Andy." Voice incredibly shy, scared almost.

"Oh." What's wrong with Andy, I wondered. "That's great, on your days off you can be whoever you want, but Andy keeps the job. See what I mean?"

"Yeah, okay."

As he walked from the counter to the cash register Smeg flaked away like old paint so by the time Andy shook hands with Rafi it seemed ridiculous to call him anything else. That's how completely Andy he really was.

They talked for a while, and the only wrong moment came when Andy pointed at me, nodding eagerly. Dumb move. He shouldn't have mentioned we knew each other, but it worked out all right. Rafi hired him.

"I am liking this guy," he said as they came back toward me. "We'll try him for rest of the week. Lilybelle, are you free a minute?"

Andy was grinning at me, and I tried to smile too, but it felt tight and dry like a Band-Aid on my face. I wondered who thought of the expression "fired." It was too perfect.

Lily strolled over leaving her half-full section, hot food up, orders in her head, no problem. In one easy move she could take care of it all.

"This is Andy who I am hoping will be our next busboy," Rafi said. "Can you show him around?"

Lily did a quick scan. She looked as if she were trying to decide whether or not to tie Andy around her waist as a belt.

"You're either on the bus or off the bus, Hee-Hee." His famous squeal took me by surprise. "I want to be good at this, Lily, better than a busboy. I want to be a Bus Man."

Lily stared at his skinny-armed enthusiasm, his too-short T-shirt coming untucked. Then she smiled. It was one of those smiles that only black women in their fifties can do, a smile so powerful it brought back childhood memories of grace before dinner, a hard kind of love. Only my childhood was different. Lily's smile actually made me remember someone else's childhood.

They walked off toward her section together, unbelievable. I had spent the last four months trying to get her to say hello to me, and Andy comes out with one comment not even particularly funny, and now they were best friends.

The syrup dispensers still needed to be filled, same ones I had messed up earlier. I began to pour from a gallon jug licking it off my hands when it dripped. The maple wasn't as good mixed in with that bitter finger taste.

Chapter 4

"Wait till you see the therapy you will get from this."

We walked quickly toward the ocean, Rafi swinging his briefcase high with every step. The beach wind flattened my clothes
against places usually kept private, breasts too small, a fleshy
stomach. I began walking backward.

"You look cute," he said, "being whipped around. I hope you
find this helpful."

"Thank you. I'm sure I will." It wasn't clear whether he had
changed his mind about firing me or not. I didn't want to ask.
We stood at the edge of the ocean, just outside the range of late-
night waves. Everything was black.

"You are knowing why we do this, right? Firearms can be very
therapeutic. Between you and me I take The Mag to work every
night. Like you, sometimes I lose my inner vision. I become
rattled. Like this." Rafi's voice went squeaky imitating panic.
"Oh my God, I'm thirty-five, and still only restaurant manager.
How could this happen? I'll never have my own business. Help!
I'm getting fat." He continued in a normal voice. "Then, I picture
my briefcase. The Mag waits inside. I feel its presence in the
hand, the recoil, and that's it. My vision returns. You will understand as soon as you have shot a well-made firearm."

What am I doing here, I thought, peering through the
damp wind.

"Are you cold? Would you like my jacket?"

"No thanks."

Rafi took off his blazer, the brown one worn every night.

"Really, you look cold." He draped it over my shoulders, and I was surprised to feel bare wool. It was one of those jackets that from the front seem silk lined, but then really the silky stuff only goes a little way.

"Tell me something." His body rocked slightly back and forth as if we were on a boat.

"What?"

"I don't know." He was close to my ear. "Tell me a secret."

"I don't have any secrets." Rafi's pockets had waxy gum wrappers, a pack of cigarettes, and something cold metal, the size and shape of my pinky.

"Come on Girl." It sounded like "Gil" and was drawn intimate from the throat.

There was one secret, a situation that was all pictures, you had to see it. I wondered if I knew the right words to make him understand, visualize, the way he saw The Mag. "Well, there is something I've never told anyone. I don't know. You have to swear not to say anything."

"I swear." Teasing, right hand on heart.

"Seriously."

He put his hand down. "Of course. Trust me."

I smiled quickly because to me my overbite always looked like Ed the Talking Horse from that old TV show. Also the secret. Always, whenever I thought about it my mind did this glossy kind of dance, skittering away from thinking too hard. "Okay. Well, this happened in New York about eight years ago. I was living on the Lower East Side with my mother, her friend Lois, and Lois's three kids." Why am I telling him any of this? I wondered. What do I want from him now? Not gum, not a Life Saver.

Rafi laid his briefcase flat on the sand and sat carefully on one side of it. "How old were you?" He motioned for me to sit next to him.

"Twelve."

"Little Gil," nodding as if that explained something, and I looked away red-faced for no reason.

"Yeah, well, my mom used to cocktail at this place called Bo Peeps. She'd usually get home around four, and I'd hear her because I was such a light sleeper."

I tried to explain exactly the way it was. The mossy apartment. The six of us. Lois's oldest kid, Zeke, was cross-eyed and scary. I used to lie in bed listening to the wet chewing sounds he made in his sleep.

"So, one night my mom came in. Now, I still don't know why I did this, but I crouched down next to the bedroom door, and opened it just a little. You know, a kid eavesdropping."

I described my mom and the way in winter her hair always clashed with her face. She wore it extreme. Work hair. Frizzed and fake black with sparkly stuff that left bits of glitter everywhere she went. Her face though was scoured bloodless from the cold, overexposed, like a bad photograph where you think, "No, that can't be you." My mom smiled at Lois eagerly with a different overbite than mine. It made her look like a hot-wired teenager.

"Anyway," I told Rafi, "Lois was sitting there on the couch wrapped in the American Airlines blanket. She had attached these paper parasols to all the bare bulbs, so the light was dim with Chinese shadows on the wall. I could still see them though. Absolutely perfectly. My mother stood there intense somehow in her dirty white coat, while Lois jumped up to make tea with that blanket dragging on the floor. Now, I had been on planes, and the blankets we got were tiny. I asked Lois about it once, and she said, really condescending, 'Oh, you have to sneak up to first class. That's where all the good stuff is.' I remember as a kid being pissed off to think of her using a blanket she didn't even pay for and then stealing it afterward."

Rafi grinned and stretched his legs out in front of him. "I've done it," he said. "Do you have any idea how much those airlines are making?" He tapped his feet together.

"Aren't you bored?" I asked.

"Don't be silly. It's a good story."

I shrugged, hoping he'd think so at the end. Hoping he'd say, "J.O., you're perfectly normal. It really doesn't matter." There was a large rock about fifty feet to our left. It reminded me of a giant arm muscle rising from the sand, the way it curved blacker than the black sky. I stared at it till Rafi said, "Go on."

"Anyway, my mother was still standing there with her coat on saying how freezing she was. So Lois wrapped the blanket around her. Without that blanket all she had was a tank top and underwear, and I remember her legs were incredibly pale. I mean like this." I leaned forward and touched one of Rafi's white socks, bunched around the ankle.

"Then Lois goes, 'What's wrong?' My mom shook her head and bits of glitter fell from her hair. 'I can't stand this anymore.' She started talking really fast. 'This whole life, this whole environment is shit. I can't raise J.O. like this. How do you think she'll turn out growing up this way? She'll turn out like garbage, that's how.'

"I sort of shivered hearing my name when I wasn't suposed to be listening.

"Lois said, 'No, J.O.'s fine, don't worry.' And my mom goes, 'It's not her, it's what she's exposed to, this sleazy neighborhood and my sleazy job. You know what that place is like. I don't know, I'm thinking of just getting out of the city.' "

Rafi slipped off his shoes. "What was this place?" he asked pouring trickles of sand from inside the heels.

"A dive."

"What dive? A swan dive?" Laughing, he spread his arms in the swan dive position, a loafer in each hand.

"No. Not that kind." My voice burned too mean. A dry ice voice. "A dive is anywhere cheap and dirty."

"Okay, than what?" He put his shoes back on. Rafi's cheeks looked rough. It was a little scary, I thought, the way a guy could grow a beard just like that.

"Lois had thick hands," I continued. "She squeezed the blanket together around my mom saying, 'Don't leave.' Then she put on this street voice. 'When you leave the Big Apple, you ain't goin' nowhere.' My mom turned her back and started rubbing her eyes. 'Come on, Lowie,' she said. Now, I'd heard a lot of things, but I'd never heard *anyone* call Lois Lowie. So then she goes, 'This was going to be a temporary arrangement anyway, nothing was supposed to get complicated.' Lois came close behind my mother and started picking glitter out of her hair. 'Life is complicated,' she said. 'Did something happen? Did Clem bother you again tonight?' "

"Who's Clem?" Rafi asked.

"I don't know. That was the only time I ever heard his name."

He gave me a look I knew from work. It was the this-story-better-have-a-payoff look.

"Okay." I talked faster. "My mother said, 'He scares me. I mean really scares me, but that's not saying much. Everyone scares me these days.' She was still rubbing her eyes. So, Lois moved even closer, right up against her back, and I could see the goose pimples on her legs. 'I just don't know what to do,' my mom said, and then said it again really distinctly. 'I just don't know what to do.'

" 'That's okay.' Lois took my mom's shoulders and turned her so they faced each other. 'I know exactly what to do.' She wrapped my mother in her arms and kissed her." I took a deep breath trying to imagine air all the way from Japan feeding my blood. Rafi was silent.

"And?" He finally said.

"And, that's all." I stood up, looking around the deserted beach. Neutral, the wind had stopped. A good place to die, I thought, and then began jumping up and down on the sand to keep from getting too morbid.

"And that's what you have never been telling?" Rafi watched me jump.

"Yup."

"Well, did you move?"

"Uh-huh, New Jersey. We ended up back in New York again though, but not with Lois."

Rafi took the gun out of the briefcase, and I stopped jumping. "To tell the honest truth, it doesn't seem such a secret. Perhaps being younger it seemed bigger."

Did he misunderstand? I wondered. Or maybe it's me. Maybe it's really no big deal.

"J.O., watch." From high in the air he dropped the gun squarely on the briefcase, thunk. "Do you know why I did that?" His accent seemed thicker. "To show you a revolver will never, ever fire accidentally. Automatics, yes. A revolver though is your friend. If you understand this friendship, it will not betray you." While talking he emptied the cylinder and reloaded, showing me how. Rafi's fingers knew about loading that gun the way you know the particular push and pull of your own house keys in the door.

I shoved cold hands back in his pockets and touched the metal thing I had felt before. A bullet, of course.

"All right." He held the gun toward me. A very gunnish gun, black with a long barrel. "This is a Smith & Wesson .357 magnum. I own quite a few firearms. This one I love. Now, I'm going to fire, then you will." With palms on knees he peered for a long time into the ocean. Empty. Then, standing very straight, Rafi fired six shots into the blackness. Bam, Bam, Bam, Bam, Bam, Bam. Perfectly spaced. He turned toward me and licked his lips.

"Listen, I read an article about one of the greatest mathematicians." Math? I thought.

"This man believes God has a book. In this book the math proofs, the theories, are all written Pure. We have math problems that are taking a hundred pages on computer, but in God's Book it's two lines. So, this guy has a saying when he sees good work. 'That's straight from The Book,' he says." Before reloading, Rafi spun the cylinder tic-tic-tic, almost a cat's purr.

"When I fire, it comes from here." He touched his stomach then flew arms outward toward the ocean. "You see? Up and out. Unbroken. When I fire, it is absolutely pure from my body to the gun and out. Straight from The Book. Do you understand?"

I nodded and smiled. "Sure."

"Good." He handed me the gun, heavier than I thought and warm. "Then shoot."

It was hard resisting the urge to drop it. I tried to squeeze the trigger like he taught me, but kept imagining a huge explosion, or worse, J.O. slips and blows off her foot. "I can't."

"Why?"

"I don't know. I'm just, I just don't know what to do." The gun was getting slick in my hands.

"Okay." Rafi moved close behind me. His fingers wrapped calloused warmth over mine, breath in my ear slow and deep. "Ready?" Spicy cologne with sweat just beneath.

He forced my fingers to pull the trigger six times. Bam! The power jumped our hands upward with every shot, a thrust you couldn't stop or control. Bam!

"So, did you like it?" Still close behind me.

"I don't know, my eyes were closed the whole time." I felt removed, buried with the bullets in the ocean.

"It's all right." He took my shoulders in his hands and turned me around. "It doesn't matter.

First he kissed my eyelids and then my mouth. It was a wonderful kiss, not removed, and I gave, feeling my lips relax against his. Rafi gathered my hair in one hand pulling just hard enough so all the roots of all the hairs tensed and sang against the scalp.

"So?" He cradled my face in his palms.

"So," I answered. "Straight from The Book."

Hugging me tight he laughed across the blackness all the way to Japan. We didn't say anything else till in the car when Rafi asked for his jacket. He sounded embarrassed, and I began to feel sick. The MG was coffin cramped and low. Too low. It made me edgy not seeing the road ahead. Silence. I stared at a scar on his hand, gleaming nasty white with Frankenstein stitches. How could I have missed that before? I wondered. He probably had a car accident the way he corners. No seat belts, I held on to the door handle.

"J.O., I'm not going to fire you if you promise to try harder at work."

"Okay." We zipped by a flashing billboard for The Hotel Monte Carlo, Luxury Nineteen-Dollar Rooms. What was that word my mother liked so much? *Ersatz.*

"But I think it's a good idea if we don't see each other this way anymore. Not prudent."

"You're right," I agreed. "I was just thinking the same thing."

"Nothing against you."

"Oh, no. Nothing against you either."

Rafi turned on the radio and squirmy violin music filled the car. Classical, you never knew what its intentions were. With a good rock song, I thought, you always knew where you stood. After a minute the music was over and they started fund-raising. Rafi changed stations. A girl group.

"What do you like? I don't follow this music. Who are these people?"

"The Pointer Sisters," I told him. A good song, the kind with flouncy harmonies you could fill in especially the do-do-do-do-do part. "Holdin' me close, but I just say no."

"The Pointer Sisters," he repeated.

"I say I don't like it, but you know I'm a lair, cuz when we kiss, ooohh fire."

Rafi suddenly stiffened in the seat. He flicked off the radio and pressed hard on the gas. "Wait a minute. Your mother is gay?"

Outside the ocean slipped from view, back on the regular freeway.

"A lesbian?" It sounded really loud the way he said it. "Now I see." He smiled enthusiastically as if just solving some complicated algebraic equation.

"Yeah, well, with Lois anyway. Later it was different." I stared out at the highway guardrail rushing by us dirty and blurred. Nervous, I didn't know what to say, couldn't explain my mother without going into all of it.

My father had been from L.A. originally and wanted to move back here most of the time he and my mom were together. She refused. "Miles left me for the sun," she'd say. "But I don't want to poison your mind against him, so let's drop the subject." Lois made her feel good, I knew that. She had a way of seeing exactly what my mother needed and giving it, little things like hollandaise.

So what's the point of meeting my father, I wondered. According to my mom the guy deserted his wife and newborn baby to go play beach blanket bingo. That was her side. I never heard his side though, he might've had a good reason for leaving.

A good reason, is there such a thing? As usual the more I thought about it the more I didn't want to.

The next night I arrived at work, hat ironed, bow in place. I told myself I wouldn't mix the specials up and spill food on people. Also, when they said "Waitress, I asked for sourdough," and I knew they hadn't, I would just apologize, and not get all flustered. It didn't happen though.

We were in the dinner rush, and I carried four coffees balanced risky up my arm. There was an old couple who kept asking which were decaf. I was hurrying, behind on orders, and dropped one on the table, one on the floor, one in the woman's lap, and one on my leg.

It burned right through the stocking and I just stood there, sucking in breath. Everyone stared.

"Oh my God." The woman got up. "Where's the manager?" Her flowered dress looked like it might be silk.

"No, please don't. I'll pay the cleaning bill. My name is J.O., I'll buy your dinner, here, let me try to wipe it off."

She pointed at the dress, irate daisies covered in brown coffee. "I want the manager."

The unemployment line would be long, I thought. And I'd still be on crutches, deep-tissue burn.

"Do you think that's really necessary, Lydia?" The husband stood too. "After all, she says she'll pay." He took his wife's elbow, and winking at me gently shoved her back into the seat.

"Thank you, thank you." I scribbled my name and address for them and ran to the bathroom.

No blister, just a red hurting. I threw my stockings in the trash and slipped bare feet back into The Sun Maiden shoes. Nurse's shoes. For a second I was a nurse, saving lives.

When we packed for the move to New Jersey my mother had sung old Beatles songs, grinning eagerly. Instead of writing what was in the boxes we drew pictures to fool each other. Eyeglasses for the box with drinking glasses. When we arrived she had pointed at the big box that had people sweating with planets and stars.

"Great," she said. "The space heater, let's take that out now."

"How did you guess?"

She laughed. "I know you, that's all."

"Oh." I laughed too, suddenly relieved. It was a warm and big relief, like coming home in winter, that first blast of house heat on your face.

In the office Rafi was doing paperwork, briefcase next to him on the desk. "Hi." His face went sweet for a second, then back to normal. "What can I do for you?"

I took a step toward him. "You can teach me how to shoot."

Rafi was quiet for a moment, hand on head, fingers drumming against the bald spot. "What happened to your stockings?" he finally asked.

"I spilled coffee on my leg."

"Oh." Fingers still drumming. "Can I have a look?"

I walked over, and Rafi put my foot in his lap. "We can go to the range. Tomorrow, are you free?" he asked bending his head to look at the burn, low near the ankle.

I nodded and then realized he couldn't see me. "Yes," I said. "Tomorrow would be fine."

Rafi bent even further till his lips rested very very lightly against the pink skin.

Chapter 5

2:45. I sat in my bedroom blowing panicky smoke rings out the window. Rafi would be here at 4:00. Maybe there was a special way people acted at a gun club, I thought, social codes I wouldn't understand. And what was our situation anyway, was this a date? I wished Samantha were home.

In the backyard Mr. Saul worked on The Car Of The Future. Welding. The frame was almost finished, "The bones," he had yelled at me passionately. "Frames are the skeleton of the car."

Mr. Saul welding was much worse than Mr. Saul sawing. Sawing belonged in the natural world, small children sawed every day. But welding was not natural. Science-fiction eye gear hid his face, and sparks—which Mr. Saul ignored—clustered yellow white around him. A couple of blowtorch burns, no problem. He reminded me of religious people I had learned about in twelfth-grade history, the ones who ripped at their own skin for spiritual reasons. Any minute, I thought, he'll weld himself ecstatically to the car by his belt buckle. I decided to take a walk to the bank.

The bank was one of my favorite places, and as usual when I got there, I glanced around the huge room for my father. There was no one who could've been him.

Standing in line was comfortable. I ran my fingers along the red velvet ropes used to keep the line organized. The ropes felt very soft. Behind me were two women in silky office clothes, their bright dresses glowing clean against the pearly bank carpeting. "We've decided to go with all original moldings," one of them was saying. "Sam wants to strip the paint and then . . ."

her voice trailed away as my turn came, and I walked up to Marilyn, my favorite teller.

"Heeey, whatsup?" Marilyn asked when I stood in front of her. I loved how she said it that way every time.

"Not much." I pointed to her stomach. "You're really starting to show now."

"Tell me about it, my whole body's getting bigger. You know what Joey says to me? He says: 'Honey, are you sure you're not having another baby out of your hips?' "

I had been there the first time Marilyn felt it move. She said, it's like you're taken over, never alone.

"Have you agreed on a name yet?" I handed over my deposit, thirty in checking, ten in savings.

Marilyn smiled, front teeth overlapping each other like crossed legs. "Nope. We just call it Acute baby." Her pink polished fingernails blurred as she counted the money, mostly singles.

"Acute baby?"

"Yeah, it's this joke we have where he puts his hands . . ." She blushed suddenly and changed the subject. "I saw your roommate on TV last night. How's she doing?"

"Fine." Acute baby, I thought, some kind of private thing they did together. Would I switch places with Marilyn right now? Would I right now? Does she get out of the car at night, walk to the door, and know she's home?

"So what's new with you?" she asked. Wham, wham, her stamp on my receipt made a good noise. A bank noise. "You look pretty, got a hot date later?"

"I'm not sure." I wondered if I should ask her whether the shooting range was considered a date.

"Well, watch out, there's a lot of weirdos around these days." Better not ask, I thought.

Marilyn fingered her necklace which was gold and spelled her name in fancy script. "Don't give away the goods too soon, see what I'm saying?"

Goods. The thought of him on the beach made a quick glittery feeling go through me, and I looked away certain it showed all over like red paint. "I'll be careful."

"Please, you never know." She handed me a bag from Mrs. Fields. "Do you want these cookies? There's two in there."

"Okay, thanks."

No one noticed me eat them in the far corner by the scale and the gumball machine. It was past 3:00, and Marilyn was taking care of the last few customers. The doors were locked. I could live here, I thought watching the sun on the floor, the way it patched yellow across the almost empty bank.

3:30. When I got home Samantha was in a bathrobe doing dishes, her arms completely wet, soapy puddles all over the floor. She liked to wash dishes the way other people wash a dog.

"You won't believe what happened," she yelled whirling away from the sink. Whenever there was news, good or bad, Samantha's face always had the same wild intensity. I was never sure what to do with my own face till I knew.

"First of all, what do you think?" Quickly stripping off the robe Samantha turned a circle in front of me with outstretched arms. "Do I look naughty?" She had on a lavender teddy, bare feet crammed into patent leather pumps.

"Very naughty." I tried to stay calm knowing Samantha would absolutely have to tell the entire story before she put any clothes on. Please, please, let it be short, I thought. Rafi was due in twenty-six minutes. I sat down at the kitchen table, chrome and glass, my legs beneath its surface looked distorted somehow. Thicker.

Samantha yanked at the crotch of the teddy which was too tight and spoke in a whisper. "Listen." Whenever something big happened she always whispered. "I got raped last night."

"What?" I jumped up and grabbed her bare shoulders. They felt warm, hot almost like the heat that comes off little kids when they've been playing. "Did you call the cops? Are you okay?"

"It wasn't that kind of rape. It was good."

"Oh." I took my hands off her shoulders and stuck them in my back pockets.

"You want a soda?" Samantha got two small bottles of Diet Coke from the refrigerator and put them on the table. They made a cracking sound, glass against glass.

"So what happened?" I asked a little confused. And tense. This wasn't going to be a short story, and out of all the things in the whole world I didn't need Rafi to see when he got here, Samantha prancing around in a teddy was probably number one. I pictured her saying, "Nice to meet you, Rafi. I was just telling J.O. about getting raped in a good way." Not out of the question.

"After the dinner and drinks," she said, "we went back to his place in Santa Monica. Nice, right on the beach. So anyhow, everything starts out normal, kiss, tongue. 'Oh Baby,' you get the picture. Then, all of a sudden he throws me on the bed, rips off my clothes, and makes me wear this."

The Samantha movie. Without wanting to I saw her shaky and pale while a man's fingers tore at her black dress. "Were you scared?"

She took a gulp of soda. "Sure, at first I was kicking and screaming, but then I don't know. Something clicked, and it was great." Another gulp. "J.O., let me tell you, we were out of control."

"Where'd you meet this guy anyhow?" Perverted scumbag, I thought, trying to put an image in my head. He would have a mean little beard and walls covered with African masks.

"On the set, but he's only there till Friday. The Rapist is a very talented actor/screenwriter," she continued, "and I think he's going out with me as a career move. Isn't that wonderful?" She jerked her arms wide spilling soda on the floor. "Power! Let me tell you I came three times all the way from my boots. Like an animal," she whispered.

I took out a cigarette and wondered about coming from your boots. It sounded vaguely illegal. Samantha had gotten me like always, even with Rafi here in twenty-five minutes I wanted to know the rest.

"Oooh, Oooh," she wiggled two fingers in the air till I put my cigarette between them. I watched as she lit it off the stove, graceful, eyebrows never burned. "So anyways, it was scary in the beginning, he's tearing off my dress and I'm thinking: 'Samantha, you're not in control here.' Control would have been a peck on the cheek and 'Good night, thanks for dinner.' Then he got to my underwear, that was the good part when I saw those lacy panties fly off the bed. Something just snapped. All of a sudden it was primal, I mean get me on all fours, baby, I'll bark at the moon."

"Samantha, come on." I turned my face away and stared at the kitchen radio. It was one of those prehistoric type of radios, large and brown. I wondered what song was playing right now.

"Maybe that's my true calling. Porn." Posing seductive against the refrigerator. "Samantha Sucks Santa Monica, hey baby, do you live by the ocean?" Voice throaty, moaning. "Oooh, I love those salt breezes against my naked, heaving flesh." Smoke came out of her mouth in a pant.

"Aren't you cold?" I asked hopefully looking at her bathrobe still on the floor. Twenty-four minutes.

"Nope, have some party eggs." She opened the refrigerator, fishing around with half her body in there. Was this something to be envied? I couldn't decide.

Samantha sat across from me. Behind her the wallpaper had millions of cozy blue flowers against a yellow background. Cozy flowers, background, glass table, red hair, teddy. I shut my eyes. When I opened them she had stuffed a refrigerated malted milk ball in each cheek. Party eggs. "So, do you think I'm sick?" she asked. "We did it again before breakfast."

I listened to her teeth crunch into malted milk. I stared at her face, freckles, eyes excessively blue. "These are so good." She rubbed chocolate off her teeth with one forefinger and licked it.

Yes, I thought. It is something to be envied. "I don't think you're sick, not at all."

"Really? The Rapist has plenty of friends. Remember, I told you about Jeremiah."

"Well, actually Rafi will be here in twenty-three minutes. We're going out."

"Rafi, The Israeli? That's great, I wish I could meet him, but I have to jump in the shower and then go audition for this play." She tossed a party egg high into the air catching it in her mouth.

"An audition?" I smiled, boneless relief. "Well, I hope you get it."

As she walked across the kitchen to the hall, Samantha squirmed off her teddy. "Your bow's next to the coffee maker. Thanks."

"No problem." Still smiling because I couldn't get over the incredible good luck of her not in a teddy, not even home when Rafi got here.

They missed each other by less than fifteen minutes. I wished I had more time to prepare—try on clothes, get rape out of my head—but there he was in our living room.

Except for the beach a couple of nights ago, Rafi was someone I had known only from work. Late-shift manager. Seeing him here at my apartment was disorienting in a good-bad way like when a whole bunch of people sing Happy Birthday at you.

Rafi quickly scanned all the high-fashion furniture that had pens and party eggs spilled across it. Then he walked over to two 8 × 10s hanging on the wall. Samantha's idea. One was her having a nervous breakdown in *Anaconda,* the play she did last year. The other was me looking as if I might have a nervous breakdown, standing frazzled in front of the same wall where the photograph was hung. In the background of my picture you could see Samantha's picture. Rafi squinted at her with the same expression she always got, a where-do-I-know-you-from? expression.

"Wednesday night, Channel Four," I explained. " 'You're Busted.' "

"This is your roommate? She is the one borrowing the bow?"

"Yes."

"Oh, okay, she's a good actress I think. Is she here?"

The way he worded it sounded like it was all right for a good actress to have borrowed the bow. "You just missed her," I said trying not to seem pleased.

We left. Walking over to his car Rafi pointed at my bright green Gremlin. "This is yours?"

I nodded.

"What is the situation here?" he asked touching the strips of gray tape that ran across the driver's door.

"That won't close, so I taped it and just use the other side."

Rafi studied the car for a long time. "Hmmmm," he mumbled. "Uh-huh." With palms on his knees he crouched thoughtfully and checked every angle. I wanted to go. The way he was dissecting the car seemed rude almost, like closely studying someone's birth defect. "Let me get this straight," I imagined him saying. "These dark red blotches actually cover half your body?"

We drove west past streets who spoke differently to me than the streets I was used to. Money sounds: Doheny, Alpine. A sign said, "The city of Beverly Hills is pleased to announce its official sisterhood to the city of Cannes." Rexford Drive, Canon Drive, Rodeo.

"Your car was in an accident," Rafi told me. "The body needs to be straightened then door will close."

Passing lots of huge office buildings and traffic now. Century City. At the end of it was a little residential stretch I had never noticed with sidewalk trees that looked comfortable against the sky. Here the street names reminded me of New England towns, Fairburne, Westholme. Westholme. Slam! For a second I couldn't breathe, and my whole body gave a little rabbity jerk like when you're about to fall asleep. My father lived on Westholme. I had known it was somewhere in this area, but never actually saw the street.

Rafi was talking about being in an airplane, but I couldn't listen. Scattered like shrapnel. On the flat space between our seats was a piece of paper with two phone numbers, and the name "Monk" written on it. I calculated, frantically adding and dividing all the digits in different combinations. Cruel seven, fat baby three. ". . . except for the time difference," Rafi said.

The Westside Gun Club. For hours I had been picturing possible gun club types, but I was wrong because the people in the gun club weren't any particular type at all. They were the same people I saw in the supermarket or at work.

"Hi, Rafi," a man behind the long counter said. He was good-looking in an average white-guy way, the kind of person who might get surveyed on the street. "Who's your friend?"

"This is J.O." Rafi told him. "J.O., this is Mark."

The door next to Mark opened and a guy walked into the room holding a big gun. "I need more ammo," he said. The guy had on a netted T-shirt, and I could see sweat on his chest. He grinned. "Hey Rafi, it's an EZ world."

All three of them cracked up laughing, and I just stood there. "Didn't Rafi tell you?" the netted guy asked me. "He used to think there was this one huge corporation in America called EZ, and that they practically ran the whole country. EZ repairs, EZ financing, EZ home improvement." The guy's voice was very loud. "Oh."

"Anyway, catch you later." He picked up the ammo and left.

These people walk around here with loaded guns, I thought. What if someone is having a really bad day?

Rafi said, "Can I get a .22 for J.O.? She should start little."

I shook my head. "Ummm, I'd like a .357. Please. If it's all right with you."

When I had fired Rafi's gun on the beach for a flash second I was tapped into the heart of something, something I didn't think a .22 could touch. Power, but not desperate like gang kids doing drive-bys. This was different. This was bigger and older than the gun itself, older even than numbers. And I wanted to press against that heartbeat. I wanted some hollow place to be filled, but it was all so scary.

Mark coughed, a cement-truck sound. He coughed again before I realized he was laughing. ".357, huh? Rafi, this lady doesn't waste time."

They chatted for a while in another language, gun talk. I looked around the room and everything seemed flattened out, colorless somehow. Cement floor, no windows. On the wall behind Mark was a framed black and white poster of a woman's body just from the neck to the thighs. She had on an extremely tight tank top, and was squeezing a gun, thick and pornographic, against her crotch. The caption said, "You can't rape a .38." Creepy, really creepy.

Mark handed me a .357, but as soon as I picked it up Rafi's sharp fingers dug into my arm. What is it, I wondered instantly overcharged and ready to dive to the floor.

"Always, J.O., always, make sure to check if gun is loaded."
Taking it from me, he opened the cylinder and peered into the
six empty holes.

Before going through the door we put on plastic ear protectors.
They made a faraway whooshing noise like between stations on a
radio dial. We went down a tight narrow hallway with reddish
walls, so tight that Rafi needed to walk behind me. At the end
was another door which was very hard to open, and I had to push
all my weight against it before finally bursting into the range
itself. Cold. Hospital bright. I took shivery air into my lungs,
realizing I'd been holding my breath.

Inside were about ten little booths, but the only other person
there was the netted guy who fired shots sweaty and grim.

Rafi helped me set up a target, and my whole body got goose
bumps from the cold air as I tried to aim. Unusually strong
goose bumps. I thought of Foxtrot, who used to say, "J.O., those
goose bumps of yours would go through steel retaining walls." It
was embarrassing. When I finally shot the first round I missed
the target entirely.

"You anticipate," Rafi said, his body warm next to me. "Try
again."

I shot some more thinking of Bic lighters when I was a kid.
Me and Lois's son Zeke alone in the house, we'd put the top part
of a Bic in our mouths and press the button spilling out butane
for about a minute. Then we'd hold the light to each other's
faces, flick it, and blow. The flame would shoot over a foot high.
Almost an explosion. I could remember exactly that rush moment
of light, knowing for sure this time I'd lose my face. And when
I didn't, I'd want that moment again. Firing this gun now, my
hands shaky as I dumped out used casings, felt just like that.

Soon my fingers were covered with smudges, and sore from the
recoil. My ears hurt also, since even with the muff things, it was
very loud.

"If you at least agree for trying a .22," Rafi told me, "it will
make your aim better. This gun is too much."

"I'll exercise my arms," I said, and reloaded.

Rafi smiled. "Well, keep practicing, I shoot over here." He walked to the next booth, moving easy. Well oiled, I thought.

The range was empty now except for the two of us. I tried to imagine The Book, and just fire not thinking about it. So far only one of my bullets had gone anywhere near the middle of the target.

Bam! Rafi's shots had perfect authority with each one timed a second apart and all six landing dead center.

"Yours even sound better," I said.

He laughed. "I have idea."

After that, every time I shot, Rafi followed an instant later which forced me into a rhythm. Him, me, him, it snapped through my body so personally I wanted to close my eyes. We did it that way for a long time.

For a while driving home the world seemed different, opened out somehow. I imagined I could look at a plate of french fries and see perfectly clear all the way to Idaho.

"You liked shooting?" Rafi asked.

"Uh-huh. I'm going to get very good at it."

He glanced at me strangely and then began to laugh. "Yes, you will, J.O. You should see your face."

When we were almost to my house Rafi stopped at a hardware store, and asked me to wait in the car. In a minute he came out with a paper bag that he laid in my lap.

"Here, I bought a surprise present for you. It'll be fun."

Inside the bag was a long piece of chain, heavy linked and cold against my thighs. Chain? Fun? What kind of surprise present is that, I wondered. I tried not to look at it or imagine me hung porno from the ceiling while his shooting buddies argued over who went first. Maybe every single guy in the world except Foxtrot is like Samantha's Rapist, I thought, and somehow I don't know about it.

We parked beside my driveway and got out of the car. "Okay," Rafi said opening the bag. "Here is my idea. With these hooks we wrap one end of chain around that lamppost, and the other to your Gremlin back bumper, then—"

"Wait a minute. The chain is for my car."

"Yeah?" Rafi looked at me.

"Oh. Thank you."

"Good. Anyway, I think we can straighten body and then your door will close. All right?"

I nodded, half relieved half cautious because this was bone surgery happening on my only car. Cars, I thought of Mr. Saul, and how you could usually hear his welding torch hissing nasty all the way from the street. It was quiet now, he must've been taking a break.

Rafi maneuvered the Gremlin till it was just in front of a lamppost, then carefully hooked up its bumper. "Okay," he said. "Now, I'll stand here while you drive forward."

I got in the car and lightly touched the gas feeling all six cylinders work against the chain. I wondered how much force it took to pull over a lamppost.

"Stop," he said.

Getting out I looked at my back fender which bulged a little, like the swollen part around a cut. "Are you sure this is a good idea?"

"Yes, I promise. Let's try again." He rehooked the chain to the actual body of the car, underneath the bumper where it was secure.

Eighth-grade science my teacher had said, "Pretend there's a rock. This rock will not be crushed no matter what you do. Now pretend there's walls closing in around it, and these walls will not be stopped. What happens when the walls reach the rock?"

This time when I began driving, Rafi yelled, "Gas, put more gas."

I hit the petal and faint popping noises began all around me.

"There would be an explosion," the teacher had said. "The whole thing would blow up."

"Harder," Rafi's voice was excited. "It's working."

Just then Mr. Saul appeared out of nowhere with his flaming welding torch gripped in both hands. There was a long hose attached. "Don't move! Don't breathe even." He stepped toward Rafi, gassing the flame higher which made it turn bright blue. "We had an agreement. On the phone you promised another ten days." His face and frizzy hair were completely soaked in sweat.

I jumped out of the car yelling. "Stop! It's okay, this is my friend and we're just fixing a door."

"J.O.? Ah, Young Lady, I'm so sorry, you gave me such a scare." Mr. Saul's welding mask was up over his forehead like the beak of some giant bird. Woodpecker car, woodpecker man, I thought. Under the beak I could see his features twitch in the aftermath of fear. It made me wonder if my own face was jumping around also.

"Who's this?" Rafi asked. He hadn't taken his eyes from the flame.

Mr. Saul noticed, and quickly turned the torch off laying it on the ground next to him. "I own this building, and believed perhaps you might be someone else. Again, I apologize to both of you. Unexpected noise often makes me a little nervous."

That's great, I wanted to tell him, but just one question. If "a little nervous" means you almost take Rafi's head off with a blowtorch, then what happens when you get "very nervous"?

"I'm Jonas Saul." He held out his hand.

"Rafi Oded." They shook.

Hearing full names made them both feel like strangers for a second, Oded, Jonas, who were these people?

"Are you treating J.O. properly?" Mr. Saul asked. "She works so very hard you know, and I must say it's good to see her finally with a boyfriend."

I stared at the sky thinking, this is it. It doesn't get more embarrassing than this.

"So, you are repairing a car. Detroit is unimportant, Los Angeles is the city of the automobile. I am currently building one that I call The Car Of The Future because it will change the world's ideas about driving and about what a well-constructed machine really is."

"Oh," said Rafi.

"Are you Israeli? Rafi is an Israeli name."

"Yes." He bent down and began fooling with the hook under my bumper.

I wished Mr. Saul would leave. He had really gone too far this time, and soon an authority might need to be called, though I had no idea how to handle it. There should be a commercial: Dial 1–800–BAD–SAUL.

But instead of leaving he began to talk in another language, Hebrew I guessed, and Rafi straightened up lighting a cigarette. Not fair, I thought. First Andy and Lily formed some deep personal connection, and now these two were having a party. I got in my car deciding Rafi would never meet Samantha. Never.

They talked for about ten minutes with the language around us like moving boulders. Rafi seemed different in Hebrew, leaner, more intense. He asked a sharp question to Mr. Saul while turning his fingers in a circular gesture I'd never seen him use. Mr. Saul didn't answer, and he asked again, demanding.

"They are full of phony baloney," Mr. Saul said. More Hebrew, more questions and answers. What is this about, I wondered.

In my car there was an old tennis ball sitting on the floor. Sometimes when I stopped short they'd roll from under the seats, tennis balls out of nowhere. I put the one in the glove compartment. Just outside, the welding torch lay facing me, and I stared at it trying to remember if my car was still chained to the lamppost.

The second Mr. Saul finally left, Rafi bent down next to my open window. "I'm sorry about that, now let's finish your door, okay?"

"What were you guys saying?"

"Not much." He smiled at me. "Stay there, I'll tell you when to drive."

"Wait a minute, what were all your questions?"

"Questions?" Rafi wiped his mouth with the back of his hand. "I'm not sure what you mean."

I looked into his eyes, the tiny black spot like a third pupil. I remembered the syncopated feeling when we fired today, the surprise present. "Forget it," I said. "Let's fix this door."

This time as soon as I started to drive there were loud popping sounds. Go, I thought and hit the gas. Hard. It didn't explode like the rock and the walls because deeply rooted metal began to move and the car actually changed shape around me. I saw the alignment shift. I saw the door slide in its frame.

Rafi yelled, "Okay, stop." He stripped the tape off the side, then opened and closed my door a few times. It worked.

"I can't believe this." I jumped out of the car slamming the door behind me. Thunk. "Listen to that, isn't it great? Thank you."

"I think I am deserving a kiss, what is your opinion?"

"Yes."

His lips were the best lips I'd ever felt, the way they moved just a little to fit soft against mine.

It was different, though, with him in my bed that night. We took off our clothes and I panicked wondering what he was thinking, and if the sheets were clean, and when Samantha was coming home. Curled naked under the blanket, I decided Marilyn had been right to warn me about giving away the goods. Too soon. My skin was covered with rough goose pimples, teeth actually chattering as Rafi laid his whole hand flat between my breasts. I pulled away embarrassed that a guy could fit his entire palm there.

"Do you have a radio?"

"On the desk."

Rafi got up and turned on classical music. In the half darkness I watched the solid line of his legs, shorter than I'd expected and moving easy across the room. Rooted. He had a large white scar that tracked along one rib all the way around to his back. This is nuts, I thought, what am I doing?

In bed again now, with floaty piano music behind him. "Are you okay?"

"Yeah, just cold." My voice sounded extremely nasal. Of course. Why nasal, I wondered, why couldn't something attractive happen when I got nervous.

Rafi wrapped himself close around me, soft chest hair, heartbeat. I could feel his body the way the sun feels when you get out of cold water. "Hey," he rubbed my arms. "It's all right, it's only me."

"I've never been with someone in an actual bed before," I whispered.

Rafi smiled against my neck, whispering back, "Actual bed is a good place."

Then we were doing it. I had been scared that sex was like some foreign language you'd completely forget without practice. Wrong. I stroked his back feeling the electric life, the secret messages in his spine hard against my fingers. Our bodies rocked. Rafi put his weight up on his palms and looked right into my eyes. Didn't look away.

He's *seeing* me, I thought getting edgy again. He's seeing straight to the marrow and past the marrow. No one had ever done that, and it felt terrifying. My hands went numb as I imagined all the blood rushing to protect major organs like when people get in terrible accidents. No matter what happens, I realized, this guy sees exactly who I am. What's wrong with just fucking?

I began to recite a list of things he didn't know about me, social security number, shoe size, the way caramel always made my mouth itch.

"Here," Rafi whispered.

He was smiling with a face so tender it somehow punched right through my fear like a can opener on a vacuum-packed can. I could almost feel the hiss. Here. Only him, only me. I touched his cheek, his neck, and finally, for the first time in my life, all the words in my brain were silent.

Lying there cozy afterward, Rafi told me stories about himself. "On the roof my first girlfriend and me would watch the sun set in Jerusalem. It is famous how the whole city is looking like it's made from gold."

"Did you go out with a lot of women?" I asked.

"None as pretty as you."

"Oh. Well." For some reason if people said I was pretty it hurt a little, but in a strangely satisfying way like poking a canker sore with your tongue.

"What? You're very pretty."

"Thanks."

He must've seen something because Rafi rolled on top of me and pinned my arms over my head. "I know how to torture J.O. now. Pretty, pretty, pretty." He kissed my face between each word.

"Let me go," I said laughing. "Do you want a cigarette?" I got up slowly and walked over to my purse.

"Do you feel safe here?" he asked.

The question was so unexpected for a second I thought it was in my head. "Safe with you?" I lit both our cigarettes. "This makes me feel macho."

"Do you observe people outside? Men?"

"What men?" Then I remembered the fleshy-faced blond guy sort of bullying around in his convertible. "What's going on?" It was getting cold there in the middle of the room, but suddenly I didn't want to move.

"Your landlord, Mr. Saul. It costs so much money for building car like this, and he was short fifteen grand. That's it. Come on girl, come back to bed."

There was a sound in his voice I didn't like, a "here kitty-kitty" sound. "Don't call me girl, I'm not girl." Outside my window the backyard lights glinted mean white on Mr. Saul's fence which had barbed wire along the top. I should've realized earlier. Stupid. "So, he stole fifteen thousand dollars. Why did he talk to you about it?"

"He didn't steal, he borrowed. And these guys are potently nasty."

"You mean potentially," I said and began blowing smoke rings I could barely see.

Rafi cleared his throat. "No, I meant potently, can I have my cigarette, please?"

I walked over and handed it to him, half gone now. "Well, why didn't you tell me this before?" Even though I'd just said it the words felt worn out in my mouth.

"I was confused and wanted to wait for right timing. Saul asked me to keep this a secret from you because he doesn't want you to worry, and I told him 'okay.' But that's wrong. J.O., I knew this man had trouble the instant I saw his face. Saul is very frightened and is breaking as soon as you question him."

I sat on the edge of the bed and looked at Rafi who had his back propped against the wall. "Well, thanks for lying when I asked you about it before." My voice came out bitchier than I'd meant. So what? How could I be sure he'd told me all of it, or that stuff like this wouldn't happen again.

"J.O., please listen. In life I am trying hard to do right things. It means a lot to me. The whole reason I pushed Saul into telling this was because of my own worry about you. I see a man scared in his own building, the same building where you live, so I am wanting to know what's wrong. And if you should be scared too."

His face still had a little of the big-eyed intimacy leftover from sex, and I could see how important to him it was that I believed. That I understood.

"Forget it." I climbed back in bed and put my arms around him saying, "Forget it," a couple more times. All gone. There was no tumor, I thought, just a dust spot on the X ray, a car backfiring, it's only a movie.

We lay there easy together as Rafi told the story. Mr. Saul had borrowed fifteen thousand dollars, but couldn't pay it back on time. Two days ago the guys—not Mafia, he'd met them by placing a newspaper ad—gave him another month. That's all, they said. Meanwhile the engine had barely been started, and Mr. Saul was convinced if they didn't get their money in thirty days they would do something awful to the car.

"And what do you think?" I asked.

He sighed and wrapped my legs tightly in his. "I think these men don't care for Saul's car, when they are wanting money they'll work on people."

After a while Rafi fell asleep sprawling out warm and loose as if he'd been sleeping here for years. For me it was different. Restless. His breath sounded very loud, and since I was next to the wall I couldn't do my usual position of one arm hung off the edge of the bed.

An hour later I was still completely awake. This is ridiculous, I thought, maybe I should go outside for some air. What about Rafi? Was it rude to just leave a person in your bed? I decided no, not if the person was sleeping. A few minutes later I stood up, put on my bathrobe, and went outside.

The air was extremely June, cool and safe against my face the way a mother's hand feels checking for fever. Everyone says you can't tell when the seasons change in L.A., but they're wrong. Only June air felt that way.

I sat on the hood of my car wishing Samantha would come home. "Why are you outside in your bathrobe?" she'd ask.

And I'd smile at her oh so casually. "I just got laid, but I must've worn him out, he's sleeping. You want to go for a burger?" Then I'd pull a cigarette from my pocket and rip the filter off before lighting it.

She didn't come home though, and I realized that being out here hadn't done much good. I was still completely restless. Finally, I got in my car and started to drive, the gas pedal gritty under my bare foot. Something about driving with just a bathrobe on felt illegal in a silly way, like sneaking grapefruits across the California border.

I pretended to myself it was random going west on Santa Monica. No radio: omens would come later. Passing through Century City at night, the office buildings glittered down at me, huge and deadpan. Beverly Glen, Fairburne. I pictured Rafi asleep in my bed with the blanket kicked around his feet. Or maybe he was awake now, and didn't know where I was, maybe Samantha had brought The Rapist home and surprised him. I almost turned back, but there was Westholme. I made a left and drove slowly down the block till I saw my father's address.

After parking across the street I took a long look at his house which was gray with pointed peaks that seemed spooky but still inviting somehow. The flower garden in front. Basketball hoop attached to the garage. The streetlights felt like moonlight around me, and I thought, my father lives here. This is his house.

I wondered if I was supposed to cry or have some revelation. There wasn't a revelation. All I felt was lonely and glad no one else was nearby because this should only happen in private. Time for an omen. I turned on my radio thinking, please let it not be some stupid tire commercial.

The Doors were singing "Wild Child" a great song because of the ending. I loved The Doors, loved Jim Morrison, but knew it was vaguely uncool, like loving Fleetwood Mac or Diana Ross. I was too young to remember Morrison being alive, so the last line of this song fed into my private hope. Secretly, I was one of those crazy people who believed he'd faked his death. Hid out in Africa like he'd said he would.

I always imagined him in some distant jungle his skin gone almost as brown as the skin of the African woman he lived with. At night he'd sing to her.

My father's roof was light gray. Someone took a lot of time with that roof, I thought. Someone was cramped on a ladder for hours carefully painting the bottom part where it overlapped the house. That picture made me lonelier than all the rest of it put together. I turned up the volume for the last line, and then said it out loud with Morrison trying to match the stone old sound in his voice. "Remember when we were in Africa."

Part Two

JULY

Rafi

Chapter 6

Rafi stood at the phone by the register calling in tomorrow's meat order. He liked the mystery of the meat company. "I talk to their machine," he told me once, "and next day, Bam, the meat is here. A year now, and I have never once been talking to an actual voice. They could be Martians."

At The Sun Maiden no one, not even Andy, knew Rafi and me were together. "Not professional," he had said. Sometimes after closing the three of us played Liar's Poker in the empty restaurant. The chairs would be up on tables, desserts gone from the display cases, and I'd sit there feeling the real room. Not for customers, this was a restaurant only for us.

Tonight had been great, July Fourth, and I'd never seen the place so busy. People had waited a long time for food, but they still tipped better than usual, pressing greasy five- and ten-dollar bills into my hand. That wasn't the best though. The best was that somehow I'd managed to turn each of my tables at least five times. Amazing. Yeah, there were a lot of mistakes, but almost everyone had made mistakes tonight.

Andy was sprawled lengthwise down the countertop eating a cookie that was supposed to look like George Washington's face. "Liar's Poker," he said. "Kiss those dollars good-bye, Babe, you're finished in this town."

"Don't count on it." I closed my eyes for a second and heard buzzing from one of the coolers. You only noticed it when the place was quiet, a good buzzing. A secret buzzing.

Opening my eyes I saw Rafi walk toward us, the way his feet turned out just a little, one hand half in his pocket. It wasn't an obvious walk, nothing you could imitate, but I'd recognize it from a million. Rafi slid onto the stool next to me and began going through his pocket for dollars. The dark sweat spot under the arm of his button-down made me smile. We'd probably take a shower later.

The first bid was mine, and I opened with "Three twos," even though I had none at all. Sometimes it was good to start with a total bluff.

"Five twos," Andy told us. That meant he had a pair, or possibly three, and was relying on my bill and Rafi's to make up the rest.

Rafi said, "Five threes," and I just grinned feeling a perfect kind of whoosh go through me like an oven when you light it. The numbers. No one had those threes.

"Show them." Sure enough, the threes weren't real, and I said, "Thank you, Gentlemen," making a big production of sweeping up the dollars.

Rafi lit a cigarette. I could tell it secretly drove him crazy that I won Liar's Poker so much. Sometimes at unexpected moments like in a movie theater, or at a red light, he'd suddenly pull out a bunch of bills. "Now, J.O., let's play." I loved it.

We had just started another game when two people knocked on the front door, a short man and a tall woman.

"Sorry, we're closed," I yelled pointing at the clock.

The man moved right up to the glass, yelling something back in Hebrew. That loose rattly sound.

Rafi laid his dollar on the counter, then went quickly to the door and unlocked it.

"Come on, it's your turn," Andy told me.

"Wait. Do you know them?"

"Nope."

As soon as they were inside the man started talking hysterically at Rafi, with wild arm gestures that almost bopped the woman every few seconds. She didn't flinch. Rafi didn't either, he just listened, nodding, his expression too tight. I wished they'd speak English. In Hebrew there was only one sentence I could understand, "Give me please the big shoes." Completely useless.

The man seemed about forty-five, sad-eyed and sloppy in an old cowboy shirt. He was the kind of guy who owned a store specializing in some rare item very few people wanted.

But the woman was not the same, waiting there calm in her high-heeled boots. Her mouth was covered with so much thick, red, glossy lipstick that it looked like a sculpture completely unrelated to the rest of her body. This woman's store would sell only patent leather and chocolate, I thought. I watched her take in our private restaurant, wet floor, Andy and me sweaty in our uniforms.

"Let's leave soon," he said.

I always drove Andy home before going to Rafi's. "Yeah, one minute."

The hysterical man was nodding to the woman now, "Okay, we wait in car," he said, heavy accent.

Rafi opened the door and relocked it when they were outside. "I have to go." He walked toward us, fast. "They were not expected, J.O., can you come with me to the office."

Even though I knew it was all right I still felt edgy for a second. Superstitious. Nothing fun had ever happened to me in The Sun Maiden office, no midnight skinny-dipping parties there, no games with pink hula hoops.

Rafi sat in the swivel chair and crossed his feet in front of him while I leaned against the wall. The room was so tiny that even the adding machine took up too much space.

"It's not a big deal," he said putting a piece of candy in his mouth. I could smell it, watermelon flavored. "This man, he is my cousin from Israel, and he was staying with friends, but things became bad with them. Tonight he stays with me. I'm sorry, but it's better you don't come over. Tomorrow we can still shoot."

A cousin. Every time I learned new facts about Rafi a little bell would go off in my head, slam dunk. Getting facts felt important, needed, like items on a scavenger hunt. "Who's the woman?" I asked.

"His wife, she stays with me too."

"They're married?" The people had seemed completely unconnected, I couldn't even picture them eating a meal together.

"Of course, why?"

"They just didn't seem married to me."

"Well, they are." His voice was too quick, almost nasty, arms folded tight across his chest. "That's it."

Maybe I insulted him, I thought. Maybe there's a Middle Eastern thing about cousins that I hadn't realized. "No offense."

"Forget it," he shook his head slightly. "I'm sorry for this rudeness." Rafi stood up and hugged me, fingers sweet on the back of my neck. "You'll come over tomorrow?"

"Yup." Our bodies pressing closer, familiar now they found their places with a liquid click. "I can feel you," I said sleazy dramatic. "Oh yes, I feel your saber of love."

Rafi laughed for a long time repeating, "Saber of love, saber of love." Toward the back of his mouth he had a gold crown which you could only see when he was really laughing. I always watched for the one glinty tooth because gold like that is a precious thing.

Outside, Andy was waiting for me on the hood of my car. "J.O., I forget how he was schooled," he said as soon as I came over. "What was he schooled with?"

I thought for a minute. "He?" "School?" Oh, it was probably a line from a song Andy was trying to remember. "I don't know what he was schooled with, you have to give me more."

Andy didn't answer. He had started wearing his brown hair parted on the side so that a big chunk of it fell across his forehead and eyes. The hair looked much healthier than a month ago, except now, especially in profile, you couldn't really see his face.

We drove east on Sunset past heavy-metal clubs that were packed, even outside, with this type of L.A. groovy person I never understood. They weren't film-deal groovy, and they weren't secret-groovy in rock clubs with unmarked doorways. These people were right out in the open showing a lot of skin, black spandex, and leather. The marquees all advertised bands whose names I thought were a little embarrassing. Whack the Weasel. It was strange, but I had never seen any of them except on Sunset Boulevard at night.

"Who are these people?" I asked Andy. "Do they have jobs? I never see them in the day."

"I used to answer phones for a janitorial supply company," he told me. "I'll bet they do stuff like that, some job where you're not seen."

I stopped the car to avoid hitting a woman who was standing in the middle of traffic, no problem. Instead of a shirt all she had on was a wide pair of suspenders. "I'll tell you right now, I'm not going if Fuckbag is there," she yelled to her friend on the sidewalk.

"Would you want her answering your phone?" I asked, "I don't know if she'd take a message. What if Fuckbag called?"

Andy laughed.

I turned left on La Brea enjoying the bubbly noise my power steering made.

"J.O., I have a question to ask you, a favor actually a pretty big favor." He paused. "Can you loan me fifty dollars?"

"That's a lot of money," I said remembering what my mother used to tell me. "Never give, or even lend things you can't afford to lose."

"I know. It's not for me, I need it for someone else."

We were in front of his building now, old luxury gone slum. I always felt a little guilty leaving him here, a building so bad that pizza places wouldn't deliver to it.

"So, how about it?" He stuck both feet up on the dashboard. "Will you be my hero?" Andy turned his head toward me, one eye showing, the other covered by hair. He had a little smile on his face that was somehow the opposite of a smile, though I couldn't pinpoint exactly what or where the difference was.

"Who's the money for?" I asked imagining desperate situations. Someone with a drug habit, maybe a girl, who was also pregnant and trying to sneak across the border.

Andy moved one foot so it dangled out the window. "I got a letter from my brother, and he wants a hundred dollars."

"You have a brother?"

"Yup. He lives in Oregon."

I wondered why he never mentioned him, all my life I'd wished for a big sister to idolize. That was impossible, but there could easily be a little sister in L.A. right now. Not as fun to imagine. "Thank you so much, Dad," she'd say and grin as he gave her the car keys for a sixteenth-birthday present. "I promise to always wear a seat belt."

My fucking car doesn't even have seat belts, I thought. Nope, no seat belts here. It had been a whole month since that night in front of my dad's house, and I had done nothing further to contact him. I felt embarrassed even thinking about it.

"Snap, hummmm," Andy told me. "That's my brother, you can't describe him in a picture. You can't say, 'Carey looks just like so and so,' for instance. He doesn't look like so and so. Buzz, Fritz, that's the way he is, that's what his name should be, not Carey. Fritzzzzz. Know what I mean? I bet you know what I mean. Anyhow, I'll pay you back, J.O. You can take it out of my tips."

I heard firecrackers that sounded like slaps from far away. "Doesn't he work?"

"He paints."

"Houses?" I resisted the urge to push Andy's hair off his eyes.

"Hee-Hee, no, angels. Carey had a little mental shakedown in college and now only paints angels. He used to paint other stuff though. I don't see them, the angels I mean, he sees them, but I never do." All the blood slowly went out of Andy's face as he hung his head upside down over the seat back.

"What happened in college?"

Andy's chin was pointed straight toward the roof, and moved sort of skittishly as he spoke. "It's the story before that counts, incidents and accidents. Carey's incident changed stuff, but if it hadn't have been that it would have been something else. Anyhow, do you think you can help?"

He's a good friend, I thought, at least as good as Samantha, and he asks a lot less. "Okay." I opened my wallet and quickly counted out the money—a twenty, four fives, and ten singles. "So you'll pay me back soon, right?"

"Absolutely, no problem. I really appreciate this, really really, what would I do without you? I mean that, I don't know what I'd do."

"Oh, come on." I pulled both feet up close to my body, knees against the steering wheel.

"Well, thanks again, J.O." Shy voice almost whispered. "See you." Andy was out of the car and halfway to his building before I could even say good night.

Now came the part I didn't like. There was a stone lion on either side of his door, both of them missing pieces and covered with graffiti. Every single time he went inside Andy would stroke first one then the other on their battered heads, pausing a second to really get into it. And as usual I watched him with a tiny sick taste in my mouth because those lions felt extremely unlucky. Ruined. What did they guard?

"Andy."

He turned, fingers still resting on the mane of the right-side lion. "Yeah?"

I didn't know what I wanted to say, and just sat there, blank, till all of a sudden the words he had needed earlier slipped into my mind totally clear. "Jumpin' Jack Flash." "I was schooled with a strap right across my back," I said, voice filled with so much relief it surprised me.

Andy started whooping around his front door. "That's it, you got it, I wish I had something festive like Hawaiian clothes or a rare cactus. I'd hand it over to you right now."

He ran to my open window, and gave me a dry kiss on the cheek, a hard kiss, so I felt its impact even after pulling away.

Chapter 7

Before going home that night I took a short drive through the hills above Hollywood. No traffic, every house was dark. With the car in neutral I coasted down switchback coyote roads, brights on, my whole body alive and focused on the Gremlin. It knocked, it squeaked on tires skin smooth.

A long way below all the lights of the city unrolled themselves as far as I could see, and I turned on the radio hoping for the perfect omen. Commercials, commercials, then the Mexican station. It was some kind of ballad, *"Yo quiero poco más."* *Yo quiero*, I want, and *más* was more, but what about *poco*? Chicken. I want more chicken? No, that couldn't be right. Did it mean something extra if the omen came through in another language?

I lit a cigarette and headed home wondering about Carey and if Rafi gave up his bed for the cousin and his wife.

Chapter 8

Going through my front door I realized tomorrow was the fifth already and we still hadn't paid July's rent to Mr. Saul. He seemed crazier every day. If my mother were here she'd tell me, "That man is getting sucked right into the swirling, black vortex." My mom liked vortexes. I didn't like vortexes and had begun to feel very sorry for Mr. Saul.

In the kitchen Samantha lay on the floor wearing a shiny black bodysuit with greenish bones painted on it. They looked like they might glow in the dark.

"Hi, why are you wearing a skeleton suit? Is that for your play?" Samantha did a play every summer.

"I don't want to go into it," she said, testy. "So, how are you? How's The Israeli?"

"Fine." I sat down at the table. Lately she'd been talking a lot about wanting to meet Rafi, and it made me edgy. Men always loved Samantha. All men. All the time. "His cousin's in town." My voice sounded like that was dark personal information only I should know.

Samantha got up and began stretching, one bare foot in front of me on the glass tabletop. "So, when do I finally get to meet this guy?" Through the tight legs of the suit I could see her runner's muscles. They looked sexy.

When you become a lesbian dwarf, I wanted to say, but instead I shrugged. "How's The Rapist?"

Samantha stopped in midstretch. "He's not The Rapist anymore, things have changed. It's much stronger now."

79

What's stronger than rape, I wondered staring at her painted-on ribs. Devil worship?

"Last night was intense, he told me how old he was, and with older people that's a big deal. An act of trust." Her voice dropped to a loud whisper. "He's forty-two, J.O., I'm involved with a guy who might remember the Second World War."

I laughed. "Did you say that?"

"Of course not." She laughed too, thick and bluesy, I loved that sound. "Anyway he's no longer The Rapist. He is now The Legend. So, why don't the four of us go out this weekend, it would be fun."

"You mean with Rafi?" I pictured Samantha laughing, touching Rafi's arm, while The Legend and I discussed legendary things. Normandy. "When are you going to tell me about that skeleton suit?" I asked.

Out of nowhere Samantha slammed her fist into the side of the refrigerator making me flinch. "Fuck the suit. Fuck the whole stupid play." Her face was in profile, and I thought she must really be feeling bad. Samantha hated her profile, guarded it like some terrible secret. "Oh God, J.O."

I waited to hear the story, part of me glad to have distracted her from Rafi, part of me guilty for being so manipulative.

"I think I'm shallow." No more profile, she was facing me now. Making movies. "I have the lead in this play, right? It's kind of experimental, but there's, you know, a story." I watched her pace the kitchen, her leotard flashy black, wrong against the yellow linoleum. "So, today in rehearsal the director suddenly decides I should be wearing this skeleton suit for the entire first act, and everyone thought that was brilliant. Fuckin' deep, you know? It's supposed to be some kind of symbol, but I don't understand. I'm the only one who doesn't understand why I'm wearing a skeleton suit."

"You didn't ask?"

She stopped short and glared at me. "Are you crazy? You never *ask*, you're just supposed to *know*. Anyway, I refuse to take it off till I understand why it's on in the first place. The problem is I'm unbelievably shallow."

"You make that sound like a bad thing," I said trying to joke with her. Not a chance.

"J.O., if I wasn't unbelievably shallow I'd know why I had on a skeleton suit. My life would be different. Okay, stop, stop, I'm miserable." She sat down and began rolling her shoulders like a prizefighter. "So, are we on for Saturday night?"

Even though I knew I asked, "What's Saturday?"

"You, me, The Legend, and The Israeli. Are we going out?"

"Well, maybe. I might have to work."

"You act like you don't want me to meet him."

My purse sat on the table, and I stared at it wondering why things always looked so clumsy next to glass. "It's not that."

"Then what is it?"

I thought about how sometimes in bed Rafi would take my cold feet and press them against his stomach. "Come here, feet," he'd say. "Little feet." Letting him get hot for Samantha was out of the question. I'd lay my dead body between them first.

"What's the problem?" Her voice was hardfisted, heavy. A cinder block voice.

"I know why you're wearing that skeleton suit." My own voice sounded desperate, but she didn't notice.

"What? Why? Tell me."

I slowly pushed my chair back, and got up stalling for time. What were skeletons? Death. "It's death," I said.

"It is?" Leaning toward me, her face wide open waiting for my next words. "Actual death? But my character doesn't die. Tell me."

"It's not an actual death." I paused, trying to think what other kinds of death there were. "It's emotional, see? Your character goes through a big change emotionally, a kind of death, and this is to let the audience know. It's foreshadow, get what I mean?" I hoped that was right since I hadn't even read the play.

"That's exactly it, you are incredible."

I smiled realizing she had new respect for me, respect that poured warm and smooth across my skin.

Someone knocked at the back door. I glanced at my watch, one-fifteen.

"Who's there?" Samantha asked.

"Hello, I wouldn't have bothered you this late, but I saw lights on." It was Mr. Saul. "Tomorrow is July fifth."

Immediately Samantha threw open the door and stood there dramatic, one hand on her hip.

"Hello, Samantha, once again I'm sorry to bother you." He didn't even blink at the skeleton suit, just went right by her into our kitchen. Maybe it's nothing special to him, I thought, maybe inside the swirling, black vortex everyone wore skeleton suits.

"You want to know why I have this on?" Samantha sat at the table carefully crossing her legs. "It's for a play. My character goes through this huge emotional death, and . . ." She talked more about symbolism and theater till I knew by tomorrow she'd think the idea had been her own. Shallowness forgotten. I wondered why I didn't care, why I loved her so much.

We wrote the rent check while Mr. Saul looked around a little greedily at our kitchen life. Sink full of dishes, Samantha's rotten potato she was trying to grow into a plant.

"It's quite nice here. I am never in my own kitchen because the car keeps me so busy, it is now three-quarters finished, however, there is a small problem wiring the electrical system. Let me explain."

No, please, I thought. I'll pay you double rent.

Bam! Bam! Bam! Bam! Firecrackers. The noise powerkicked into my muscles so close it was like the range, the same scorched kind of fear.

Mr. Saul practically dove for cover. Then he grabbed a steak knife from the sink and was halfway out the door before I could say anything.

"Wait! Stop! It's only firecrackers, just some kids that's all."

"Perhaps." He stared down at the knife held too tight in his shivery fingers. "But there are many terrible people."

Mr. Saul ducked quickly out the door and I stood there, anxious, wondering whether to follow. "Do you think he'll be okay?" I pictured a bunch of bored sixteen-year-olds looking for trouble.

" 'Okay' is a lot to ask for," Samantha said. "How about 'not dangerous.' "

Going out after him I thought, this is dumb because if the firecracker kids already left he doesn't need me, and if they were still here what could I do anyhow. I walked up to the fenced edge of his yard trying to find him in only the light from our kitchen window. The Car Of The Future sat about fifty feet away with four posts and a roof around it. I could just make out the beaky hood had been left open. After a while Mr. Saul appeared from next to the car and began poking at its front end, his body almost shapeless in the dark.

"Hi." Samantha came up to the fence beside me. "Any excitement?" Her suit glowed bright green, especially the rib bones which were the exact color of numbers on a digital clock.

"No," I said.

All at once Mr. Saul made a terrible sound, a whimpering so pained and personal I told myself it wasn't him, I told myself dogs. Or someone's TV. But no dog sounded that way and I ran across the yard yelling. "What's wrong? What happened?"

He was sort of bent over with his back to me. "They shot it," he said. "Those men shot my beautiful car."

I peered into the darkness hoping he was just paranoid again. He wasn't. The shots had ripped four jagged holes big as quarters right near the tip of the open hood. For a second my mind refused to take it seriously, and I thought, these guys would be great at the range with four shots to a small, dark target from at least fifty feet. Then I remembered this had nothing to do with the range because the range was fake. These were true-life shots. Not fake. Not fake, I thought again, fear in my lungs like broken glass.

Samantha pushed by us. "They actually shot it? This is unbelievable." She stuck her fingers in the bullet holes and wiggled them around.

"J.O." Mr. Saul's back was still turned. "Come drink a cup of tea with me. Please."

Something about his hunched shoulders gave me a sick, yanked-open feeling like seeing a bad freeway accident up close. Too real. "Tea? Yeah, okay."

Mr. Saul's apartment reeked of oil and every surface was covered with car parts or books about car parts. Two big spaghetti pots filled with some kind of liquid took up most of his cluttered table. I could see blurry chunks of metal soaking inside.

"Please, have a seat." Mr. Saul was heating water in the microwave, his voice far away, muffled almost as if packed in invisible wool. "You probably know I'm in a great deal of trouble." He handed me tea in a blue mug with large polka dots. I covered them with my fingers. Polka dots always made me a little sad, they tried so hard.

"Rafi told me about the guys you borrowed money from," I said. "This was them, right?"

"Yes." He reached into one of the spaghetti pots and stirred the metal inside. It made watery clanking sounds. "Rafi insisted that I tell him my true situation that day, he knew something was not right. Smart man." Drops of gray liquid flew around us as he took his hands out and shook them. I saw some go in my tea.

"J.O., I was very worried you might move if you felt there was danger. Now, I cannot blame you." He started to massage his temples, closed eyes twitching like people when they dream. "So, do you plan to leave?"

"Of course not, don't be silly." Where would I go anyway with five hundred dollars in the bank, I thought. Better here than a building like Andy's. "Why don't you call the police?"

"No police." Eyes snapping open he hit the table hard enough to make stuff on it jump: screws, some wire, a brand-new toothbrush. "I will not have police, who might steal my idea."

That kind of made sense, though I couldn't picture any cop in the world wanting to steal the woodpecker car concept. "Wait, what about maybe getting another mortgage or bank loan to pay the guys back."

"Young Lady, what do you think?" Mr. Saul smiled, but it seemed frightened and twitchy on his face. "I already owe to the bank, and even to Ruthie my sister with only one arm. These men were a final resort."

I looked down at the toothbrush still in its plastic package. *Extra Length,* the package said, *for hard-to-reach bacteria.*

Mr. Saul continued. "I sold all of it you know, the silver, my wedding ring." Carefully rolling back the sleeve of his sweatshirt he leaned toward me saying, "This is what remains."

It was the biggest, goldest watch I'd ever seen, way too beautiful for his cheap plastic strap which must've been new. "My father's, J.O., there is no other quite of its kind in the world."

I saw. The watch sat like a huge dinner plate on his wrist with fancy numbers drawn in a language I didn't recognize.

"Recently, I began to wear it for luck, and I tell you that this watch they will have to kill me for." Mr. Saul's smile looked a little less frightened now, almost satisfied, as if the idea of dying because of a watch was much better than dying because of some money. "I gave them a partial payment, but still they call at night. They shoot." He grasped my shoulder with dry fingers strong, but shaky.

"Do you understand my whole life is going into that car?" His grip tightened. "It is the product, J.O., everything. All I am. Some people get old and go to Miami. The Car Of The Future is Miami. This car is the sun." Pausing he let go of my shoulder. "When it is finished I'll take you for the very first drive."

I smiled and said, "Thank you," wanting to believe it would happen that way. I didn't though, not for a second.

Back in my bedroom I put on a tight black T-shirt (too skimpy for outside) and began to exercise. Lifting cinder blocks. I stood at the mirror and concentrated on pumping cement harder and higher than the night before. The added strength in my arms had made The Mag easier to handle.

At the range some days power slammed through my body so strong that a tearing would start deep inside. In high school we learned about Indians and how one type had a sacrifice where they ripped the person's heart out and held it up to the sun. A few times shooting The Mag I'd thought, "Now, Now," feeling both actions near me—the ripper and the person being ripped.

But the feeling was never completed. Some pinpoint opening stayed just out of reach, and no matter how many times I fired

I couldn't quite squeeze through. Cinder blocks above my head, and down again, above my head. I thought about action. All the heart-ripping Indians in the world weren't going to help me dial the phone.

Chapter 9

It was very hot when I left for Rafi's the next day, a breathless kind of heat that made driving the Gremlin feel like being trapped inside someone's closed fist. I turned on the radio wanting to hear slippery music. The Allman Brothers would be good. Duane Allman's guitar always sounded wet.

Nothing. There were only staticky voices too faint to make out, and I moved the tuner dial hoping it wasn't broken. My radio had never sounded this way.

"You aren't hearing me," someone said with other voices fuzzy in the background. "If you listen I can help."

Shit, oh, shit, I thought pressing back against the seat as far from the radio as possible. Maybe it had finally happened, a supernatural omen straight from the core of the universe. That's when I noticed the button was set on AM, and my face went bright red even though it was only me in the car.

"So, my wife believes it's Jeff's own fault," a man said, dry-mouth tense. "She feels we've already spent too much money on rehab places, and there comes a point when you should just wash your hands."

Not knowing AM I leaned forward and tried to frame the voices in my mind, an artsy commercial? No, too realistic. Maybe it was some type of radio soap.

"What about you, do you still have faith in Jeff?" Another man, not tense at all.

"Yes, but my wife gets mad if I even bring up seeing him."

They spoke awhile longer, and the guy decided he'd stand by

Jeff who was his son from a previous marriage. "That's right," I told him. "Lose the wife."

The other man said, "I'm Glenn Friedman. If you're in the L.A. area call and tell me what's on your mind."

Omens don't get any bigger than this, I thought. He's a shrink, of course, it's a call-in shrink show. Whispering the number he gave, I pulled up to a pay phone and began to dig sticky quarters out of my change purse.

Glenn Friedman was busy, I redialed, busy again. Fifteen minutes later I was still at it, the July heat on my skin like oily fur. This is ridiculous, I told myself. You're standing here being broiled alive in the hope that a total stranger will get on the phone so you can tell all of Southern California your most personal problem. Real smart.

The phone booth was right in front of a Popeye's Chicken that had someone on the sidewalk in a huge Popeye costume giving out fliers. Most peopled ignored him. The costume's plastic arms and snarly plastic head shimmered a little in the heat.

Four more tries, I decided. That's all I can take. Busy, busy, then on the third try it rang, and a woman picked up right away. "Do you want to talk with Glenn Friedman?"

"Umm, yes."

"Great, your name?"

I hadn't thought of that, what if someone who knew me was listening, or worse what if my father heard? "Samantha, my name's Samantha."

After a few more questions she put me on hold and Glenn's program played through the phone. "We broke up," a woman was saying. "I threw his Siamese fighting fish down the garbage disposal."

They talked about it while I waited, smoking like crazy to keep my hands from hanging up. The street was crowded and bright. I watched Popeye who for some reason began hitting himself pretty hard under the chin and behind his neck. Yellow fliers covered the ground. Maybe Glenn Friedman actually is my father, I thought, and he's using a different name for the radio. No, that's stupid.

After the fish woman was done Glenn said, "Our next call is Samantha."

It took a second to remember he meant me. "Hi." My voice sounded incredibly young, too young almost to dial a phone. "I've never met my father," I said, "or even spoken with him. I keep messing it up."

"Well, what scares you so much?"

"I don't know."

"Yes you do, it's in your voice."

I thought about telling my secret fear not just to Glenn Friedman, but to anyone else who had their dial tuned. Say the words, I thought, it'll be good practice for when you actually call your dad. Talk.

"Are you afraid of possible rejection?"

I kicked the metal bottom of the phone booth. Talk.

"Samantha?"

I glanced at Popeye who had taken his head off and was holding it under one arm. He looked exhausted. The guy's straight brown hair and large features reminded me of Andy, and then I was saying it. "My father might not know who I am. It's been too long."

"Hey." Glenn's voice was so nice I wished at that moment he really was my dad. "Don't you see how that's not real? No one in the world would forget they had a child, of course he'll know who you are. Samantha, I'll bet that contacting him, no matter what happens, will put your life on a whole different track. Action will set you free."

From this spot I could see through the glass door of Popeye's where a long line of people waited to be served. "Action will set you free," I repeated. It was a comfortable sentence like one of those rules from physics. An object in motion tends to stay in motion. Matter can be neither created nor destroyed.

I decided not to mention Glenn Friedman to Rafi who was in a funny mood anyway. Distracted.

We went shooting, and I hoped the idea of free action might

improve my aim, but it didn't. I wished for the millionth time my hands were bigger since the rented guns all had gigantic grips.

Traffic was heavy when we left, neither of us talking much, just getting roasted in Rafi's convertible.

"I have to stop somewhere," he said. "Okay?"

"Sure."

He shifted into third without even touching the clutch, a complicated trick using RPMs. I thought of The Woodpecker Car. Mr. Saul's action, the action of a lifetime, had made consequences choke tighter and tighter around him, not free at all, and I was pretty sure things would get worse.

"What do you think of this?" I asked. "Last night the guys that Mr. Saul—"

Rafi laid sweaty fingers on my arm. "I want to be hearing your story, but first let me get this errand finished so I can give you true attention. One second, Okay?" He pulled up in front of a pawnshop.

"Here?" I asked.

Windows streaked with dirt, the flashing sign said, "Monkowitz's: Fa$t Ca$h For Your Valuables."

"Yes. I want to be in and out quickly, all right? Especially if this guy is making manipulation."

Following Rafi through the door, I breathed in dust and the smell of old leather, my eyes not adjusted to the gloom. The store was crammed with too much stuff, most of it worth money. VCRs, crystal, a drum set, two violins, ski equipment. One entire wall was taken up by a large table covered with neatly folded sheets and towels. MONOGRAMMED LINENS, the sign said. WE HAVE MANY INITIALS.

"Hi Rafi." The guy behind the counter was short and wore a Raiders cap. His yellowish brown eyes were set very deep as if giant thumbs had pushed them back in his head.

"Monk, this is J.O."

"How you doing?"

"Fine."

Next to Monk stood a stuffed pinto pony, easily the grimmest animal I'd ever seen. Decayed fur, broken-off tail, but the worst was this pony had only chewed-up holes where its eyes were supposed to be. "Good. Rafi, here's the latest." He handed over a piece of paper that I tried to get a look at, but Rafi put it away too fast. Some kind of list maybe, it was hard to tell.

"So, J.O., are you learning to shoot?" Monk's seamless features all worked together blending cheek to jaw, jaw to chin, so I couldn't really see a straight edge anywhere. I wondered what kind of manipulations he made.

"Yes."

A door at the far end of the counter opened, and an extremely pretty blonde, about eighteen, came over with a small silver statue in her hand. "Monk, where'd you get this, it's gorgeous. Oh, hi." She smiled noticing us.

Rafi said, "Hi, Liz. This is J.O."

Liz looped one arm around the pony's neck stroking dead, raggedy ears. "Hi there," she said still smiling enthusiastically. "Are you Rafi's girlfriend?"

Monk laughed, and I glanced carefully at Rafi not sure what to say. "You know, that's some pony." Why didn't she ask *him,* I thought, so I could get an idea also.

Liz began to comb patchy brown mane between her fingers, her waist-length hair getting mixed up in it. "Thank you, he's mine. Monk gave me my very own pony." Giggling, she kissed the top of its head, and I had no idea how much of this was a joke.

"That new piece is good," Monk said to her, "let me show Rafi and J.O."

Liz handed him the statue, a dragon, and Monk put it on the counter. It was a detailed dragon, about six inches long with fangs and a mean silver tongue that reminded me of horror movies. The innocent family takes it home, and that night their pony disappears.

"Push down on the head," Liz told Rafi.

He reached forward, but Monk got there first moving one pointy finger right between the horns. A small flame shot from the dragon's mouth.

"It's a lighter," Liz said. "Isn't that great? There's even an engraving on the bottom."

Monk picked up the dragon and turned it over. *"To Mrs. Tremen,"* he read, *"with love from all of us at The Middlebury Country Club.* Well, I'd guess her club days are finished."

I watched him push the dragon's head so the flame popped out again and again. It made little clicking sounds.

"What do you think, Butterscotch?" Monk asked Liz. "Keep or sell?"

"Keep." She kissed him on the neck and walked away, blonde hair whooshing clean.

"Look at that ass," Monk said softly. "Let me tell you, Liz is sweet."

I stared at the jewelry on black velvet inside the display counter. Earrings, cuff links, a pearl necklace. They were good pearls with a shine, an almost yellow richness that made me feel suddenly messy. Not sweet.

"Liz is the real thing too, raised in New England with little sacks of herbs in her underwear drawer." He laughed. "Yeah, she's great, but I like the heat. Some women have a kind of heat that Liz is missing, for instance I knew this Cuban girl a while ago who was mystic. Plugged in. You wouldn't believe . . ." he paused. "Never mind."

"What?"

Monk was staring at my mouth so I wiped it thinking there might be dirt. There wasn't and he smiled. "You don't want to know."

"We should leave now," Rafi said putting his arm around me. "Work tonight."

I rested my elbows on the counter and leaned toward Monk. "Yes, I do want to know, come on." It was the first time I had ever ignored anything Rafi said to me. This felt incredibly important though. All my life I had wanted to be one of those beauty girls like Liz who caught light and held it, but now I saw that because I wasn't, grown men would tell me secrets they'd never tell Liz. Secrets I needed to understand.

"I like J.O.," Monk said to Rafi. "She has heat."

Rafi moved behind me his hands clasped tightly together over the bottom part of my stomach.

"When a woman's plugged in," Monk told us, "there's no limits. If you fuck certain women up the ass for a really long time they can get to another place." He paused lighting a cigarette off the dragon. "It takes about two hours, but with the right woman something will click. They can tell the future. Prophecy. No shit. It's very intense, Liz couldn't handle that, you know? The power's just not in her."

"Oh." I tried hard to keep my face perfectly normal. The idea was so scary, but just what if it were true. Who's future did they see, their own, or the world's? And what about men. Did it take a special man also?

Rafi's hands were digging into my stomach, voice sarcastically patient. "Perhaps we leave now."

"Does J.O. want to leave?" His eyes on me, Monk pronounced my name as if it were in quotes.

He's just making trouble, I thought. And anyway two hours was ridiculous, no one could stand it. I'd seen baseball games that barely lasted two hours.

Without a word Rafi took his hands from my stomach and walked toward the door.

"Good-bye," I said to Monk.

He still had his eyes on me, just *looking* in this way that made a thick fuzziness settle throughout my body. My hands felt huge. I backed up a few steps, then turned quick, hoping to never see Monk again.

Outside it had cooled down a little, but you'd never know from touching the baked car seat. "How are you?"

Rafi was easing out of a tiny parking spot, eyes squinted almost shut as he tried to avoid scraping the car parked in front of us. "What is this word *luke?*" he asked finally inching onto the street. "I have only heard it used with warm. Can you be lukeangry or luketired? Right now I am lukeRafi."

At the light we stopped next to an orange Bug with a frizzy-haired woman inside twisting around on her seat.

"So, how do you know Monk?"

"I met him one year ago. Today he was idiot, and I am sorry for introducing you."

I watched the woman's body suddenly drop completely out of sight. No one else was in the car.

"You want to come over while I get ready for Sun Maiden?" Rafi asked. Thursday, he worked, I didn't.

"Sure."

At the green light the Bug pulled ahead of us, and I saw a pair of sheer panty hose fly out her window and land on the street.

The stucco ceiling in Rafi's bathroom always reminded me of those pointy things that grew inside of caves. I sat on the closed toilet seat while he took a shower, my skin moist and blurry in the steam.

"Classical is astonishing," his voice was loud over the rush of water. "But for me Israeli music, the Yemenite, is best. I wish a few of these songs were the sound track to my life."

Clothes were scattered on the floor, striped T-shirt, khaki shorts with something white poking out of one front pocket. The paper from Monk.

"J.O., I should get you tape of this music because I think you are interpreting wedding and bar mitzvah bands, right? It is different, I can't express."

Reaching into his pocket, careful, the piece of paper steam-limp against my fingers. So easy, he'd never know.

Rafi began to sing wordlessly, "Do-do-do-do" and I pictured soap gliding on skin, the way his bald spot seemed bigger, endearing somehow with wet hair.

Kicking the shorts across the bathroom I asked, "What was that piece of paper Monk gave you?"

Silence, only water.

"Rafi?"

"You must be careful with Monk, you know? This guy is very much sleazier than I am, and I'm a sleazy Israeli." He laughed. "The shop is nothing, he makes fortune selling unlicensed guns."

"To who?"

"Anyone, gang kids mostly."

I stood up and leaned against the Formica counter, shiny white with streaks of fake gold. "If I ask a question do you promise to tell the truth?"

He was quiet, and I counted the seconds thinking, please, if you can't promise this what am I supposed to say. Five seconds, six.

"Yes, I promise."

"Are you selling guns with Monk?"

The water went off abruptly and Rafi opened the shower curtain, his wet naked body catching me by surprise. "I am not this way. I am not killer. In '73, J.O., I almost lost my mind." He touched the scar, the big one, that began at the edge of his chest and sliced left all the way around to where I knew it ended, hook shaped, just before his spine.

"Why?"

Smiling sort of crooked he grabbed a towel from the rack. "War in Israel." Out of the tub now, wet hair in swirly patterns on his skin.

You're pretty lame, I told myself. What did you think happened to him in '73, a surfing accident? My own huge secret, the father thing, felt silly compared to a war. I leaned over and kissed his cheek, his ear. Rafi had beautifully shaped ears, they reminded me of the kind of flower you only see in photographs. South Idaho Star Blossom.

"If I ask a question, are you promising to tell the truth?" His hands on my hips, pulling me toward him.

I counted silently, five, six. "Yes, I promise."

"Will you come into the other room and make love with me?"

"Okay." I paused. "But I don't want to know the future."

Rafi's gold crown showed when he laughed. "That's good, neither do I."

Chapter 10

I wanted to talk with Samantha about Mr. Saul but she was napping, sprawled across her sheets in a blood-red cotton dress, one pale arm flung outward. It was the most dramatic nap I'd ever seen. Late afternoon, I stood at her door wondering if she'd talk today. There had been no sleeptalk for a long time.

"Hello." I moved toward her feeling the air, padded and heavy, that comes off sleeping people.

She groaned, turning restlessly on the bed and I bent down close. "Tell me."

Another groan and then she said, "Seven out, line away."

The words were so fast and loud I jumped backward almost tripping over a pile of clothes. "Who? What line?"

Samantha sat up, eyes open now, but staring at nothing. Infinity. "Bet the hard ten, bet the come, the field, the point, bring it out, make it come out with a hardways bet."

"Forget it," I told her and left the room disappointed. My ideas on sleeptalk were probably wrong after all since the words never seemed to fit with anything.

On our kitchen table was a bag of party eggs and I ate a few, the malt too sweet, gritty against my teeth. Lighting a cigarette I wondered what to do tonight. Maybe call Andy, we'd go to dinner.

"What time is it?" Samantha walked in looking anxiously around the room. "What did I miss?"

"It's 5:30," I told her, "and you missed everything. The birthday party, the assassination attempt, the poltergeist."

She laughed and grabbed a handful of party eggs. "God, I'm

starving, 5:30? Shit. I'm supposed to meet The Legend at 6:15, he taught me all about craps so now we're going to Vegas. Look how wrinkled this dress is. Want to come?"

"To Vegas?"

"Yeah." She walked to the sink and quickly shoved her head under running water. "I'll give you a hundred dollars gambling money if you loan me your black jeans."

At this time of day the sun always made a big patch of light in the shape of a cowboy hat on our floor. I went over and stood in the middle of it. My body still had a loose weight from the sex with Rafi, and I wondered if fingerprints were left on skin. I imagined both of us covered with each other's invisible marks, smudgy stroked tattoos that would never blur like the ink kind.

Rafi had left for work before there was a chance to tell him about Mr. Saul. "Samantha, listen." How might he have reacted, I asked myself. Buy a gun? Ignore it? Call the cops? "What do you think about Mr. Saul's car getting shot?" I wanted to make this casual because Samantha had no feeling for him. No reason to stay if things got bad. She could afford much better anyway, a solar-heated home in one of the canyons, pine-tree quiet. Good-bye, J.O., wish you were here.

"I think it's incredible." She took a dirty measuring cup from the sink and threw it high into the air. "Gunshots, cars, hunted men, I can use it for my acting. This is so exciting."

You'd never know she'd just been asleep, I thought, trying to organize myself by looking out the window at the sun. Her excitement made me angry. Mr. Saul deserved better than having his problems used to feed someone's TV career—sitcoms, not even good TV.

"This isn't exciting at all," I said. "It's horrible. Mr. Saul was up here getting the rent, otherwise they might've shot him also. Not exciting." Why do I keep repeating that, I wondered.

Samantha shook her wet hair spraying drops of water on my arm. "Oh, come on, you're just as jazzed as me, only you won't admit it."

"That's not true."

"Yes it is." Her voice was loud and thick, a voice with no

muffler. "Look at me. Look right over here and say you don't feel any excitement, if you can do that, then okay, I'm wrong."

Samantha's face seemed thinner somehow, whittled down to nothing but clean hard bone and colors. White skin, red eyebrows. It was the power face she had for acting big scenes or telling a good story where I always saw the pictures.

In today's picture, very clear, both of us dive to the floor as shots rip through the window, Bam Bam. "J.O., don't," Samantha screams, but it's too late. I'm on my feet committing some amazing act of bravery so the bad guys are killed. Mr. Saul is saved. "My daughter's a hero," Miles says on the eleven o'clock news.

"See, I knew it." Samantha laughed. "Don't tell me you're not loving this, it's written all over you. Now what are we doing 'cause I have to hurry, yes or no on Vegas?"

Inside the cowboy hat patch of sun I closed my eyes. "No, but thanks anyway." I breathed in deeply, soaking in the spots of light, the private smell of Rafi still remaining on me, and my own cement-pumped muscles which felt huge. Capable of fighting evil men to the death. "I want to talk with my dad tonight," I told her. "It's been a long time since I called him."

Samantha left about twenty minutes later, and I walked into my room. What if the guy's a jerk? I thought, sitting cross-legged on the bed. What if we just don't get along? I concentrated till the New Orleans photo came to me clear. He had been half leaning toward my mother with a goofy smile, as if her presence and the city street was all he ever wanted. I pictured the shiny black hair down to his waist, hair that went with ancient tribal secrets. I picked up the phone.

"Hello?" My dad's voice sounded distracted, eating dinner maybe, or reading.

"Miles Warren?" I asked.

"Yes." In the background a dog started to bark.

I looked around my room wanting to hold this exact moment forever, cluttered desk, the poster from *Psycho*. "This is J.O."

The dog's barking was really close now, and I heard scuffling noises. "Hold on a sec," my dad said. "Ryan!" A pause. "Can

you get him out of here, please? I'm trying to talk on the phone."
The barking continued, it was playful, not angry, and I imagined
a Great Dane puppy with its paws on my father's lap. "Ryan!"

"Coming, coming." Someone else was in the room.

"I think he needs a walk," my dad said, "and please take the
scarf off his neck. It belonged to Grandma."

Grandma? I had completely forgotten there was another set of
grandparents who might even be alive.

"I'm sorry." He was back on the phone. "We just got a new
puppy so it's been kind of nuts around here. Now, who is this?
Jo? Jo who?"

"What?" I lay down on the bed with a rush buzz in my ears.
The phone stayed near my leg.

"Hello?" it said.

I hung up. Glenn Friedman had lied, people forget. My stomach began to hurt, first a little, and then really bad with a thick
dirty taste in my mouth. Was it wrong not to explain more? I
wondered. Maybe I should call him back. I rolled on my side
about to throw up all over the bed if I stayed there another
second. Feet on floor, move.

Wandering into the kitchen I opened the refrigerator and
watched my hand go into cold white. It trembled. It looked like
someone else's hand. "Stop shaking," I said and picked up a beer
with fingers so numb it was hard to tell where they ended and
the glass began. Obviously J.O. was dead and buried in his mind.

I sat on the couch feeling calm, completely blank. Lobotomy
blank. On the end table was a clock and I stared at the second
hand jerk and pause, jerk and pause. I practiced holding my
breath. I figured out how many hours it had been since my father
last saw me, exactly a hundred eighty-eight thousand, six hundred
seventy-six. It got darker.

Across the room was the framed 8 × 10 Samantha had insisted
we hang up. Even in bad light I could tell how hunched my
shoulders were, staring anxiously at the camera—Like me, oh
please, like me. Then I was over there smashing the picture on
the floor. "FUCK YOU," I yelled and ran back into my room.

I threw the almost-full beer bottle against the wall over my bed, but it didn't break. Jo? Jo who? Beer spilled. I grabbed the phone and with one hard pull ripped it loose, yeah okay, my body hit the desk. Salvation Army bullshit, I thought pushing the whole thing over on its side. Crash. Papers fluttered, an ashtray broke. I picked Heather Peeps Haber up off the floor and tore her in two pieces. She was so old it was easy.

Running back to the refrigerator hacking little screams began to come from me so I bit the inside of my lip. Shut up, shut up.

Six-pack, I raised the first bottle high and shattered it with all my strength against the tile edge of our sink. Brown glass exploded. I smashed another one, another, my T-shirt soaked mealy with beer. The fifth bottle sliced open my palm as it broke, come on, fucker. Poke my eye out. Jo? Jo who? No pain someone else's hand.

On the way out our back door it really started to bleed, squishing around inside my closed fist. The evening street was very quiet. I smelled a barbecue.

In the Gremlin heavy metal blasted from my tiny speaker so loud I couldn't even hear the song. Red light at La Brea, but I just leaned on the horn and went straight through. No problem. I drove east on Franklin with the speedometer trembling at seventy though it didn't feel that fast. Red light at Highland. The traffic was too heavy so I stopped there barely making it since my brakes weren't used to such short notice. Knees on seat. Resting.

"Hey." The guy in the car next to me leaned over and unrolled his passenger window. '57 Eldorado, I knew since it had been my mother's dream car. This one was blue and white. "Are you okay?" The guy had long hair, early forties maybe, and was peering curiously at me.

I hit the gas. Cars screeched, honking and people yelled stuff out their windows. I turned up the radio.

After driving around Hollywood for a couple of hours I finally ended up in front of Andy's house, the first time I ever visited anyone unexpectedly. Yeah, so? He buzzed me in not even asking who it was, real smart. Andy's hall smelled like mildew and disconnected TV noise came from behind almost every door. Most of them were on different channels, gunshots, laughter, *"Donde están los niños?"*

Andy opened the door with Fear on his shoulder, her scaly rat tail going all the way around his neck so I saw the tip of it on the other side.

"What's wrong? What happened?" His eyes narrowed as he pulled me quickly into the apartment. "Is that blood on your shirt?"

"Beer." I felt so tired then, a deep tired like even my skin weighed too much.

"Uh-uh," Andy said, "that's blood at the bottom."

"Could I just sit for a minute?"

The one-room apartment was crampy dark and smelled like Fear's cage. Andy had always found some excuse not to let me up here, and now that I knew why it made me feel even worse. I wouldn't have cared. Sitting on his dirty plaid couch I felt every detail of every spring straight through the thin cushion.

"Well," Andy said.

Different-sized paintings were jammed together on his walls, their harsh colors swirled too much, too manic. A couple of them had hundreds of intense blue slivers like pilot lights all across the canvas. Beautiful, but not nice.

Andy said, "Your teeth are chattering, are you cold? I have a parka. Want to put it on?"

"Yeah."

"Ummmm, do you see angels? Carey only paints angels."

"No." I closed my eyes.

His parka was one of those greenish ones with fake fur on the hood though this fur had worn off. It looked like soggy bread. I zipped the front and pulled the hood up loose dark around my face.

We sat in silence. Andy flicked the TV on and off purposely turning his back to leave me alone. I played with triangles in my mind because they were very straightforward, you could picture measurements and find the hypotenuse. After a long time he asked timidly, "What do you want me to do?"

"My father doesn't know who I am," I said.

"Yeah? Neither does mine."

"No, I mean for real. He doesn't remember me." Then I started to cry, not the kind that makes you feel good, but the kind that hurts more each tear squeezed out slow and hot.

"Is he crazy?"

"No." I told him all of it, my own voice foreign to me as if it were on tape. The parka felt sticky slick against bare skin. "It's so humiliating," I said, "to have your own father erase you."

Andy leaned over and poked my arm. "You're sitting here, right? Who handed your father the Eraser Empire? Nobody erases you unless you say okay, get it?" One of Carey's paintings was right behind him so it seemed as if the blue sparks were showering down on Andy's head. They were very vivid against the gray of his T-shirt, the washed-out brownness of his hair and eyes. "So, listen to me, J.O. He's got the Fluff n' Fold life now, the butcher-block life. Some kid with a soapy name. Well, you've got a life too. People know you, you have weight and take up space. I know you. See what I'm saying?"

"I guess." I got up and walked over to the only windows.

On the ground three floors below was an empty swimming pool with enough light nearby to read the words spraypainted across its bottom in big black letters. "No Diving HA-HA."

Andy came up next to me and spoke quietly. "My dad thinks I'm some kind of freak, J.O., some kind of natural phenomena. He's wrong. I may not have The Beard or The Girl, but I live here. This is me. I live here." He laid his bare foot gently on top of my sneaker, then pulled it away as soon as I looked at it. "Want to get yogurt?" he asked. "You could order a topping that has a lot of sugar. It might be cheerful."

I took off the parka not feeling especially better, but back in the world anyway. Things had consequence again. "All right, let's go."

Andy insisted on bringing Fear who crawled around under his shirt like a moving growth as we drove to Melrose. The yogurt place was an almost empty bare room with lots of black and white tile, and a man playing guitar in one corner. Above him a sign said JOIN US FRIDAY NIGHTS FOR A MUSICAL CELEBRATION OF THE SIXTIES. The guy was fat cheeked and balding with tiny scabs all over his head. Hair transplant.

In New York my mom had briefly dated a man named Malcolm who was having a hair transplant, and she'd always warn me before he came over not to mention the scabs. "Don't even look at them," she'd say. "He's emotional." Malcolm's doctor had explained how some of the new hairs would attach themselves, but some wouldn't. My mom told me Malcolm's big fear was ending up with weird hair patterns on his head, stripes or a bull's-eye.

Now this scab man started in on "Heard It Through the Grapevine," not really getting the opening chords. Yogurt guitar.

We sat at the black counter and ordered. "What size?" the woman asked, a blonde who moved around in a boneless kind of way as if put together by garden hose.

"Small," Andy said.

We watched her gush our yogurt from the metal machine.

"This is stupid," I told him after we paid. "What does yogurt have to do with the sixties?"

Andy laughed. He held some in front of me on a spoon, strawberry, it looked very bright. "Yogurt keeps you alive forever." He brought the spoon up to his shoulder and Fear licked it. "Sometimes," Andy said, "it bugs me that I don't know history. Do you know history?"

"What do you mean?"

The scab guy went into a Motown medley, and I wondered if he thought this was a good career move. On my shirt the blood had dried dark, its shape reminding me of a cowboy hat. What else was shaped like a cowboy hat? I couldn't remember, and wished for the parka again. My hand hurt.

"Okay, this is a secret." Lowering his voice Andy spoke right into my ear, "Why are we supposed to remember the Alamo?" I could feel his breath. "Everyone says, 'We lost big time in Vietnam,' right? So, did we lose for real or are they just being deep? History. I don't know what happened. Did they do Vietnam in your school?"

"No." That war was vague to me, and it suddenly seemed very depressing not to know about a war in my lifetime, a war my father could've fought in. For a second I thought I might start to cry again.

Andy ate the rest of his yogurt in three big bites his spoon rasping against the Styrofoam bowl. "Bad news, we don't know anything, Hee-Hee." On his ear was a glass eyeball, a real one he'd turned into an earring. It swung. "J.O., my brother called after I sent that money to tell me that now he wants paint and clothes."

"Paint and clothes?"

"Yeah. Only red, yellow, or orange cotton, though the paint has to be all different colors. Oil base. He said he was doing some things around the house and didn't want to go out."

I propped one foot up on the next counter stool. It felt good to be dealing with someone else's problems, problems I hadn't caused.

"Anyway, I said I'd send the stuff because he's my brother. He wants red clothes, he wants paint, I'll send it. Then he hangs up and I thought, this is too weird, so I called back but he wouldn't answer. It just rang and rang."

"That doesn't sound right, what are you going to do?"

Tearing up the Styrofoam bowl he dripped strawberry yogurt that almost glowed against the black counter. "I'm not sure." Andy continued ripping the bowl till it was in tiny pieces. I looked at his profile, straight hair over one cheek, lips tight, concentrated. "Carey's talking the spider language again which makes no fuckin' sense but also does. To me. I hate that. I hate being able to understand him because I don't want to live in spider country. I don't want to be around if he really goes up."

The Motown medley ended. Andy stood, walked over to the scab guy and after they talked quietly the guy nodded.

I picked up my yogurt and held it near my face, melted vanilla with Oreo pieces on top. Up close the cookies reminded me of the winter junkyard with Foxtrot. Smashed cars covered in snow. "What are you going to do about your brother?" I asked when he got back.

The guy began playing music I recognized right away even though it sounded off-key. "I walked forty-seven miles of barbed wire," Andy sang along too loud, "got a cobra snake for a necktie."

I pictured his brother alone in a distant Oregon shack talking some spider language. "You can't just leave him there."

"Come on take a little walk with me baby, and tell me who do you love?"

"He could really be in trouble, is there anyone to call?"

"Who do you love? Who do you love?"

I got up and threw my yogurt away.

Driving Andy home I almost asked to sleep on his floor because I didn't want to face my empty apartment. The beer, the desk, the broken glass. But that felt kind of awkward, and anyway waking up to Carey's paintings wouldn't be much better.

I dropped him off and headed south on Highland. At night especially traffic moved together in clumps of five or six and I pretended my clump wasn't random, we were all going to the beach. I turned on the radio. Instead of music a strangled buzz came out of the left speaker which must've blown from being played too loud before. Worst omen possible, I thought, shutting it off.

Driving along Beverly now I glimpsed the old building where The Spanish Kitchen used to be, a restaurant Samantha told me about. I stopped, backed up, and parked in front of it. The Spanish Kitchen was a legend, a real one, not like most L.A. legends which felt temporary because you had to know movies and stars to understand them. I walked over to its boarded-up front covered with graffiti and about ten layers of those sticky posters. The sign was still there, letters missing. I wished I could go inside.

A long time ago The Spanish Kitchen had been this cozy, normal restaurant owned by a guy and his wife. After the guy died—Samantha vaguely thought he'd gotten shot in a robbery— his wife just locked the doors and never let anyone in there again.

It wasn't always boarded up though, so you could actually see inside till a few years ago. Nothing changed. There were tables set and ready for the next day, specials listed, toothpicks in a little holder by the register. The woman, if she were still alive, lived right behind the place, and Samantha said she must be crazy.

About six feet off the ground were some windows not boarded over, and I jumped up trying to see inside, but they were all painted black.

His voice had been stranger-friendly when he asked who I was as if I belonged to his present life, someone with the dog's obedience school maybe, and it was just a question of placing it. The woman's not crazy at all, I thought, leaning back on splintery boards. I flexed my cut hand to get some pain happening. Snap back. It didn't do much good though, I couldn't go home, couldn't stay here.

Rafi and Lily would have closed up The Sun Maiden by now, doing side work with the rich smell of tomorrow's pies just baked around them. I hadn't wanted to call Rafi all breathless and needy, but just dropping by might be okay. Rafi, I thought, the word steady in my mind like a hand on the small of your back. Rafi Oded, Raphael, Rafi. I walked to my car.

The Sun Maiden parking lot had just been repainted last week, fresh white lines that almost glittered off the pavement. I went up and knocked on the glass doors. Rafi was behind the counter laughing like crazy, with one hand clutched against his stomach, while the other waved frantically in the air as if saying, "No more, no more." I couldn't see Lily.

It took three more knocks, loud ones, before Rafi finally noticed me. He got a Danish out of the microwave and walked toward the door, his lips saying, "It's J.O." I couldn't hear through the glass.

Rafi unlocked the door with a blue key ring that had a Dodger insignia I'd never noticed. "Come in, what are you doing here?"

"Just dropping by." I saw Lily sitting at a booth, her stocking feet propped on the opposite bench. "Hi," I said.

She was holding a joint, a roach really, pinched between forefinger and thumb. The air smelled spicy from pot. But I wanted pies, I thought, feeling like a dumb little kid as Lily silently held the roach out, eyebrows raised. I shook my head because pot made me ridiculously self-conscious.

"I'm allergic," I told her. "It gives me seizures." Being too nervous for pot sounded extremely wimpy, but seizures were real, they were a box you checked on application forms.

Lily took a final hit off the roach, licked her fingers, and put it out.

"There's blood on your shirt, what happened?" Rafi asked biting into his Danish.

"Oh, this? Just a scrape." My voice was nasal. Swallowing, I hid both hands in front pockets as if they could look at the cut and see up narrow veins straight to my heart. See the whole night.

Rafi pointed at my shirt. "It's like flying saucer," he said, "the shape of the stain."

I changed over to back pockets, smoother on my palm. "I thought it was more like a cowboy hat." Who is he? I wondered. What am I doing here?

Lily stood up and made a snorting noise. "You people are disturbed. Come here, J.O., let me try to get that blood off."

I followed her behind the counter almost gagging on my own thankfulness. Lily's back was very large and very straight. I wondered if she ever had kids. It was the kind you could ride on, and for a second that's all I wanted to do, be carried piggyback with my chin on her shoulder, arms wrapped tight around her neck.

I slept at Rafi's that night. When he asked what was wrong I told him my speaker had blown, I said complete music was important, and I had lost all the bass lines. He didn't believe me, but let it go anyhow. I was glad. No way would I tell him about the phone call, the fact that my own father didn't recognize my name is not something to tell a person if you want them to think you're special.

In his bathroom I took off makeup, a cigarette burning on the sink edge. I'd been smoking too much, and now there was pressure in my throat as if a hot fist were stuck there.

In the other room someone was talking Hebrew on Rafi's machine, an angry voice that said, "Fuckin' DMV" at least three times. I blew smoke at the mirror watching it flatten then spread across my reflection. The next message was a woman. Rafi turned the volume down, so I opened the door a little trying to hear, but it was too soft.

"Anything exciting?" I walked out of the bathroom oily eyed from cold cream.

Rafi's hand jumped to erase both messages. "I'm not sure."

"Please."

"J.O.?"

"Please," I said again, the word all wrong, whispery.

Rafi put his arms around me, and I hugged back feeling secrets multiply foreign and furry like space creatures between us.

I woke up the next morning picturing Marilyn. The picture was so strong I decided instantly to go to the bank because Marilyn would help, she knew things. Woman things: vertical stripes make you look thinner, and if a man is attracted he will unconsciously show the palms of his hands. Good useful things: baking soda in your cat box soaks up the smell, bay leaves in your cabinet get rid of weevils.

Rafi was still asleep, so I got up quietly and wrote a note saying I'd see him later at work. In my car I turned on the radio, hoping that somehow the speaker had magically fixed itself overnight. It hadn't.

The cool bank air felt wonderful on my skin, sweaty, no shower, and as usual I automatically paused in the middle of the big room to look for my dad. Stop it right now, I thought, don't waste your time.

"Heeey, what's up?" Everything about Marilyn was swollen huge, even her fingers. "How you doing, J.O.?" Her wedding ring hung from a gold chain around her neck.

"Okay." I handed over my thirty-dollar deposit. "How are you?"

"Great, not so tired anymore, and Joey's picking up freelance computer work like crazy. We spent a fortune on this gorgeous crib yesterday but it's worth it Joey tells me because 'that crib belongs to my first child and will be a family heirloom.' " Marilyn grinned, her cheeks going chipmunky.

"Yeah, well." There was a silence while I looked away from her to the harmless blue bank paintings. Talk, say something, I told myself.

"How's you and Rafi?"

"Fine, great." Trying to smile and at the same time check how many people were behind me I asked, "Do you ever imagine stuff?"

"What do you mean?"

"Well." The line was short so I went into it, my voice rushed and grateful. "Lately it feels like Rafi's been hiding something from me, no that's not right, 'hiding' sounds too sneaky. I think there's a part of his life that he hasn't told me about. But who am I to know his whole life, right?"

"What has he done?" She tied her long hair into a knot loose around her face, and put elbows on the counter, listening. "What exactly makes you think so?" Marilyn's voice had gotten leaner, professional almost.

I told her about Monk and the piece of paper, but left out Liz, ass fucking, and the guns. "When I asked about it," I said, "he changed the subject. And then last night there was a message from a woman on his machine, now maybe I'm paranoid, but something about the way he erased it, well, I don't know. It's probably just me, I mean she could've been his niece."

"No." Marilyn put the NEXT TELLER PLEASE sign up across the counter, and I felt ridiculously flattered. Hot stuff at the bank.

"Listen, do you love this guy?"

I just stood there a few seconds afraid to say it. Stupid, what could happen, I thought, there were no Love Police who were going to come and take me away. "Yeah."

"Well then, here's the deal. I'd bet money he's seeing another woman, and if you want I'll give you the best advice you're ever going to get."

I nodded.

"Lay back." Pieces of hair were falling from her knot, and she shook her head so all of it came down. "Don't cling to him, don't ask where he's been, just let it go." Touching my arm softly, her wrists were dimpled like a baby's. "The boy chases the girl till she catches him, see what I'm saying?"

"Yeah, I guess." I remembered how once at Rafi's house when I had no clean clothes he washed my cotton underwear in the sink then dried them with a blow-drier. "I don't mind," he had said. "My hands on your underwear is good." The thought of him being that personal with someone else's underwear, probably black, maybe crotchless, made me feel sick.

"If you stay relaxed about it he'll come back," Marilyn told me. "They usually do."

"You think?"

She smiled, meeting my eyes a beat too long. "I know."

At home Samantha's car was parked in the driveway which meant she was back from Vegas after staying up all night probably. I wished I had made it here before she saw the kitchen. Opening our front door I wondered if spilled beer went through any kind of violent chemical change when left on linoleum for too long.

"J.O., is that you?" Mr. Saul called from the backyard.

"Yes." Amazing, I thought. He can hear a door being unlocked from fifty feet in the middle of the day. I walked toward the yard happy to put off facing Samantha and the mess for another few minutes.

"Hello, hello, hello, Young Lady." Mr. Saul stood next to a little house that was not there two days ago. A silver house. He had nailed sheet metal across the four posts and roof protecting the car so now it was closed in completely. "I heard noise last night." Mr. Saul unlocked his fence so I could walk into the yard. "It sounded terrible."

"Oh, that was just a stupid accident, I dropped some stuff."

Even though his hair had grown out frizzy almost to his shoulders, Mr. Saul still seemed formal to me the way older people do. I wondered if it was because his generation were formal all their lives, or if maybe after reaching a certain age you automatically got better manners. "Well, this is something," I said. His windowless shed glinted low and dull in the sun like a cheap government project.

"Actually, I'm quite proud." He led me over to the door. "Try to get inside."

I stood in front of it relieved he'd stopped asking about last night. The door had no lock I could see, only an old brass knob clashing with the rest of the metal, thickish metal, I wondered where he'd gotten it as I gently tried to turn the knob.

"Really, Young Lady, you can apply more effort than that."

I turned harder and pushed. Nothing.

"If the men who worry me are this generous I will have no problems. Put strength into it."

Taking a step back I slammed my shoulder hard into the door, and Mr. Saul must've seen something because he touched my arm. "How are you, J.O.?" His fingers felt like dried grass. "Is your friend Rafi treating you nicely?"

I stared at a bunch of wires crinkled in a snarly little nest on the ground. "Fine."

Bending slowly toward the door Mr. Saul paused with his face about a foot from the knob, and said, "Let J.O. see how you work." Click. It turned easily and I felt a rush of heat as he pulled open the heavy door. "It hears my voice. This lock will not respond to anyone but me."

"You made it? Yourself?"

"What do you think, my Aunt Zena made it? Of course I made it myself." He slammed the door. "When you are willing to take the time you can do many things, let's see, I began this lock perhaps one month ago. I only wish I had finished before those men shot the car."

"But it's voice activated, didn't that cost thousands of dollars?" I touched the knob, almost overjoyed he'd invented something sort of normal. A lock had real uses, it wasn't embarrassing.

"*Ha!*" he said with such force I jerked my hand away. "If anyone should tell you this costs thousands of dollars you tell them, '*Ha!*' Brains. Brains is what it costs." Mr. Saul's navy blue T-shirt said, SNAP-ON TOOLS in white letters, a shirt that made him look stronger the way cops and army guys seem stronger in their uniforms.

"Anyway," he told me, "the lock is just silliness. If it weren't for my problems I would not have even bothered." As he leaned back against the door I noticed how long Mr. Saul's eyebrows had gotten, poking out from either side of his face. I wondered if they'd cast a shadow. "I paid part of the money, and they said it would be all right for the time being." He shook his head slowly, eyes closed. "I don't believe them."

"Do you think they'll try to hurt the car again?" Part of me kind of itched to meet these guys, mean enough to shoot an old man's invention, rich enough to loan thousands of dollars, and weird enough to loan it to Mr. Saul.

"They may try, but I will tell you this." Bending toward the lock he clapped his hands, and said, "Open my friend," smiling at the click. "I may not be a strong man, however I can build a strong house, so unless they have wrecking machinery The Car Of The Future is secure. Now, if you'll excuse me the electrical system still needs work."

I felt the heat like a living thing with claws as he went into his metal shed, popped on a light, and began to hum.

When I got upstairs Samantha was at the kitchen table eating a bowl of Captain Crunch, her legs tucked underneath her to avoid the beer all over the floor. Other than that she completely ignored it.

"How you doing?" My feet crunched on broken glass as I opened a window to get rid of the bad smell.

"Good," she said. "What time are you coming home tonight?"

I counted the drops of dried blood in a line close to the door. "I don't know, why?" There were six.

Samantha looked me over very carefully as if she were one of those guys at a county fair who try to guess your weight. "You have artistic vision, right?"

"I don't think so." It sounded like a question that really meant, "Will you be a row of hedges in my play?" "How was Vegas?" On the table next to her was the box of cereal, Captain Crunch grinning wacky in his pirate hat.

"This is it, J.O., I'm in love. Big-time love." Spreading her arms apart she showed me how big the love was.

I got out the sponge mop and started filling a bucket with water. "The Legend?"

"No, no, no, it's much bigger than that now, he's not the legend anymore. He's . . . The Messiah."

"The Messiah? But just a few weeks ago he was The Rapist." Samantha frowned at me. "We've grown a lot since then. J.O., I want to marry him and bear his children. First we'll have a girl named Angel, and I'll stand at the back porch before dinner yelling, 'An-gel, An-gel, come inside now, honey, your suppah's ready.' " Her voice was loud and staged Southern.

I began picking up splinters of glass feeling kind of stupid about what I'd done since it hadn't made a bit of difference. Quit the self-pity, I thought, and learn from Samantha who can get anything like magic because she doesn't care, doesn't need it.

Samantha said, "I want to ask something."

In the noontime light her hair looked very red, and I remembered going with her about two weeks ago to get it redyed. The hairdresser had been this quiet, extremely hip Japanese woman who intimidated me like crazy, but not Samantha. "Hold out your hand, and I'll show you the perfect color," she had said. No problem. The hairdresser had waited with her palm open while Samantha dug around inside her purse finally coming up with a box of paprika. "Here." She had dramatically dumped almost half of it in the woman's hand. "Beautiful, that's exactly how I want my hair to be."

Now, she asked me, "Why does Captain Crunch always shred the roof of your mouth? I mean is it actually shredding or do I only feel it that way? Could he tell from kissing me?"

There were two unbroken bottle necks under the table and I crawled to get them. "I don't know."

"Eat some and tell me if it shreads your mouth, okay?"

"I'm not hungry."

"Oh come on, just one bite, pleeaase?"

I scooped a little onto her spoon and brought it halfway to my face. The milk was yellowish from pieces of floating cereal that I could smell chemical sweet even over the smell of beer. "I really don't feel good."

"Oh, all right." Samantha opened her mouth wide, and I fed her the bite of cereal. "What happened here anyway?" she asked.

"An accident. Tell me about Vegas." I picked up the sponge mop glad just to have her talk. Watching Samantha was like watching TV.

"Vegas Schmegas, listen to this, The Messiah sold a screenplay to a big producer with Paramount, and let me tell you it's none of this five-thousand-dollar option stuff. We're talking major pesos, piles of Krugerrands."

The beer pond seemed to stretch endless across the floor so I purposely didn't look at it as I dunked my mop in the bucket.

Samantha continued, "Anyhow, while we're driving back The Messiah asks if he can sleep over tonight, so I said, 'Sure, you'll meet my roommate.' Then he says 'Oh? What does she do?'"

I froze, mop in hand, and turned complete attention to her. "What did you tell him I do?" This could be worse than hedges, I thought. Much worse.

"Here, let me help you." Samantha got up and walked around the beer. "Well, let's face it, he's really hot right now, and I'm only a semiregular on a sitcom everyone knows is going into its final season." She picked up a roll of yellow paper towels from above the sink. "I had to tell him something, so I said you're in UCLA, that's all. Film school."

I watched her toss paper towels down on the beer one by one. They fluttered in the air.

"So, he started asking all these questions about your thesis film, hey, I had no idea he'd get that involved."

I poked my foot at the soggy brown hill of paper towels on the floor. "My thesis film? Samantha, I'm only twenty."

"That's okay." She dropped another on top. "I said you were *gifted*."

"Great, just great." I gathered up all the useless towels and threw them in the wastebasket. "What am I supposed to say to him? I don't know anything about movies." I pictured The Messiah cross-legged on our couch, his halo so bright we all wore sunglasses and sat on the floor.

"Come on." Samantha went to the table and poured another bowl of Captain Crunch. "It's easy, just act really visual. Film students always act visual."

"How do you act visual?" I began mopping and the sponge immediately flopped out of the metal holder.

"Say things like, 'Look at the shape of that doorway, my DP would love it.' "

"What's a DP?" I fought to keep the nasal fear out of my voice; maybe I could sleep at Rafi's. No. Lay back, don't cling. Trying to cram the sponge onto the metal part again, I realized it belonged to a completely different mop.

"Anyway, what he'll probably ask about is your film, so maybe while you're at work tonight just think of a plot. Student movies aren't that long, just have a few ideas ready." She poured the milk and took a big bite.

"He'll know it's a lie, I can't do this." I tried to think of a story line, any story line, but my mind was blank. I couldn't even remember movies I'd seen in the past three weeks.

"You know what your problem is?" She mushed the cereal around in her bowl getting it soggy. "Lack of confidence, and just because you have low self-esteem I'm in trouble too. Well, that sucks. I'm asking for one little thing here, one little movie plot, which I'd think of myself except I don't have that kind of vision."

"Well, I'm sorry I can't do it."

Samantha didn't answer because we both knew that all this was just talk, I would do it.

When the floor was clean I went into my bedroom, broken stuff all over, disconnected phone. I looked at everything not sure where to start or even if I wanted to start. At least put the phone back together, I told myself. Don't become a crazy person.

Grabbing the wire I bent down and stuck its little plastic end part in the wall jack. My phone was ringing. Unbelievable. For a second I just stared, thinking it had broken somehow, and would ring forever like those toilets that won't stop flushing. I gently picked up the receiver. "Hello?"

"J.O.?" It was my mother. "You sound weird."

"I'm not weird."

"I didn't say you *were* weird, I said you *sounded* weird."

"Oh." I sat on the floor kicking aside half an ashtray. "How are you?" Since moving to L.A. I'd only spoken with my mom a few times, though we weren't really on bad terms.

"Lonesome for you," she said. In the background I heard a squeak which meant she had just sat down in the big green chair.

I looked around my trashed bedroom. "I'm lonesome for you too," I told her.

"How's the job?"

"Fine, good." I wondered if I should talk about Rafi, but then decided, better wait. He was only five years younger than her.

"J.O." My mother paused dragging on a cigarette. I heard smoke come out. "What's in L.A. that you don't have here?"

I kept quiet.

"I can't believe the only fruit of my loins moved three thousand miles so she can get a tit job and wear deodorant tampons."

Even on the phone I knew my mother's eyebrows were jumping up and down with every word. An upset thing. "Mom." On the floor next to my foot was the Swiss Army knife she'd given me last year. The knife was a good one. Options: a magnifying glass, tweezers, miniature hacksaw. I held the tweezers in front of my face not sure what to do.

"So, did you speak with your father yet?" Her voice had gone up about ten octaves trying to be careful.

I closed my eyes. I started to pluck my own eyebrows where they met slightly at the bridge of my nose. "Someone shot the landlord's car," I told her, "The Car Of The Future. You'd like Mr. Saul, the guy's—"

"Have you seen him?"

My eyes were tearing, but I contined to yank at the hairs anyway. "I miss you so much," I said.

On the phone my mother began to cry. "You won't like him, J.O., he'll disappoint you. I promise."

I cleaned the entire room after we hung up. Passionately. My hands worked on their own fixing the tipped-over desk. I vacuumed behind furniture, scrubbed moldings, and wiped the inside of the light fixture. It took four hours, and when I was done the room felt strange, sort of plucked and pale like the way kids look after a haircut. I forced myself to think about Samantha's movie. Maybe a woman coming home to find a dead stranger in her bed. No, that would be too long.

Chapter 11

In The Sun Maiden dressing room I buttoned my uniform still thinking about a student movie for The Messiah. A waitress movie maybe. The camera could follow someone all night with lots of weird angles and different speeds to show how waitressing, when it's brilliant like Lily, is also art. No. That wouldn't work, I thought, leaving the dressing room. Where's the story? What's the climax?

Rafi was hurrying up the stairs and we almost bumped into each other. "J.O., you're here early."

Just seeing him I got a wet little poke. "Yeah."

He checked to make sure no one was around then quickly took my face in his hands, scrunching it together. "I have surprise for you, but I need keys. Your car keys." He kissed my nose leaving his lips there for an extra second.

"My keys?"

"Yes, I will be gone for a while with your car, but it's not too busy."

Rafi followed me back to the lockers and waited as I dug through my purse. Even though the dressing room was empty it felt wrong to see him here, a place meant only for women. "Why do you want the car?"

"If I told it wouldn't be surprise." Putting my keys in his pocket, he smiled. "You will love this. I'll see you later."

As he walked to the door Rafi reached around and absently scratched his back. Something about the way he did that—body arched, long fingers groping for the right spot—made him seem absolutely genuine. Unplanned.

"Rafi?"

"Yes." He turned.

I took a deep breath. "Are you seeing someone else?"

"Me? No, of course not. Why? Are you?"

"No." We stood there awkward for a few seconds. Downstairs the restaurant geared up for a Saturday night, and I heard Mexican music coming faintly from the back kitchen. "Mexico," I said, just to say something.

"Yes." My keys in his pocket jingled as he played with them.

Five plates up my arm. The trick to becoming a decent waitress, I had finally learned, was to set up a song in your head, a chant, and then let nothing exist outside it. No father, no cars shot, nothing. Saturday was the best night here because families stayed out later, and people were on dates. Since Rafi was gone with my car it was harder than usual to keep up, but I found the chant anyway. Got inside. "Hot open turkey, both four tops want a check, iced tea, two eggs over, sourdough, decaf, Enrique, she says this burger is raw."

Andy ran by me carrying a bus box crammed so full he could barely see over the top. The little ponytail he wore at work stood straight out behind him.

"Three set-ups on nineteen," I yelled.

He skated across the few feet of wet floor near the kitchen yelling back, "Shit, where's Rafi?"

The room was noisy, and sweat poured down my ribs. Real sweat, work sweat, not the toxic kind from sitting around nervous. I served a family their dinner: fried chicken, Moby Dick, and two kiddie plates. A polite family, they all said thank you. It's like we're doing a dance, I thought, and now everyone knows their part because it's been the same in restaurants for hundreds, maybe thousands of years. "Enjoy your meal." I grinned, finally belonging to The Sun Maiden.

Rafi came back around 7:30, and for once I saw him only in work terms. "Andy's buried," I said as he walked in the door, "we need another busboy on Saturdays."

He began to help clear tables with a rubber bus box propped graceful on one hip. It stayed busy all night. I remembered Lily saying once that July Fourth week was almost like Christmas.

Right after we closed Andy came behind the counter where I was scooping spoonfuls of grape jam into little paper holders for tomorrow.

"Hi," he said.

"Hi." Without the rhythm of customers to take it away I had started thinking about my dad again, wishing for him to appear in the restaurant right now. "J.O., I'm Miles," he'd say.

Then I would get the perfect kind of breezy politeness in my voice as I turned toward him, "Miles? Miles who?" Yeah, right.

"Will you give me a ride to Venice?" Andy asked. His thin face hung loose with exhaustion so that for a quick instant I saw exactly how he might look as an old man.

"What's in Venice?"

"My mom. I want to explain some stuff to her, you know, what I told you about my brother Carey. New stuff too. It won't be fun at all, but can you drive me?"

"Okay." This is good anyhow, I thought, since it gives me more time to come up with a movie lie for The Messiah. Maybe a father . . . No.

Before leaving we played a few rounds of Liar's Poker which I won easily. "Someday, girl," Rafi told me, "I will beat you at this game."

"Keep dreaming, Oded. And I'm not girl."

Rafi purposely waited till Andy was changing clothes before he asked if I wanted to go to the range tomorrow. I said yes, but the secrecy was beginning to get to me. A lot. What did he think would happen if people knew we were together, riots in the street? Even though it was dumb I wanted to be seen kissing him because if Rafi just ignored me all at once, pretended we were never a couple, there would be no one to say, "Yes you were. I saw you."

Andy came out wearing a man's suit vest without a shirt. He had a doll's arm attached to the belt loop of his jeans, its stiff plastic fingers resting against his leg. Whatever happens, I thought, his mother will be interesting.

Outside I let him into my car, and walked around to the driver's door. "Hey, great," Andy said when I opened it, "you didn't tell me you got a new car stereo."

For the first time in my life my mouth actually dropped open in shock. I turned on the interior light completely wordless. The stereo was beautiful with shiny buttons, knobs, and levers that clashed wonderfully against my low-tech dashboard. There was a fat envelope propped up on the windshield, and I grabbed it trying not to let Andy see.

"What's in there?" he asked.

"A tape." It was Israeli. On a small sheet of paper Rafi had written: *Enjoy your music. My father used to always warn me how it only takes one second for destroying a thing that took a lifetime to create. I want to be careful to you. I want you with me.* I stared at his block-heavy letters, afraid if I looked up again the stereo might be gone.

Andy touched a sleek button saying, "This must have cost one point five million dollars."

"Not quite that much." Pulling out of the lot, I kept both hands on the wheel because this moment, the moment just before turning it on, should be stretched long as possible.

Andy leaned against the door facing me. "Not that much? This didn't come from Micky's House of Chicken Skin, it's a top-of-the-line Blaupunkt. Are you a hit man?"

"No." I turned on the radio and sound flooded through the car unbelievably thick, but still crisp and clean. "Three hundred sixty-five degrees," The Talking Heads sang. "Burning down the house."

"J.O., you tip me out every night so I know how much you make, and with speakers and installation that thing cost a lot of money. Where'd you get it? I want some, Hee-Hee." He thwacked the doll's arm against the seat. "Make the next right."

There were details in the music I'd never heard, drums like bright red flowers blooming on the dash, hidden harmonies that crept around us lush and green. Andy's right, I thought, this had to be pretty expensive. Rafi purposely didn't have credit cards, and though The Sun Maiden paid him okay, I knew this kind of money wasn't just hanging around his back account. Also, what did that note mean? What did he have to be careful of?

Andy began buttoning up his vest. "You should trust me," he said. "I'm taking you to meet my mother and the exterminator. That's trust."

"Rafi gave it to me." As soon as the words were out I felt really bad. You just betrayed your own boyfriend because you're too suspicious, I told myself. Suspicious of what? A beautiful gift. A guy who seems to care.

"Rafi? Why would Rafi buy you a car stereo?"

Street names came watery now, Navy, Brooks, Ocean, Marine. We were in Venice. "I guess because he likes me."

"*That* way?" Andy pulled the rubber band from his hair and stretched it between two fingers. "He likes you *that* way?"

"Yeah. I think so."

"Make a left here." He shot the rubber band hard, stinging my thigh.

The Talking Heads went into "Once in a Lifetime," which meant the station was probably playing a whole set. Good. "Please don't mention it," I said, "no one at work is supposed to know."

We didn't say anything after that except Andy's directions twisting through small dark streets. Venice wasn't really familar to me, but I always thought it had a different feeling than the rest of L.A. Sort of unraveled. I'd heard more and more ex-rock-and-rollers-who-now-wear-suits had moved here with magazine houses and babies dressed in black. To me though it still seemed like a border town where rules didn't count in quite the same way.

Andy sang along with the radio smacking the heel of one hand against his forehead like David Bryne. "Same as it ever was, same as it ever was."

Finally we pulled up at the back of a small apartment building with a two-car garage next to it. Getting out the air felt harder, the ocean taste flat blue salt in my mouth. I stepped toward the building.

"No, in here," Andy said knocking on the splintery garage

door, one of those lift-up ones. It opened to waist level, and he ducked down to get inside. I stood there a second, then followed.

A garage seems like a big place to keep a car, but it's not a big place to live especially with no windows and the only air coming from a ceiling fan and some vents in the door. The place was amazing though. Thick beige carpet, track lights, and a life-sized wax statue of someone I almost, but not quite, recognized. Next to the statue was a bulky crew-cutted man sitting on a leather couch. Midfifties maybe, he had on a green jumpsuit with BUDDY stitched in red script above the left pocket. Click. I looked at the statue again. It was Buddy Hackett.

"Hiya, kids," the alive Buddy said.

Across the tiny room was a woman who must've been Andy's mother, though their features were very different. This woman wasn't just beautiful, she was stunning, with white-blonde hair reminding me of the fuzzy stuff that grows on dandelions. I watched her flip two burgers on a hot plate in the corner. They sizzled. They smelled so strong it felt like another person in the room, so that including both Buddies, Andy, his mother, the meat, and me there were six of us packed into this garage.

"Mom," Andy said, "this is J.O., J.O., my mom Tina." He bounced on the balls of his feet, even more fidgety than usual.

Tina walked over in two steps and shook my hand. Her small fingers made me think of Christmas tree ornaments, the blown glass ones that snap if you breathe too hard. "It's nice to meet you," she said. "Andy's told us good things." Quiet voice, but full pouty lips that would always make her seem sexy even if she wasn't feeling sexy. "Would you like a hamburger?"

"No thank you."

"Have a seat kids," Buddy said from the couch. "My casa is your casa."

We sat down, Andy sideways in an easy chair, and me next to Buddy. He smelled like roach spray, and I realized his green suit was an exterminator's uniform. I wondered why he had it on so late at night.

Tina came over with two plates, gave Buddy his, and sat on the floor to eat. One nice thing about living here, I thought, is you could just lie in bed, paint all four walls, clean up afterward, and cook dinner without really having to move.

"Oh, hey! You're that J.O.," Buddy said suddenly. "I got it now, you're the girlfriend Andy's been telling us about."

Andy shrunk backward into the easy chair with a desperate pleading expression crinkly around the eyes.

"Yeah," I said. Was I smiling? Should I smile?

Buddy picked up his hamburger. Hanging on the wall above the hot plate was a framed butcher's chart of a cow showing the different cuts of meat. I glanced from the burger to the cow trying to figure out where it came from.

"So, when are you going to move in together?"

Andy slid both hands up over his face, and I didn't know how to react, didn't know what he'd told them. "Move in? Well, it's hard to say." Pause. "So, do you like being an exterminator?"

"Love it." Buddy nodded, he had a big head. "The bug puzzle. Extermination's a whole lot more complicated than people think because bugs are part of The Triangle. Let me make it perfectly clear for you right now." I could hear real passion loose like ball bearings in his voice. "Okay, listen up, there's us, there's bugs, and there's God, right?"

Andy pulled his hands down. "I need to tell you stuff about Carey," he said leaning toward his mother. "It's important. He's got problems again."

Tina didn't answer or even move. Her shiny jumpsuit was the exact color of the carpet, and it made her seem like she might dissolve, become a puddle of beige on the floor.

"I need to tell you now," Andy said.

Buddy punched my shoulder. "Uhh, I'm going up to the roof for a smoke, want to come, J.O.?"

I wasn't sure. A roof sounded wonderful, meatless air, bugless air, and also maybe Andy wanted to be alone with his mother. On the other hand it would mean sitting with Buddy in pitch darkness while he made the bug puzzle all perfectly clear for me. "Do you guys want to be alone?" I asked Andy.

"It doesn't matter," he said.

"Well then, I guess I'll stay here." I turned to Buddy feeling kind of bad. "I want to hear about this. Really."

"That's okay," he said. "Tina, honey, give me a kiss."

In a second she was sitting on his lap facing him. I moved my eyes away, but still heard the secret rustle of clothes, their lips smooshing together too much right behind me.

"So," Andy said. "So, so, so, so."

Buddy got up, opened the door to waist level, and I realized now if you opened it any higher it would hit Buddy Hackett in the head. The statue reminded me of Monk and Liz's rigor mortis pony, though this was a much happier kind of thing.

As soon as Buddy was gone Andy took off his sneakers and began to wipe them with a piece of grimy tissue from his pocket. "Carey calls all the time making demands. He says, 'Here's what I need. Write this down.' "

My thesis movie for Samantha, I thought. A mother and son in the garage plan a kidnapping. I wondered if The Messiah was at our apartment yet.

Tina tipped her face up toward the ceiling fan, and I watched the breeze move her hair around. I thought of dandelion fuzz again, making a wish and blowing so it scatters. Don't use this for the movie, I told myself. It isn't yours.

"Carey wants to spontaneously combust." Andy spit on the tissue and continued scrubbing his shoes. "For real. He believes that by living a certain way he can make chemical changes happen in his body. He eats sulphur. Now, I'm not Mr. Bunsen Burner, so I don't get all the exact methods, but Carey's plan is to leave the earth in a giant ball of flame. Snap, crack, good-bye. And it has to happen all by itself, no Bics flicked for my brother."

"Spontaneous combustion," Tina said softly. She picked up her burger which was untouched, then put it down again.

Above us I could hear Buddy clomping around on the roof.

"Has Carey always been into fire?" I asked, not exactly sure how I was supposed to act. Do I mind my own business? Do I ask questions?

They looked at me, quick, both of their faces skittery with

such unexpected fear that I got it too, like biting on a dime. "Well," I said. No more questions.

Tina grabbed at her hair with one hand and pulled it down around her neck. "Let me give you some money for the things he wants."

"Buddy money," Andy said, putting his shoes back on. They were covered with streaks where he'd tried to clean them. "Easy insect money. Carey told me he shaved every hair on his body, yip, yip, he said he shaved his cat too. Your money will burn." Tying his laces much too tight, I thought they'd break the way he jerked them.

Tina asked, "What are you going to do?"

Andy moved next to me and rested his forehead on my shoulder, more personal than he'd ever been. It felt strange, I was used to Rafi.

"I guess if he gets worse," he said, "I guess I'll go up there and try to put him in an in-stit-tu-tion again. Bad word, bad word."

I pictured a bald angry guy and his bald angry cat walking around a shack in Oregon. You couldn't get me up there for anything, I thought.

Tina asked, "How's five hundred?"

I looked down to my palm, the jagged half-moon cut was barely even closed. Easy insect money, I thought. Lying my cheek against Andy's head I wished I had magic bones to build a full circle around him.

"J.O." Tina reached across the coffee table, her fingers sudden and startled on my arm as if she'd been pinched. "I'm doing the best I can." Her touch felt alive like water with electricity zapped through it.

"Of course," I said smiling. Polite.

Buddy's footsteps pounded hard across the roof again, and we all looked up at the cracked shaky ceiling.

Chapter 12

We drove out of Venice in about five seconds because for some reason I never understood the way back is always faster than the way there. Andy hadn't mentioned the girlfriend thing, so neither did I. I thought it must be pretty embarrassing for him and didn't want to make it worse.

Driving east on Santa Monica Boulevard with the wide-open beach feeling faded behind me. Andy was quiet.

I asked, "What would happen if we just kept going east, past Sunset, past downtown? Would we reach the end of L.A.?"

A grayish tennis ball rolled out from under his seat, and Andy began tossing it around the car. "We'd reach gangland first, bangland, hangland."

I remembered how strange L.A. seemed to me when I first moved out here. The little things. On the freeway sometimes there were signs that said PARK AND RIDE and I used to drive by them wondering, park where? Ride what? Maybe in California, I had thought, people are on the freeway so much that they built actual rides like Coney Island for when you got bored. And even after I learned what it really meant "Park and Ride" still reminded me of Ferris wheels. L.A. was a Ferris wheel kind of place. I wondered what part of it my father came from. "Where does your father live?" I asked Andy.

"San Francisco. His neighborhood's bad, but it's sunny. That's all I know. Can I have this?" He held out the tennis ball.

"Sure."

"Thanks." The smile Andy gave me was not quite wide enough to show his crooked teeth. "In my mom's whole life she did only one thing, and that's leave my dad. Even before she met him she was saving up strength to leave." Andy grabbed a pack of matches from the dash, and began trying to set the tennis ball on fire. Bits of old fuzz smouldered then went black. It smelled really bad. "Then when mom met the Buddy Man she left my dad, but doing it took all her blood away. My dad's a real-life vampire. He takes blood. Not mine though, I still have mine." Shoving his wrist in my face Andy showed where the blood was.

"What about Carey?" I asked. "Does he still have blood?"

"Carey's off to one side with this fire thing."

I nodded, making a right then fast left to the skinny part of Santa Monica just before my dad's house.

"Where are we going?" Andy threw the tennis ball, spotted black now, out the window.

I turned onto Westholme feeling that my blood was gone also, tapped from my hand last night so there were only empty veins crisscrossing hollow blue.

My dad's house looked pretty much the same as a month ago, cozy, not Spanish like the houses on either side. A white Honda Prelude was in the driveway, and I pulled up right behind it. "I want my blood back," I said.

Andy shoved his thin hair behind his ears, and something about that was comforting like clothes warm from the drier. It was a habit I recognized, seen him do a bunch of times. "Open your door." My voice had gone nasal.

He did and so did I, pushing it wide. With both doors open the car felt exposed, disassembled around us the way a gun feels when its cylinder is open in your hand.

I put on the Israeli tape Rafi gave me, then cranked the volume loud as possible. A man's voice began, a haunted cobblestone voice. Whatever the words meant didn't matter, only this voice skinning back mysteries too old for me to understand. Rafi's music. My ears began to hurt as I saw light come on in one of the upstairs windows.

Someone was there. No, not someone, my father. He stood looking down at us, and it was too dark to really see a face, just his white T-shirt with a pattern I could barely make out across the chest. A round pattern maybe.

Everything felt too raw and real, the inside of my mouth, the car door cutting sharp into the air. I turned my head away from him, and the song had guitarish instruments now, quicker.

There were lots of flowers in the yard, more than last time. I got out of the car and walked over to two bushes near the front door, squishy lawn under my feet. One of the bushes had pale yellow flowers like a bunch of withered suns. I don't want to see withered suns, I thought, and turned toward the other bush.

It was five feet maybe with purple-pink flowers. In the dark they looked blackish. Behind me the singer held one note, jagged, hollow, his voice shivery on the high part. Omens.

I grabbed the bottom of the bush which felt wet. Yanking hard I didn't really expect it to give, but it did a little, shifting in the soil. Another yank, and the whole thing came right out of the ground. I had to catch my balance as roots tore surprisingly delicate in my hands. The black dirt hole reminded me of missing teeth, and I looked up at the window, but he was gone.

Andy was sitting blank faced in the car. I forced the bush across both our laps, and just waited there for a second, breath coming in gulps. Feathery leaves were everywhere, they blocked the windshield, they twined in my fingers.

"Let's go, he probably called the cops." Andy had to yell into my ear because the music was so loud. His voice sounded strange as if from the other end of a long skinny tunnel.

The flowers had drooped almost instantly, and I pulled one off the bush and put it against my tongue silky and bitter. Better not eat it, I thought. Poisonous maybe.

I turned my headlights on the house, the kind of house they use in an insurance commercial. My movie again. In the movie the flowers are magic. They make you disappear. The girl doesn't know this and eats all of them, so that when the boy turns to tell her something she is gone. Wiped off the earth.

"J.O., step on it." Andy yelled.

Wiped off the earth, I thought gathering the bush up and holding it tight against my face and body. The purple flowers had no smell.

Part Three

AUGUST

The Car
Of The Future

Chapter 13

General Motors was not interested in The Car Of The Future. Neither was Chrysler or Nissan, Ford or Toyota.

"I don't understand these people," Mr. Saul told me. We were sitting in the car. I was drinking iced tea and he was fooling with wires inside the dashboard because even though the car was finished, Mr. Saul still liked to pick at it the way some mothers are always picking at their children's faces and clothes. "One month now it has been ready. What is the problem?"

I rolled the iced-tea glass across my forehead enjoying the cool wet. Six o'clock in August, it was just now possible to think about other things besides how hot you were.

"These car companies are stuck in the mud," Mr. Saul said, hard to understand since he was holding two wires from the dash in his mouth. I checked to make sure the power wasn't on.

It had been a surprise to me that the car even worked, though Mr. Saul was superstitious about driving it. He thought other people might see and steal the idea. I was superstitious about riding in it also, but not for the same reason. To me the woodpecker car was held together only by the strength of Mr. Saul's faith, and if he stopped believing, even for a second, the thing would fall to bits no matter where we were or how fast we were going. Right now the car had one mile on it.

I looked out at the four bullet holes jagged on the bright yellow hood. "So what are you going to do?" I asked.

He bent down very slowly and began putting the wires back in underneath the dash. "At night I have seen advertisements on the television. They say, 'Do you have an invention? We can help you.' So maybe they can, I will try."

"But what about the guys you owe money to?"

"Ah yes." Dropping the wires he turned his head toward me. "They are not behaving so crazy now, perhaps they are waiting till I sell the car, you know these men understand I have no money, they are different than Mafia."

I didn't believe that, not even a little, and Mr. Saul didn't either I could tell by the ragged way he looked at me. "They can't hurt the car," he said. "My lock will keep them out."

Wake up, I thought. These men will break your arms and legs because there were two things you had to remember about ruthless assholes. Number one they would always be ruthless and number two they would always be assholes.

I looked at my watch, six-twenty. "I have to leave," I said feeling like it was a lie, but it wasn't. "Rafi's picking me up soon."

"Go on, make yourself beautiful for your boyfriend. Are you eating a nice dinner?"

The car door squealed when I opened it, a nasty squeal I thought, it doesn't like people getting out. "We're going to a play." I didn't mention that it was Samantha's play since Mr. Saul might feel bad he wasn't invited even though they never got along. Samantha had given me three tickets insisting that Rafi come so she could meet him. I was taking Andy also.

"A play is very nice," Mr. Saul said picking up the wires again. "Have a wonderful time."

I went inside, glad not to be there if he electrocuted himself. In my bedroom I lifted cinder blocks awhile not only for The Mag but also for Rafi, who liked my muscles. Sometimes he'd hold my arm—bicep in one hand, fist in the other—and say, "Clench," and when I did he'd turn my fist back and forth. "Feel the mouse. Feel it run."

Outside the window I could see most of Mr. Saul's yard. The bush I took from my father's house a month ago was planted near his fence where it had almost died at first, but now was doing fine. Besides the car, which was usually housed, those flowers were the only real color in the yard, glowing so bright that every time I looked over there my eyes had to adjust a little. If the sun were purple it would be that color.

I put the cinder blocks down wishing I had gone to the range today. My aim was getting better and better. Rafi thought I should have a gun of my own, even said he'd loan me money to buy something nice, but I didn't want it. Not yet. Actually owning a gun seemed like a huge statement, "I got this gun, what do you got?" a statement I wasn't sure about backing up. Rented ones felt different though. They never left the range so were safer, diluted somehow by the hundreds of people who had used them. When it was really time for my own gun I believed I'd know.

In the shower I thought about Samantha's play, she would meet Rafi this time, no avoiding it. Maybe before tonight Samantha would suddenly get a huge boil on her chin, too huge for flirting, and Rafi would say, "Nice girl, it's sad about this boil." Mean, I told myself. You're a mean, mean woman.

I still hadn't actually met The Messiah because when I got home that night with the flowers and my thesis movie, they were already in her room having sex. Loud. Samantha had made throaty groaning noises while The Messiah said, "Oh you sweet fuckin' thing, I need it baby, I need it." I lay in bed wanting to listen and not wanting to at the same time. Neither Foxtrot or Rafi had ever said anything like that, and I wasn't sure who was normal.

Opening night in a packed theater. The three of us were seated on folding chairs tight up against the stage so that our faces would be level with the actors' knees. Samantha's play was called *Dot, Dot, Dot,* and the program said it took place in Dot Dugan's living room. The stage was completely empty though except for one beanbag chair and the words DESERT SYMBIOSIS painted on the back wall in huge red letters.

"Where's Dot's living room?" Andy asked me. "They could've done some furniture, right?"

"It's a metaphor."

"Oh."

I'd learned from Samantha that anytime you told someone there was a metaphor they usually felt stupid and dropped the subject. That was mean, I thought. "I don't know where Dot's living room is," I said, "in fact I don't even know what symbiosis means."

"Symbiosis," Rafi told us, "is I get something from you, you get something from me."

"Like using?" Andy leaned across my legs toward him. "Are people going to use each other in this?"

The lights dimmed. When they came up again a woman was onstage sewing a flowered lavender skirt that looked very familiar. Then I realized it was mine. Samantha had borrowed it a couple of weeks ago. When she entered, the other woman completely ignored the fact that Samantha was wearing a skeleton suit.

"This desert sun is hot," the woman told her and continued on my skirt.

I'm getting that back, I decided, it can't be good to have the same thing sewed night after night. I wondered if Rafi thought Samantha looked sexy.

"We need to talk," she said.

The other woman threw my skirt down. "Bloodsun, ozone, talk is useless."

Next to me Rafi made a sound like when you swallow the wrong way and it goes up your nose. I kicked him.

The play was very hard to understand, mostly because besides Dot all the characters were named Placebo, and unless they were sitting I could only see them from the waist down.

During intermission we went outside to smoke and lean against Rafi's car.

"Festive play," Andy said getting out a clove cigarette. He'd been smoking them for a couple of weeks, and I thought he liked the idea of being addicted to cloves better than the actual taste. "You want one?"

"No thanks."

Ever since he found out about Rafi and me Andy watched us differently than before. The little things. I was trying to quit biting the skin near my fingernails, and when Rafi saw me do it he'd grab my hand, "Have some gum," he'd say. And Andy would be staring, his face gone pierced and hungry.

Young, hip people from the audience came out to stand on the sidewalk, a certain kind of woman with long straight hair, an intensely beautiful face, and no makeup.

I had a theory why there were so many gorgeous people in California. In the 30s and 40s the prettiest girl and cutest guy from every town across the country came out here to be stars, and when they didn't make it they married each other and began a whole tribe of good-looking people.

"Listen," Andy said. "I want to talk about my brother. Can we talk about my brother?" His nose had a sweat shine on it, eyes watery from trying to speak with a cigarette in his mouth.

Rafi shrugged, and I said, "Sure."

"All right, but this is kind of private. It's a back-door conversation, there must be a back door." Grabbing our arms he led us around the side of the building into an alley behind the theater. A dumpster was there with a small pile of nasty gray something next to it that could have been meatloaf or could've been a washcloth.

Andy tucked his thin hair behind his ears and took a deep breath. "I need to ask Rafi a favor. It's asking a lot. I'll never ask this much again." He was talking to me as if I had to give permission.

"Whatever," I said leaning back against the dumpster which felt warm from being in the sun all day. I didn't care that it was probably filthy.

Rafi moved his feet slightly apart and squinted at Andy. "Yes?"

"My brother Carey, you remember Carey, right?"

"Spontaneous combustion," Rafi said.

Andy had been telling both of us about Carey for over a month now, his crying, his late-night phone calls, threats and demands.

About twenty feet away across the alley was the back of a pizza place, and I watched a teenage kid in a white uniform come out, probably on his break. The kid, who completely ignored us, dramatically held a small orange sponge ball between forefinger and thumb. He moved it, twisting his hand around. The sponge disappeared.

Andy swallowed. "Carey won't use the phone except to call me, and he never leaves the house. I need help." He rubbed his arms.

Yeah, but what do you want from Rafi, I thought. The kid's sponge reappeared. Magic. He grinned, practicing banter I couldn't quite make out as his orange sponge changed to blue, and was gone again.

"Listen." Andy's eyes flicked quickly between Rafi and me as if he were reading. "Carey says to send him stuff almost every day. 'Don't interfere,' he says, 'I'll set you off, I'll send you up.' Fire. That's what he means, fire, and I think I should go up there and get him into a hospital even though it'll suck." Andy began itching his head like he had fleas, and for a second I thought he might cry.

There was noise from the theater as people began taking their seats again. None of us moved.

"Will you come with me Rafi? I know you have guns and stuff, and it might be like that. Will you come to Oregon with me."

I pictured Rafi's guns: two little Berettas, a stumpy rifle, and The Mag.

There was a scratchy sound from inside the dumpster right next to my leg, rats, I thought trying not to scream. People named Kimmy screamed at the spider in the tub, people named J.O. did not scream. "Can I have one of those cloves?" I asked Andy. Cloves burned long and slow and left a harsh sweetness on your lips, the right kind of sweetness I thought, to act against the rats, against the magic.

Andy handed me one saying to Rafi, "So, what do you think?"

"I think charging into this man's house, your brother, and trying to put him in hospital is a very big action. Maybe you should take some time before doing this, are you sure he's really needing so much help?" Rafi's voice was gentle, low.

From his shirt pocket Andy got out a photograph—the instant kind with a black back—and handed it to Rafi. "He sent me this yesterday."

"Oh no," Rafi said. I moved next to him to see. I didn't say anything.

The picture showed a small cat that had been set on fire, its body half running, half rolling on the floor, face turned toward us. The cat's mouth was open. On the white border at the bottom Carey had printed one word, *Ignition*. I touched Rafi's sleeve. The cat's body was kind of curling in on itself, losing shape and form, but still alive. You could tell. I laid my hand over the photograph so it wouldn't be out in the air anymore. My other hand found Rafi's wrist and squeezed and squeezed till he put his arms around me.

"Well," he said after a long pause. "Well. I need time for deciding."

Andy held his hand out to get it back, the skin around his nails chewed even worse than mine. "Please."

"When?"

"This weekend, I want to fly up on Saturday."

But today is already Wednesday, I thought, did the cat know before it happened? Did it come to him to be petted?

Rafi stepped toward Andy, his face pumped with a blank toughness, a cop toughness I'd never seen on him before. "You can't take guns in a plane. If I go, and that's 'if,' we have to drive."

Andy nodded quickly putting the picture away. He didn't look tough at all. "Okay, so we'll leave Saturday morning and drive straight through, and I'll buy all the gas and food. Listen, whatever you want is all right. If you want to play word games, Botticelli, we'll play or we'll just be quiet. Whatever you want."

Rafi said, "Slow down, let me think."

I looked over to where the teenage kid had been, but he was gone. I looked at Andy's pocket. "The play's going to start soon, can you guys talk later?"

They both turned slowly toward me, distracted and surprised.

In the second act of *Dot, Dot, Dot,* Samantha wore a tennis dress, and Rafi spent half the time staring at her legs and the other half staring into space. When it was over the three of us went backstage along with most of the audience. Everybody seemed to know at least one of the actors.

Backstage was a bunch of tiny rooms with too many smells, fast food, sweat, ammonia, old clothes. I lost Rafi and Andy right away in the crowd, and suddenly all I wanted was Samantha, wanted her voice to say my name so much it didn't matter about introducing her to Rafi anymore. "Excuse me, please, where's Samantha?" I asked the woman who sewed my skirt. Offstage I could see she was aging fast, but only around the eyes and neck like metal statues that have shiny patches where people have touched them.

"Samantha's gone, she left a minute ago with George. Do you know George?"

I shook my head and turned away from her almost running through the mass of people till I was outside.

Rafi and Andy were waiting in Rafi's car. It had gotten dark. The car was extremely small for the three of us, but my Gremlin had a slow leak in one of the tires so I was trying not to drive it. Piling in on Andy's lap with my head jammed against the roof, I listened to their conversation.

"All right then," Rafi said. "I just have to make sure about leaving work, get my nights covered." He paused. "That's it."

They're going, I thought, then other thoughts blasted through in dizzy bursts like those old movies that show events by spinning around newspapers. Danger in Oregon. They leave in three days. Does Carey have a gun? I pulled my knees in tight to avoid hitting the shift stick.

"You're my hero, Rafi, absolutely my hero."

Andy's legs felt very fragile underneath me.

We went to an Indian restaurant on Wilshire that used to be a camera store, you could still see the camera sign and display window. Inside felt cramped with dark tapestries all over the walls and ceiling. They talked about Carey from the moment we sat down.

"He's had help? Therapy?" Rafi asked.

"A long time ago." Andy ate in quick little motions, his eyes never leaving Rafi's face. "Since Oregon he's stopped talking to anyone, Oregon, oar gone, lose your oars in Oregon."

"How does he live? Does he have job?"

"No job. My dad supports Carey 'cause he feels guilty, Carey's an angry guy, and everyone knows who's fault that is. I'm not angry, so no money for me."

"What do you mean angry?" Rafi asked. "What else has he done?"

"Can we please talk about something else for five seconds?" My own voice surprised me, too shrill against the tapestries. "You have the whole drive."

They both gave me a look as if I'd caught them in the middle of some secret transformation. Going liquid. Changing forms to slide under the crack in the door.

"I'm sorry." Rafi touched my shoulder. "What is it?"

"Nothing. I wish this was still a camera store, that's all. I wish I could buy a camera right now, and take good pictures of both of you."

Chapter 14

I never told Rafi that his apartment made me nervous. With the empty walls, beige drapes, and rented furniture it felt as if no one really lived there. I sat on the couch. It was a doctor's office couch, the kind of doctor who invents his own field, like hat therapy, and then buys extra bland couches to make it all seem regular. Rafi was on the living room floor using The Gutbuster. He had ordered it from some late-night TV commercial, and used the thing so much that there was a carpet blister on the small of his back. The Gutbuster made a chirping noise which I listened to combined with the chirping birds outside.

"Those birds sound nice," I said. Early for them, it was only one o'clock.

Rafi grunted. Secretly I hoped his gut would stay the same, solid and paunchy, a gut with no agenda. He stood up and began some twisting exercises that looked designed to shoot the major organs right out the top of your head. "Look at this sweating. What did you say before? Oh yes, the birds. You know I had a feeder on the terrace, but then I read article that said when you feed birds they slowly become dependent. They know only you for food. If I go away or move the birds will starve, and I don't want this."

He had stopped exercising, and I walked over to put my arms around him. "So you don't feed them anymore?" Salt in my mouth when I kissed his neck, his body slippery like wet glass.

"No."

I went over and stood near the couch. "Why are you going? Andy's a good friend, but this is insane." I pictured the cat trying to outrun its own flaming body. "I mean something really awful could happen."

"I know." Rafi folded his hands in the air in front of him, fingers clasped tightly together. "But my life is sticking like these fingers, J.O., and yes, Sun Maiden is good job, but where is the future?" Springing his hands apart toward me. "I want it this way. Open life. I want to find partner and make my own restaurant. You know I have some money saved, not much, but we'll see." He reached one foot out and hooked it around the back of my leg in a way that was personal and very shy. Not like Rafi. "Certain situations in my life are drowning me, and I want to change this. Break the spell. I believe going with Andy will give a fresh start, fresh in my life and fresh for us. That's it. I am serious about you, J.O., are you aware?"

I shook my head trying not to grin like a maniac. Serious. He'd used the word *girlfriend* before, but never *serious,* and even though he hadn't actually said "I love you," I thought *serious* was getting pretty close.

"You want some seltzer?" Rafi walked into the kitchen. "The flavored ones were on sale so I bought ten bottles. Crazy, right? Oh, no."

"What?"

I heard the hiss of a bottle being opened. "Book work tonight, I forgot."

One of The Sun Maiden accounting books was on the coffee table in a maroon loose-leaf binder which I picked up and balanced on my head. The books had become too much for the one person they had, so Rafi was helping till the owner found someone else. He hated it.

"There is twenty dollars and change that's gone," he told me still in the kitchen. "I swear these numbers have disappeared into outer space."

I tipped my head forward so the notebook fell easy into my hands. "The best thing about numbers is they never disappear, I'll find it for you."

It was unspoken between us that he brought home the books for me to work on. I loved it; sometimes Rafi would say, "You are born animal with calculator." Secretly, I hoped to be the person they hired, and was waiting for the exact moment to bring it up with Rafi. Sitting on the couch I opened the binder across my lap expecting to see numbers lined up on the page like a friendly army. Instead, there was a big scrap of paper stuck in the front of the book. A list of women's names. They all had phone numbers scrawled alongside them, and one name, Cynthia, was circled with the words "talk to Monk" written next to it.

I looked up and Rafi was at the kitchen door holding a seltzer bottle. "I forgot that was in there, please close the notebook."

"Who are these women?"

"Close the notebook," he repeated, voice completely flat.

I slammed it shut and got up almost yelling, "Who's Cynthia? What's going on?" This was the moment I'd been so scared of, the moment of proof that Rafi really was doing something. "Are you pimping for Monk? Is it drugs?" Paper proof, right in front of me, and I had thought there would be anger, or incredible hurt, but all I felt was relief. Paper proof. It was real, not in my head.

"I am never a pimp and don't do drugs, you know this." He took a long swig from the seltzer bottle, and I watched his throat jerk. "These women have nothing to do with you. With us. I am clean to you J.O., I have never lied and never been cheating." His face was squinty careful in concentration, each word hand-picked the way you pick the best cantaloupe.

I walked over to the window, opened it, and looked out at the nighttime street. Very quiet.

Rafi said, "It's not that I don't trust you, but too many people aware of this business could be trouble for me. Already there is trouble."

I watched a car peel down the block toward us, a dusty Camaro. What business, I thought, porn? Are Rafi and Monk moving guns around for Israel? But then who are the women? Girls. There's a bunch of little girls being held for some horrible reason in Monk's apartment. Stop, I told myself, you're completely losing it.

Outside the Camaro slammed on its brakes unexpectedly, raising squealy goose bumps up my arm. Two black guys jumped out.

"Is what you're doing illegal?" Dumb question, but I didn't know how much was okay to push without crossing the line, or even if there was a line.

"Illegal, yes." Rafi came over and stood next to me. "But it's not at all like you're thinking. It's mundane." He smiled a little, new word.

The guys began to box with each other in the empty street, laughing, one of them yelled woo-woo-woo to the rhythm of his arms piston quick. "Hey, your moves are primitive," the other guy said, and I wondered what made them want to leap from their car and start boxing at this hour.

"What are they doing?" Rafi asked.

"What are you doing?" The top of his arm had a small, delicate scar that reminded me of lace, it looked like you could just brush it right off. "What's illegal and mundane?" I whispered, touching the scar which was bumpy rough under my fingers. "Shit."

Rafi pulled me against him and I smelled sweat and Flex shampoo. "I'm *with* you, you know. The other is unimportant, and I'm asking as your boyfriend, as someone who is caring very much, to let it alone. Soon, I promise to explain. Soon. Things will work out, J.O., you'll see. J.O." He paused. "What does this stand for anyway?"

"It's my name."

"Woo-woo," the guy said.

"But these are letters, they must stand for something."

"Rafi?"

"Yes, my Sweet Baboo?"

I loved being called Sweet Baboo, the name Sally from *Peanuts* always wanted Linus to call her. "You're not going to leave me for a more thrilling life, are you? Fugitive of justice." I kind of laughed. Ha-Ha.

"I will never leave you." Rafi clasped warm hands around my back, and I automatically leaned into it. He jerked upward, bones popped loudly, three different places. "That's a promise, I will never, never leave you. Okay?" Fingers cupped strong around my chin, crack, crack, my whole neck loosened. "Okay?" he repeated.

Outside, I heard the guys get back into their car, still laughing.

Rafi's breath was long and slow, and I tried to sync my own breathing to his exactly, tried to imagine myself as a Believer, like the song. What I always wanted. "Okay," I said.

Rafi drove me home right after breakfast the next morning because he had to get ready for Oregon. Check his car. Buy a map. See about taking off two nights from The Sun Maiden. "We'll still go shooting tomorrow, all right?"

"All right." We said good-bye on my driveway where, once again, the Gremlin's tire had gone flat. I had tried to buy another one, but the Goodyear people said you shouldn't get them single. It's unbalanced.

Gray clouds were humping around the sky, and I wondered if it would rain as I walked in the back way past Mr. Saul's yard. He had a stranger with him.

"Hello, Young Lady," Mr. Saul said, "this is Mr. Cunningham who is interested in the car."

Mr. Cunningham was staring at The Car Of The Future with a suspicious baffled expression. His face looked the way I imagined FBI guys to be, and I wondered if this was the type who might crash Rafi's door open at three in the morning for whatever was illegal and mundane. "Anything you say can and will."

"Won't you come inspect the car?" Mr. Saul had on the oldest, blackest suit I'd ever seen, all wrong next to Mr. Cunningham who was tieless, casual, but very plotted at the same time. The kind of guy who secretly has his shirt tucked into his underwear.

"I'm J.O." I walked into the yard. Even from six feet away I could smell Mr. Saul's suit, which smelled exactly like a vacuum cleaner.

"Let me show you the engine," he said fingering his light blue bow tie that had cheerful little red cars on it.

Mr. Cunningham glanced at his watch. "I don't have as much time as I thought, maybe we can reschedule this next week."

"Please, just a few minutes. I want to show you my coolant system." Mr. Saul reached in the car window to press a button, and I jumped as his recorded voice came loudly from inside the dashboard. "Hood is open! Hood is open!"

Mr. Cunningham rolled his eyes at me, half smiling, and that's when I noticed one of my purple flowers stuck in the buttonhole of his sports jacket. The flowers from my father. All of a sudden I was furious, not for me, but for Mr. Saul, who waited patiently next to the engine in his sad black suit. You don't smugly roll your eyes at someone's life invention.

"See you later, Grandpa. The car looks great." I leaned close to Mr. Cunningham, speaking soft and intimately, "You should probably be careful about that flower."

"What?" His small hand touched the buttonhole startled.

"That bush belonged to my father who died last month." Whispering now. "Grandpa's been a little crazy with grief, he actually pulled a shotgun on the neighbor last week just because she touched one of the leaves."

Mr. Cunningham yanked the flower out, and dropped it as if it had suddenly burst into flames. Spontaneous combustion, I thought. "Anyway, if I were you I'd at least look at the car since, believe me, you don't want to make him angry. And please don't mention the bush."

"Of course not." Mr. Cunningham smiled a strained yearbooky kind of smile and turned quickly toward Mr. Saul. "Now, let's see that engine."

I picked the flower up off the ground. "If you need me, Grandpa, I'll be upstairs." Mr. Saul didn't hear, he was busy talking about coolant in jumbled desperate words that barely made sense. I couldn't stand to listen.

"You're Busted" had been canceled for next season, so Samantha was trying not to spend as much money. She wasn't doing it very well. When the air conditioner broke instead of getting a repair, Samantha went out and bought six large fans that whirred all through the apartment. It had taken weeks to get used to everything flapping around, my hair always tangled. I wasn't worried about her running out of money though. Samantha threw it all in one huge checking account, which I balanced for her, so I knew that even without a job for two years she'd be okay.

I walked into my bedroom, hot but very still. Time for an omen, I thought switching on the desk radio to KLSX. I wanted an omen about Rafi and Andy. Oregon.

The Grateful Dead poured out easy thick like honey, *"Well, I don't know, but I've been told, if the horse don't pull you got to carry the load."* I loved how they never sounded upset about anything. *"Well, I don't know whose back's that strong. Maybe find out before too long."* It's about secret strength, I thought, Rafi and Andy will find secret strength in Oregon.

Samantha ran into my room with a *TV Guide* almost screaming, "J.O., it's happened! It's awful!"

"What?" I grabbed her arm, not to be calming but because I wanted a hit off the power. Her secret strength.

She opened the *TV Guide* right in front of my face to a full-page ad for "All That Glitters." A new nighttime soap. Samantha pointed to a woman right in the middle of the picture, a very pretty redhead with cheekbones that sucked up the camera. "That's her. George, this guy in my play said we look alike. Do we look alike? I swear, J.O., I'll kill myself if you say yes, I'll open up a vein right now."

"You don't look anything alike." Automatic answer. The truth was they did a little except Samantha's extreme features would always cast her as the Wacky Best Friend, and this woman wasn't wacky at all. She was the Beautiful Hostage type. "Who is she?"

With all her strength Samantha hurled the *TV Guide* at my open window, but I reached out grabbing it from midair. Bam, quicker than thought. I laid the magazine on my bed, and she sat down next to it.

"I haven't told you, but The Messiah's been breaking dates with me lately. Opening night, and he didn't even come to the play because he said he had work to do, but I knew something was wrong, J.O., I just knew it." She began tearing the *TV Guide* into little pieces and raining them over my floor. "So, afterward me and George bought a pizza and he knocked on The Messiah's door pretending to be a delivery man. We even borrowed the pizza guy's hat to make it seem more real."

"Pizza? But didn't The Messiah just send George away?"

Samantha began jumping up and down on my bed which made loud creaking noises. "George is smart, he goes, 'Oh, I must have made a mistake with the address, can I use your phone?' 'No problem,' says The Messiah, and lets him inside." Jump, creak. "So, George informs me later how Miss All-That-Glitters was sitting right on the couch with tits out to here and fuck-me-fuck-me pumps. You can always tell by their shoes, J.O." Samantha drop-kicked one of my pillows across the room with a look on her face that frightened me, it wasn't supposed to be there. The look said, "Help, I'm losing."

Ever since I'd met Samantha she'd been telling passionate stories and slamming things around, but every time, no matter how upset she got, part of her was always in the background having fun. All the stuff was just entertainment. We both knew that. Now, suddenly it felt different because she really believed, and I could see the fear on her face.

"Listen." I jumped up and stood next to her on the bed. "Do you love this guy?"

A nod.

"Do you love him with the white hot intensity of a thousand suns?" That was a saying of my mom's, and I hoped its drama would somehow kill Samantha's worry, the lump in her flawless confidence.

"Yes, I love him that way." Whispering now, a good sign.

"All right, then I'll tell you exactly what to do to get him back." Telling Samantha what to do felt foreign, it clashed against all my instincts like when your car is skidding, but you know you're not supposed to use the brakes. I leaped off the bed and stood facing her. "Stay very calm, don't ever push for his secrets. Don't cling. The boy chases the girl till she catches him, I swear it works." You *hope* it works, I reminded myself.

Samantha was violently shaking her head. "No way, J.O., no way, I'm obsessed. That woman is The Beast, get thee behind me."

We both looked at the pieces of *TV Guide* littering my floor, and Samantha abruptly jabbed her hand at them with pinky and forefinger extended. The sign against the evil eye.

"So, what are you going to do?" I asked.

"Make a grandstand play." She let her whole body fall straight backward onto my bed. "I'm going to tell him it's either her or me. Love is rare, J.O., and needs protection so it can bloom." She made blooming motions with her hands in the air.

"What's illegal and mundane?" I asked it very fast thinking if the words hit a perfect spot at just the perfect moment, Samantha might speak the answer.

"What? The Messiah's not illegal."

"This isn't about him." Too late, the moment was over, but I hoped she could come up with something anyway. "Just tell me the first idea in your mind when I say illegal and mundane."

Still lying on my bed Samantha pulled both legs toward herself like two upside-down Vs. "My mind is blank except for The Messiah, do you think he's actually having sex with Miss Glitter-Tits? What do you think he says to her while they're doing it?"

"I don't know, I don't know. Listen, I'm going to the bank, do you need party eggs?" I need Marilyn, I thought, she would take the edge off all of this. I loved when she said, "You can bank on it," groaning at her own bad joke. Today, I decided, I'll ask about her parents, especially the father who probably has a pet name for her, a name he's called her since birth. "Scooch" or "Tykies" or "Tiger."

Samantha sat up with the same expression as before, a kind of wrinkled nervousness. "So, I'll talk to him tomorrow, and this will be good, right? Tell me you think it'll be good."

"I can't do that," I said hating the weak look on her face, and my own meanness. "I think it's a lousy idea." It was the first time I'd ever not given her what she wanted, and as I left, too sudden, I knew something horrible was going to happen.

Outside the air was incredibly humid, and after I'd walked about a block it started to drizzle. Very bad omen. Everyone on the street looked around as if it were a joke or fallout maybe, because August rain didn't happen in L.A. Ever.

The bank was crowded with a long line of people peering

uncomfortably through the gray military light. I got on the back of the line and looked for Marilyn, but her usual place was taken by someone new, a seal sleek kind of woman with perfect skin. Maybe Marilyn's in the bathroom or on a break, I thought. Yeah, that's got to be it.

I walked over to the row of desks along the far wall—loans, new accounts—everyone was busy with customers except one man on the phone. "Excuse me."

"Yes?" Fat with a long, fancy mustache.

"Is Marilyn here?" The air felt cold against my damp skin, and I looked around the bank, foreign now without her. I realized I couldn't remember Marilyn's last name, only that it was long, began with "Cz" and I probably couldn't even pronounce it.

The man shook his head and spoke into the receiver, "I want full coverage."

I swallowed feeling the nasal creep into my voice. "Where is she, please?"

"Maternity leave." Impatient now he began wrapping his mustache around the end of one finger.

"She had the baby?"

"Yes," he said, and then into the phone, "Fire, theft, the whole works."

Outside was still drizzly, and the cars and buildings seemed smeared a little, as if they were made from a material that lost its hardness when wet. I wondered what my father was doing this second. I missed Marilyn. Crossing Fairfax I stepped over a patch of oil on the street which made me remember that oil and mercury are the only liquids without water in them. That's how this rain felt with the mercury silver sky, oil on Fairfax. Did my father forget on purpose, I wondered, maybe he hated my mother and wants nothing to do with me. Enough, that's enough. I almost said the words out loud because getting into "poor me" was much easier than getting out again.

As I came near my house two men, one tall, one short, were walking from around the back where Mr. Saul's yard was. Even at seventy feet away I recognized the big blond one. I stopped.

On the sidewalk now, they headed toward me while tossing

something back and forth between them. The blond one had eyes that slid all over, he checked stuff out and then dismissed it as if the world were a giant magazine he was flipping through. When they got closer he did it to me, I could almost hear him think, "Woman. Standing there. Young."

Got to move or it'll attract attention, I thought, so I took a step toward them, thirty feet away. The other guy, not-blond, caught whatever they were tossing and said, "Cheap shit," in a voice surprisingly high. His body reminded me of one of those dogs you see barely contained by their leash, a chunky dog with every muscle twitching and thirsty. His world wasn't a magazine, it was a meat locker.

Almost there, and I stared straight ahead trying to seem forgettable since I was going to have to walk right between them. As we passed each other the thing being tossed sailed through the air in front of me, an unusually large watch with a blue plastic band. Mr. Saul's. Okay, so he gave it to them as another payment, no problem, I thought, going past my house and down the block since they weren't gone yet. He's all right, you're all right. Bullshit. But it kept me moving, my head turned back around careful, easy, every few feet till I saw them get in a car at the corner far behind me.

"Mr. Saul?" I ran toward our house screaming his name. Nothing. "Where are you?" In the yard now and the gray sky behind his shed made it look like those things in graveyards, mausoleums, and I thought, no, no. "Mr. Saul." Silence.

I ran around to the back of the shed where he lay half propped against it. Blood. On his face, nose, and mouth, the bow tie hanging crooked with more blood and dirt all over its hopeful little cars. I kneeled down next to him. "Don't move, I'm going to call an ambulance."

Mr. Saul opened one eye, the other was swollen shut, and made a weak coughing noise. "J.O., help me check the car. They may have hurt it." His voice had a funny lisp because both of his front teeth were completely gone.

I rocked back and forth on my knees. "I'm sure the car is fine, we'll check it later, okay?" I stared hard at his forehead, the only part of his whole body that didn't seem beaten.

"I have to see my car." Trying to get up he scrabbled his feet around, one hand braced against the building, the other buried in his pocket. "If you will not help me then I will do it myself."

"Don't, okay, just . . . I'll help you." This is wrong, wrong, wrong, I thought with the only first aid fact I was sure of flashing in my head. Never Move An Injured Person. Sliding my arms around his back I lifted from under his shoulders, surprisingly heavy, and Mr. Saul made a strangled noise almost letting go.

"Please lie back down, the car can wait."

"No. Help me."

I staggered, half dragging him to the door, and by the time we got there tears were coming from his closed eyes, though he didn't make a sound. Bending very slowly close to the lock Mr. Saul said, "Are you all right?" Click. I fumbled the door open with my foot, and somehow managed to get the light on without letting go of him. Inside, the bare bulb put glary shadows across the car, but it was fine. Untouched.

In the hospital lounge I called work to tell Rafi I would be late.

"Don't worry about coming in at all," he said, "unless you want. Will Mr. Saul be okay?"

I glanced at the only other people in the room, a couple of guys, kids, they looked about thirteen, who were playing chess very intently with their portable board on the plastic couch between them.

"Well, he has four broken fingers, a lot of bruises, and something ruptured in his nose. They knocked out three teeth also, Wham, just like that." I thought about how those teeth had probably been from the late twenties, their secret ridges and smooth spots known only to him. "The doctor wanted him to stay at least overnight," I said, "but he won't so I'm taking him home."

One of the chess kids made a move and nodded quietly at the other.

"Is there anything I can do?" Rafi asked.

"How about blowing their heads off."

Both boys looked up at me. I turned my back.

"Well," Rafi said.

"Well," I answered as Mr. Saul shuffled slow and dazed into the lounge.

Back at his house we went into the bedroom where I sat awkwardly on the edge of the bed not sure if I should stay or leave him alone to rest. "Mr. Saul, you have a sister, right?"

He sighed leaning back against the pillows. "Yes, Ruthie. She lives in Washington, the District of Columbia."

The doctor had bandaged his fingers so they held a Styrofoam ball and I looked at his wrist above it, at the pale place where a watch used to be. "Have you thought about going to visit her for a while?" The air felt itchy bright. Mr. Saul's wife had loved yellow, collected it the way other people collect stamps, so his bedroom walls and furniture were all yellow along with various knickknacks. Ceramic cat, a pair of bronzed baby shoes. "You could take The Car Of The Future to Washington, it might be kind of fun." The words came out raspy, as if yellow had gotten stuck in my throat.

"No. I am not about to drive that distance."

"So take a plane." I glanced at his wrist again which seemed almost see-through without the watch. "Please, Mr. Saul."

"Never. That car is my product. Would you leave your new baby to go across the country?"

I laughed and looked away. "Some people might."

"I am not those people." His one eye hard on me. "Anyway, I don't like Ruthie, I don't like the government, and I don't like the zoo. You know in Washington they think their zoo is so wonderful, but it's not a good zoo. Pandas, ha."

The doorbell rang, Shave and a Haircut.

Both of us jerked about a foot and the underneath part of Mr. Saul's eyes started twitching as he touched my hand with his good one. "Will you see who's there, please, J.O." Wheezy breath, his fingers tight on mine. "Remember there is an iron security gate, but I still wouldn't open the door."

It rang again.

"Don't worry." I stood and walked into the living room my legs completely soft. Forget about saving for a new car, I thought, and forget about this spiritual statement crap, because I need a gun. Tomorrow I'm taking my money out of the bank and buying a gun. I touched the doorknob deciding it would be useless anyway once they saw how bad my hand shook. My whole body. "Who is it." Trying to sound tough. Yeah, right.

"J.O.? Rafi sent me over with some soup, how is he?"

"It's The Sun Maiden," I yelled to Mr. Saul, and then opened the door for Andy. "Hi."

"Are you okay?" He was separated into a million dots by the black security gate.

"Uh-huh." Leaning forward I rested my forehead against it, eyes closed. "Tell Rafi thanks."

"I will, and you know what? He let me drive his MG over here, that car is beyond festive. Can I be Rafi when I grow up?"

I opened the gate so he could hand me the white to-go cup which had soup spilled down one side. Yankee bean. That's right it was Thursday. "Sure."

"See you later maybe." Andy ran down the driveway and leaped into Rafi's convertible without even using the door.

Back in his bedroom I gave Mr. Saul the soup, but he said no. "You, eat, I'm too tired." His head was sunk deeply into the yellow pillows.

I wanted a cigarette but opened the soup instead, brownish beans and liquid that was almost the exact color of the bruise across his eye.

Instead of going home I decided to work after all hoping the brightness and people would kind of weld things together again. My Gremlin's left front tire was getting low every few hours now, and though I had put in that liquid sealing stuff yesterday, it didn't help. I stopped at a gas station to fill it. Turning onto Sunset I wondered should I call the cops, no, because if the guys found out they might mess up Mr. Saul even worse. A car cut in front of me at Crescent Heights, and as I stopped short my rearview fell onto the seat. It was only attached by duct tape anyway. I tried to stick it back again, but the tape wouldn't hold, and people were honking, and then I started to cry.

At The Sun Maiden Rafi hugged me right in front of everyone. It felt so incredibly good I was embarrassed for myself. Lily and Ann had split my section which was turning over fast so I walked right in to a new table.

The corner booth, a father and daughter. Even from far away I could tell she was angry, but he wasn't, he just seemed tired.

"Hi," I said walking up to them hesitantly. "Ready to order?"

They both ignored me. The daughter was maybe eighteen in bright lipstick and an antique dress with pictures of playing cards all over it. "You're wrong," she told her dad, "it has nothing to do with age." She leaned toward him their profiles identical like facing quarters. "Can't you see that?"

"Should I come back?" I asked.

"What we have is real love," she continued, oblivious. "His age is not important."

The father sighed. "But honey," he said looking down at the table. "Mr. Bimmler was *my* chemistry teacher."

"I'll come back," I told them.

Andy was behind the counter doing Lily's butters because she always tipped him extra. "Did Mr. Saul like his soup?" he asked as I came over.

"Yeah, thanks." I had no idea why I lied.

The cold pats of butter were supposed to be stacked evenly in a plastic container, but instead Andy was building a cabin. It was going to take a long time. I watched as he made windows using toothpicks for frames, his skinny hand aimed each pat carefully one by one. "Bad news, Carey called to say he just set fire to the shed next to his house." He dropped another pat, another. "Must have a cell-u-lar phone 'cause I could hear the flames like giant wings, whoosh, whoosh." Turning from the butter Andy flapped his arms in slow motion, lips pooched out like a beak.

"Aren't you scared?"

"No, not with Rafi along. His Mag is the golden gun, the stun gun, wouldn't you say?"

I glanced over at Rafi deep in thought behind the cash register, and as I looked he got a pen from his pocket and began writing quickly on a napkin. I wondered what it was.

People came and left and somehow I managed to get inside the chant—half decaf—vinegar with his soup—separate checks—extra lemon. I still worried all night about Mr. Saul though. They could kill him in his bed. Right after we closed Lily offered to drive Andy home if I finished her salt and peppers which was fine since it meant being alone with Rafi. He was in the office ordering meat.

When they were gone I brought all the shakers up to the counter, and began refilling salt out of a half-gallon plastic dispenser. I held it three feet above the shakers to practice my aim. The dispenser opened on a metal lever that I tried hitting with my thumb for just a split second so the perfect amount of salt would stream into each shaker. The kind of thing you do when you're alone. I wondered about really buying a gun especially since you had to wait ten days before they released it. A lot could happen in ten days.

"Shit." My thumb hadn't been quick enough and one of the shakers overflowed salt onto the wet counter. Putting the dispenser down I began to wipe it.

"Hey, J.O., go baby go."

It was Monk right there in his Raiders cap and a black sweatshirt with the sleeves cut off. I stopped wiping. "Monk, I thought the door was locked."

He laughed, coming up to the counter. "You thought wrong."

Having Monk here at my job, my place, gave me the same feeling as when I saw the guys with Mr. Saul's watch. A whiplashed feeling, shocked from the socket. "Want me to call Rafi? He's upstairs." Why are you asking permission I thought, just do it. But I didn't, I didn't say a word.

"Your earring's tangled." Monk's pushed-back eyes stared at me when he spoke as if it were all code for something else much more important. He reached his arm out, and I flinched. "Stay still, J.O."

As Monk untangled the earring I felt the weight of his hand too close to my face, a high-pitched pressure like guitar feedback. I looked at his boxy chin. "I'm calling Rafi."

He smiled. "Go ahead."

"*Rafi*," my mouth was woolly slow on the word. "Monk's here."

Rafi came downstairs in about five seconds and I walked over to him, got his arm, and pressed it around my waist.

Monk took off the Raiders cap, longish hair curlier than I'd thought, it moved around like a bunch of Slinkys. He said, "We got to talk. Now."

"Can I see you first?" I asked Rafi still gripping his arm. "It'll only take a second."

"Sure." He glanced at Monk. "We will be in office, stay here all right?"

Monk put his cap back on and touched the visor in a salute, but he was making fun. It's all an act anyway, I told myself, he probably can't perform unless someone spanks him first with a waffle iron.

I followed Rafi into the office angry at myself for thinking that. The thought wasn't like me really, it was like Monk, he put it in my head.

In the office Rafi sat on top of his desk while I stood. "Monk makes me nervous," I said.

"You and me both."

Above us one of the fluorescent tubes was burning out, making a fritzy noise that seemed very loud in the quiet office. I took a deep breath deciding not to say a word till I found some leverage. A small thing. In New York there were some Greeks who lived next door, and the men would always hold little pieces of string with wooden beads attached, flipping them around in their hands. Leverage.

Rafi propped his feet on the chair in front of him, glimpse of red above one shoe. That's what was needed because I knew he owned only one red sock and couldn't remember where it came from. His other one was probably black. Just a detail, but it was enough for leverage somehow, the intimacy, the fact that no one but me would know or even care about his socks.

I said, "What's Monk doing here?"

"Please. It's business, and I'll explain when I can." Rafi's lips were beautifully shaped and seemed pinker than usual. Alive.

"I'm sorry," I told him. "But I can't deal with this. Whatever 'business' you have going with a bunch of women scares me. Oregon too. Whatever it is I can handle, I mean that, but what I can't handle is the secrecy."

Rafi got up and cradled my face in his hands, the fingers so warm and near I just about said, "Forget it." But I didn't, I jerked away.

"All right, J.O., we'll make deal. As soon as I'm coming from Oregon I'll explain the whole situation. But now is no good. Nothing is definite, and my vision, my inner vision is a blur."

I glanced down at his sock again. "Are you hurting anyone?"

"No."

"Are you lying to anyone?"

A pause. "Me personally, no."

I pictured him in Oregon, and Mr. Saul being killed and Samantha having a nervous breakdown. "I'm sorry." Trying to keep my expression completely neutral, I curled my toes up hard enough to make them cramp. "I need to know before you leave. I really need this from you." Grandstand, I thought. The exact thing I told Samantha not to do.

Rafi lit a cigarette even though you were never supposed to smoke in the office. His face was closed to me as he took detours and made choices. I could almost see him thinking in Hebrew. "You believe somehow I will not be coming back from Oregon, don't you? Well this is not a belief from today, J.O. This is thinking like Neanderthal." Shutting his eyes he held the bridge of his nose between forefinger and thumb.

"Who are the women?" My voice came out cold, almost flat, though I didn't feel flat. I felt breathless and terrified because the problem with grandstands is you always had to follow through to the end.

"Let me see what Monk wants."

"Oh, Monk," I said half sure he could hear us even though that was impossible.

Rafi opened his eyes and I stared at the tiny black spot. I'd like to take that thing from his iris, I thought, and throw it on the floor where I knew it would hiss and burn a hole right to the basement.

"Tomorrow we'll go shooting and I'll tell you," he said. "How's that? I'll tell you everything tomorrow, just let me see the story with Monk."

"All right." My shoulders relaxed with a kind of thunk, I hadn't realized they were hunched practically to my ears.

Rafi put his arms around me rubbing the back of my neck exactly the way I liked it. "One game Liar's Poker," he said. "Then I have to go."

"Come on, not now." I didn't want to play Liar's Poker, didn't want to bluff and maneuver anymore tonight.

"One game, girl. It's good faith."

We got out our dollars and began to play, Rafi going first with two threes.

"Three threes," I said fast to get it over with.

"Three fives."

I concentrated on my dollar, one five there, and then the flexing feeling began in my head, so I knew he had the rest. "Four sixes," I said.

"Five sixes," Rafi smiled.

Flex, I mentally reached for the numbers (six was a scrappy guy who always won arguments) but nothing was there. For the first time in my life I couldn't feel a number. I looked at my dollar again, two sixes, that meant Rafi needed three in order to win. Possible, but not likely. "Show them."

He handed me the dollar and sure enough there were three sixes. I tried to smile graciously giving them both back to him. "Well, you won."

Rafi looked confused. "I beat you at this game?"

"Yup." I held my fingers out for his cigarette and took a drag on it feeling completely disoriented. Homeless. The numbers had deserted me because that's what happens when you start needing to win.

Rafi glanced from the dollars to me and back to the dollars again. "But I don't understand. You always win at this."

I shrugged and went to the door. "So, I'll see you tomorrow, right?"

"Yes."

"And you'll tell me?"

"I will. Yes."

We stood in silence for a few seconds as Rafi folded the dollars separately into tiny squares. I watched first one and then the other bill get smaller and smaller, seeing it too tightly, the hair on the backs of his hands, thick wrists turning. "Good night." I left before he finished, not wanting to see my dollar, already mostly gone, disappear completely inside his pocket.

Downstairs, I walked quietly out the back door to avoid facing Monk again. The Gremlin took a while to warm up, so I sat listening to the radio, "Fat Man." "The fat man always wins," Jethro Tull sang. I lost my virginity to Jethro Tull music, the second side of *Aqualung*. It had been Foxtrot's favorite album.

Leaving the parking lot I looked through the glass Sun Maiden doors to where Rafi and Monk were at a booth with a bunch of papers on the table between them. As I watched, Rafi swept his arm violently dumping the papers to the floor. Monk laughed. I wondered who the fat man was.

Chapter 15

Friday morning. I wandered through the apartment waiting for Rafi to call, but he didn't. It was hot and windy from Samantha's fans, and I sat in the kitchen feeling stuff I was afraid of dive-bombing around me like squeaky little black bats. Rafi and Andy in Oregon tomorrow, Mr. Saul, Rafi today.

When he called, I decided, it would be smart to answer the phone just right. "Hello? Oh. Hi." I practiced getting the exact sound in my voice, cheerful yet very distracted as if I'd just figured out some brilliant way to make a million dollars with nothing but six feet of garden hose and an old banjo.

It rang. I walked slowly to my bedroom glancing in the mirror before I picked it up. "Hello?" Perfect.

"Young Lady?" It was Mr. Saul. "What are you doing?"

"Nothing."

"Oh. You sound busy."

"I'm not."

A pause, and I asked, "Is there something I can do? How are you?"

"Not so good." A wheezy kind of sigh. "The man that was supposed to see the car today never arrived. My fingers hurt."

"Do you want me to come over?" With all our windows open you could hear my phone from Mr. Saul's house.

"No, no, no. That's all right."

"Well, okay."

"Okay."

He hung up. I went back to the kitchen and drank iced coffee for a while trying to remember the exact details of every scar on Rafi's body. Shoulder, back, hand, ankle. Finally I called him myself, pretty dumb, but we had to get moving if we were going to spend the day together. His phone rang—ten, eleven, twelve—not even the machine. Maybe he changed his mind and doesn't want to tell me, I thought, picturing Rafi shirtless, using his Gutbuster with the unplugged phone tucked away in a closet. No, that was paranoid, and he would have to see me at work tonight anyway. What's illegal and mundane?

I waited three more hours, then went to the range by myself. Rafi had never stood me up before, and on the way there I half expected to see him around every corner *doing* something. What? A secret identity, an illegitimate child. Pulling into the gun club parking lot I checked for his MG, but of course it wasn't there.

The range. For the last month I'd been inching out the target a little more each time, and now it was as far away as the wire pulleys reached. The man: a faceless silhouette, big shouldered, a bull's-eye around his heart. I fired playfully at first, shooting in eyes, nose, and ragged mouth. I made a row of shirt buttons, perfectly spaced.

Then in one smooth click my body caught the motion, slid with it, and all that existed was me and that rented Mag. I shot The Mag, and The Mag in its strength shot me, firing dead center over and over. But still the last piece was missed. Only a woman and a gun, because there was no third part today, no straight-edged magic part that I usually felt but never could quite climb inside. It was good anyhow to have real skill. I shot till my arms were so numb I could barely lift them, fingers cramped and bruisy.

When I got back home at ten to five, the Gremlin's tire was really, finally, completely flat. Running in for my hat and bow, I decided to ask Samantha to loan me the Nissan tonight.

She was in her bedroom naked in front of the mirror with a bottle of black nail polish in one hand and a container of baby powder in the other.

"Hi. Can I borrow your car to get to work? My tire's flat again."

Samantha turned to face me, thinner than I remembered, her collarbone jutting out as fragile as the wishbone on a chicken. "The Messiah's coming over, and I'm telling him to give her up. Should I be Angel Woman or Filth Woman?"

"I'm late. I've got to go." My hands still throbbed from shooting which I hoped wouldn't slow me down on a busy Friday. I wondered if Rafi was there yet.

"Angel Woman or Filth Woman?" she repeated, the two choices in her hands thrust toward me incredibly significant. Offerings.

"I don't know."

"Yes you do. Tell me."

Just pick one, I thought, or you won't get to work till midnight. "Umm, Angel Woman, okay?"

Without hesitation Samantha dropped the black nail polish on the floor and began showering herself with baby powder. "Keys are on the coffee table."

The Sun Maiden dressing room was empty, so I practiced my Rafi attitude. "You stood me up!" No, too pushy. "What happened?" A little better, but how would Marilyn handle it? Walking downstairs I decided she would just ignore him, make him come to her. Yeah, perfect.

In the restaurant something had gone extremely wrong, I could almost taste it like tinfoil against your fillings. It wasn't that busy, but everyone acted jagged as if it were. Even Lily looked anxious.

A man and woman walked over to me, and it took a few seconds before I recognized Mr. Jallo, the owner who I had only met once the day I was hired.

"Hello there," he said peeking at my name tag. "J.O., I'd like you to meet Rita, who will be your new manager."

Rita gripped my hand, still sore from The Mag, and squeezed it. She looked almost exactly like Mr. Jallo, big and pink.

"Where's Rafi?" I asked pulling my hand away.

Mr. Jallo said, "America's Guest no longer works here. That's all you need to know."

They both smiled at me. I smiled back, though it was really hard. Make it conversational, I thought, like you're just curious. "But what happened?"

"Was Rafi a friend of yours?" Rita stopped smiling.

In my mind I saw him stomped by skinheads or unconscious over the wheel of his flaming car. "Was? Is he dead?"

I didn't mean it as a joke, but she laughed, "Kaw-Kaw-Kaw." A horrible sound. "As far as I know the man is perfectly healthy."

"Oh. That's good. Well, I better get to work." I turned away and almost ran over to Lily who was with a table. "Lily, can I talk to you?"

The table, three comedian types in paisley shirts, stared at me.

"One sec," Lily told them and walked a few feet away.

"What happened?" I sort of clutched at the shoulder of her uniform slick against my fingers. "Where's Rafi?"

"I hoped you would know."

"Uh-uh." I shook my head with humiliation that throbbed dirty and unfair like a punch you're not ready for. "He never called today." I sneezed.

"Bless you." Lily reached out and carefully straightened my hat. "It'll be fine," she said. "You'll see."

But I didn't see. During the dinner rush I completely lost control of the entire section, and Lily had to take two of my tables. Time seemed to move forward in lunges. It was eight o'clock for about six hours, and then a flash instant later it was eight-thirty.

At nine Rita told me I had a personal call.

Rafi, I thought, heading quickly for the phone. He would explain everything, "I love you, I'll never never leave you, come away with me."

"I don't usually permit employees to take calls," Rita said, "but I made an exception because whoever it is sounds awful."

"J.O.?" Samantha was sobbing so hard I almost couldn't understand her. "You have to come home."

"What happened?"

"Mr. Saul's guys trashed your whole car and the front of the building."

165

"Where is he?" I shut my eyes to blot out Rita who stood too close. Her pinkish face reminded me of the shade of crayon you used to color in skin that never really looked like skin. My hands itched.

"He's in the hospital, come home."

She hung up and I told Rita my grandfather had been in a terrible accident.

"I'm sorry," she said. "Leave now and call in tomorrow for your new shifts."

I could tell she didn't believe me, not for an instant.

Chapter 16

In her bedroom Samantha packed a suitcase with movements too slow, almost drugged. "I'm not staying here. It's unsafe. I'm never staying here again." The room reeked of baby powder.

"Just tell me what happened." Without wanting to I pictured the front of the building and my car. "Were there two of them?"

Samantha nodded whispering, "I can't tell you or I'll cry again." It wasn't the usual drama though, this whisper came broken from her throat.

"Just talk and don't picture it," I said watching as she threw stuff in the large suitcase, completely disconnected. A dictionary, a backgammon set, two necklaces. The room's only light came from a tassled lamp that put rainy-shaped shadows on the walls.

"They tried to break the doors, even his security gate." She took a deep, shaky breath. "They got mad. One of them kept yelling, 'Where's our money, asshole, I'm gonna fuck you up.' I thought they'd get in, J.O., I really really did." Samantha began pulling clumps of fuzz from the chest of her white angora sweater, way too heavy for August.

"Did you call the cops?"

"Yeah. They were here in twenty minutes which was too late, but good anyhow since they brought an ambulance for Mr. Saul. He had a heart attack." A pause. "I need to leave." She struggled zipping the bulgy suitcase.

"How's Mr. Saul?" Maybe if I'd watched out for him more, I thought, warned him, except what would that have done?

"I don't know, he's at Hollywood Presbyterian." All at once Samantha kind of collapsed on top of the suitcase which made a crunching noise as stuff inside broke. "The Messiah's with that woman I told you about, the 'All That Glitters' woman. He left me."

My stomach fisted up and I thought, just breathe. Breathe. "I'm sorry." I walked over to the bed. "Here, sit down."

Sliding to the floor she kneeled tightly, face squeezed between her hands. "Her name's Sabrina, and we do look alike, we really do, in fact the only difference between us is Sabrina's dumb and has no talent. The Messiah left me for me, but an easier version. Samantha Lite." She began rocking back and forth, white knuckled from holding her own head.

In a second I was over there, my arms around her shoulders. "Don't touch me, J.O."

A warning, but I ignored it and pulled her close, fingers stroking her hair. Samantha bit the back of my right hand, hard, really hard, I felt her teeth break skin, prickly burning from my fingertips all the way up through my shoulder. I sort of scuttled backward across her floor, not easy with all the mess there.

On my hand the circle of bloody teeth marks almost looked good like the print of a special cult, the Bitten-By-Samantha Cult. Almost, I thought, but not quite. "What the fuck is wrong with you?" I put my mouth over the teeth marks wondering why it was always my hands that got hurt and if there was any antiinfection stuff in the bathroom.

"I'm sorry, I'm so sorry, I don't know what I'm doing." Samantha's eyes were flashcube bright and pale because she didn't have on her blue lenses. "You know what? The Messiah is the first person I ever really loved. Ever. I mean that. There's something wrong with me, J.O., I don't love anyone."

"What about your parents?"

"I feel like I'm dying." She picked up the suitcase.

As she walked to the bedroom door I watched her bare feet with all the bones shifting on every step. I tried to remember how many bones were in the human foot. A lot. "Where are you going?"

"To George's, I'm sleeping on his couch."

I thought of staying here carless with broken windows in the living room and Rafi gone, Mr. Saul gone, Samantha gone. "Don't leave."

"I have to, it's not safe anymore."

On her nighttable was an empty glass and a hammer. Everything is lethal, I thought. Her bed heavy oak, silk scarves, an aerosol can of fly spray. "Please don't leave me here alone." I held my hand out with the bite mark toward her.

"Come along if you want, George is all right." As she wrestled the suitcase out of the bedroom it made an awful scraping noise against one wall. I always hated that kind of sound, ratchy, like feet on stiff snow or opening the freezer door when you haven't defrosted.

I said, "Rafi will call, I can't leave."

"Oh." She walked down our hallway which was dark.

I followed. "Samantha listen, George's house isn't any safer because nothing's safe. I mean nothing. Come on, just stay here."

"Don't get deep." Her angora sweater almost glowed in a way that wasn't comforting. Bone white, Halloween.

"Come on," I said again, but she didn't answer.

Samantha was my protection, I thought. Her stories, the colorized version of her life had always been wrapped around me like a striped blanket that made extra layers of warmth wherever I went. But not now. She was stripping away from me in sunburned patches. "Please." I didn't care how pathetic I sounded. "Please, please, everyone's gone. I don't know where Rafi is. He's gone."

"I'm not living here another second." She opened the kitchen door and stood in the harsh half light of Mr. Saul's yard. "Can't do it, not for anyone." Samantha's face had a grainy blankness like mug shot photos. No expression.

I watched her drag the suitcase down our broken-glass driveway. My disembodied car door was lying in front of her, but instead of going around it Samantha just tromped right over the metal. It'll be okay. Rafi will call, Rafi won't leave.

I stood there for a while opening and closing my hand so the bite mark would move around. What do I do? The water heater next door was grinding. Stones were inside, little rocks, Mr. Saul had told me once. You have to flush it out. What do I do? I sat down on the kitchen floor, sat very still.

In the next hour or so I talked to Hollywood Presbyterian (Mr.

Saul was "stable") then got in bed. With the covers over me, I began trying to sing the whole *Katy Lied* album straight through without hesitation. Rafi called during "Bad Sneakers."

"J.O.," he said. "Monk's friend Liz went to Sun Maiden and they told her you had emergency. How are you?"

"I don't know." I stroked the light green phone, the color of a desert where you could taste the chemicals. "I feel like I'm aging in dog years."

He laughed, fake, not really him. "We have to talk."

"Yeah."

Rafi was in Monk's pawnshop and wanted me to come over there, but I didn't have a car anymore.

"Take taxi," he said. "I'll pay you back."

We hung up and I got out of bed, not easy, and began putting on my shoes. Sun Maiden shoes. That's when I realized I still had on my sweaty uniform, hat, name tag, all of it, but instead of changing I just tied the shoelaces. Waitressing was a kind of grace. Not only light-on-your-feet grace, it went further than that, and now, with the way things were, I needed every drop of grace around.

The cab company said fifteen minutes. Twenty-five minutes later there was still no cab, so I called again practically begging the guy to hurry. "Soon, soon," he told me. "Be ready in front of the house."

I ran outside to where the Gremlin sat tortured and trashed on our driveway. I stood blinking in long rhythms. There was too much to see all at once, better this way, blinking, so you got it in freeze-frame pieces. Every window smashed. Body rippled with dents. Bumper guards, my stupid, sweet bumper guards lying scrap-metal twisty on the lawn.

I remembered in June when Rafi fixed my door, and the way the whole car had become wonderfully fluid, changed shape around me. Driver's door. Now, it sat about six feet away, torn right off the hinges. How did they do that, I wondered. They must've opened it wide and then rammed it with their car. More quick photographs. There were two lawn chairs mangled outside Mr. Saul's door. Front windows broken. Scooped-up lawn.

I wondered what the odds were of so much falling apart at the same time, it seemed almost impossible. And I hadn't even talked with Rafi yet.

After brushing piles of glass off the seat, I got in the Gremlin and curled my legs up. Still no taxi. This car had never left me stranded, never not once. I put the key in, and almost laughed when it immediately started since the reason I left it here in the first place, a flat tire, was now the most minor problem on the whole car. "Sorry, sorry," I kept saying as I backed in tiny jerks down the driveway. The Gremlin didn't like being driven, it made horrible clacking noises with chunks of metal and glass falling off like old skin except there wasn't any new skin underneath.

Chapter 17

I drove very slow with the tires mushy flap-flap in my ears. The sound kept me quiet though, focused, since I knew if I stopped concentrating on it for one instant I'd make noises of my own and not be able to stop.

Once my mom told me the difference between fear and anxiety. Fear is when you see a black widow on your leg, and anxiety is when a black widow is crawling loose in the room, but you don't know where. She was wrong.

I didn't have any idea what the fuck had happened, what these spiders were, but *anxiety* was way too tame a word for the panic I felt.

Sitting high on one knee I peered frantically though the only unbroken spot on the windshield. About four inches near the roof. Better be careful of cops, I thought. Definitely illegal to drive without a door. It also felt frightening, even at twenty miles per hour there was harsh wind and noise and left turns that practically pulled me out of the car. Don't look at the ground, my head chanted over and over. X ray exposed. Doorless.

Chapter 18

Monkowitz's Fa$t Ca$h For Your Valuables was pitch dark when I drove up in front. Before getting out of the car I automatically reached for a door handle, ha-ha, hoping Rafi didn't see me from the window. It was pretty pathetic.

He must've been watching though, because just as I got to the entrance he opened the sliding gate thing and yanked me inside.

The only light in the store came from its neon sign, but even in the dark I could tell Rafi looked awful. More than tired, more than nervous. Some kind of cornerstone was gone from his face, and he stared at me scattered weightless like birdseed. It's the heat, I thought, he's lost the heat. No, that's impossible.

"You're late," he said.

Waiting for the bullet is worse than when it comes, I thought, but that wasn't true. Monk's cash money presence around us, and the dark, and the grittiness on Rafi's face all told me this would be really bad.

"Rafi, I waited and waited, but you never called today, and then I went to work, but you weren't there, and I was so scared." I put my arms around him and leaned into the back-cracking position hoping he'd do it. He didn't. "They almost killed Mr. Saul. I was so scared."

Rafi gently pushed me away. "Why are you late? This was a wrong instance for being late, J.O., because I am out of time now. It's very important I meet Monk, and can't stay for talking."

Behind the counter I could just make out Liz's stuffed dead pony, cut with pinkish light from the neon outside. I grabbed his arm. "Where are you going? Please, don't just leave, please.

Samantha left, she's gone and I couldn't get a cab, and I'm sorry. Please, Rafi. I'm sorry." My own begging voice disgusted me, a voice with no guts, no strength, no nothing. Still hanging on to his arm I took a deep breath.

Rafi smelled like five things, each completely distinct, but taken together it made one big smell that was only his. Cigarettes, Flex shampoo, sweat, bubble gum, and wool blazer. I inhaled again because there was another smell on him that felt not quite in the world. Toxic. A evil black forest smell, or the air inside a tunnel that stretches miles and miles beneath the ground. It's fear, I thought. I'm smelling fear.

"Why are we in Monk's store, please, just tell me that." I glanced over at the pony again which looked even worse in pink neon, as if someone had tried to make it more cheerful.

"Monk is living upstairs but doesn't trust anyone there alone, not even Liz. Too much guns."

"So where is he?"

"I am supposed to go meet him in five minutes and should not be late. J.O., this is hard, nothing was supposed to have been happening like now. I am not aware to how I should tell you."

I leaned against the glass display counter, cool on my back. I covered my face.

"Okay, a woman who lives here in California is needing money. Maybe she was fired, maybe just young, or loser. Whatever. Monk and sometimes Liz find these women and I find the husbands. Israelis mostly, but not always. The husband will give the girl good money and pay Monk and me also for this service. That's it."

"I don't understand." I watched as Rafi came and stood silhouetted about two feet from me, hands at his sides, feet spread a little apart. There was no light on him at all, just a faceless man shape.

"Monk and I are marriage brokers," he said.

Marriage brokers? I thought. That's the secret? And for a second I believed this would be like one of those sitcom episodes where it's all just a surprise party in the end. "What do you mean?" I walked over to a table in the middle of the store. It was covered with stereo receivers, though I didn't know till I touched them. "People get married without meeting each other first?"

"It's not for love, J.O., it's greencard."

I moved my fingers over the different stereo knobs and buttons. There was something else there also wedged between two receivers, so I picked it up. A camera. "Greencard." The word felt completely alien to me.

"Yes, greencard." Rafi still stood in exactly the same place, facing where I'd been. "So husbands can live here in the States. Citizenship."

"Are you married?"

He laughed. "It's funny, that's your first question. No. I am divorced nine months."

The camera was fancy, the kind that came with a twenty-page instruction manual full of diagrams that looked like they belonged to something completely different, the solar system or a pair of lungs. I looped its strap around my neck feeling all the shadowy times with Rafi begin to click open one by one. "Wait a minute, that guy in the Sun Maiden a month ago. Your cousin. He's not really your cousin, and the woman was a greencard marriage, right? Why did you lie? You didn't have to lie."

"No, no." He sat heavily on the floor. "This man was a favor. He is my sister's husband's brother, and so I helped him with the papers. But he is asshole. He caused so many problems for me and Monk, but mostly me because he never even met Monk. Here is the bad part coming now." As Rafi lit a cigarette, the match showed a piece of his unshaven cheek very bright before he put it out. "My cousin and his wife had interview with immigration which is normal, since immigration wants to check if people are really married for love. They didn't pass."

I remembered how wrong the guy and his wife had seemed together and decided I wouldn't have passed them either.

"Why didn't you tell me?" My hands needed motion so I pulled the lens cap from the camera, but it slipped between my fingers and fell out of sight onto the pawnshop floor. What color was the floor in here anyway? I couldn't remember.

Rafi said, "I wanted to wait till I was out of the business. This is difficult business, not something people should know, and I decided to tell you about it after I quit. Three more marriages.

But then this guy made problems." His cigarette glowed as he dragged off it.

"Problems," I repeated. The wheedly edge had come off me and was replaced by sarcasm. Good. Sarcasm never begged. "You just didn't trust me, did you?"

"Always, J.O., I always trusted you. I am cherishing you." Rafi's voice was frightened into a kind of swamp water stillness, and I told myself calm down, you don't have all the information yet. It was impossible though. He had held back from me all along but gave to Monk. Monk the mystery. Monk the ass fucker.

I walked up behind him with the camera bumping heavy on my ribs. "Cherishing, does that mean it's okay to lie? I'm twenty years old, not some fucking little baby you can lie to."

As he jumped up to face me, Rafi's hip slammed against the glass display case making things rattle inside. Monk's things. "I never lied to you. Never. Lying is aberration, I am clean to you, Girl. I'm also very very sorry for these problems. It wasn't supposed to turn this way."

"What way?"

Silence.

"What way?" Behind the case where Rafi stood I could see there were shelves, but not the stuff on them. Everything was blended together in the dark.

"Immigration did four interviews with my cousin and his wife. At the last one they separated them." A line of pink neon fell across Rafi's cheek like a burn as he walked toward the window. "When he was interviewed all by himself they came strong—'What is your wife's favorite food? Tell us about her mother. Sugar in her coffee? What did you get for birthday? Does she sleep sound at night?' Avi, my cousin, is weak man, so finally he told them all of it. Even my name and phone number." Rafi braced both hands against the wall and just stood there as if holding it in place. His body was the direct opposite of when he shot, a body with no spin to it, no—what was the word? Velocity.

"They were at my house, J.O., maybe still, they came to Sun Maiden. I'm sorry, I know this is a shock. I'm sorry. Monk drives me to the airport soon. I'm going to Israel. I don't know how long, maybe six months, maybe more."

Slam, out of nowhere physical pain hit me so hard I grabbed my stomach. "No." The camera hit my knees as I bent over, stupid tears grown old before they're shed. "But you promised you'd never leave. Remember? That night in your house you promised, and I believed. Why did you do that?"

"I'm sorry, J.O. This is a federal crime, and they will put me in jail. Jail. I don't want to take a chance becoming caught, they are not playing. I have to get to airport."

"Rafi." I shook my head, but it was a huge effort, couldn't think, couldn't get air. The room was filled with underwater strangeness, and except for my stomach which hurt like a car alarm, it felt as if I were trapped inside an old home movie, the silent kind, not video. Kids wearing crew cuts, kids in the wading pool. A slow, stifled ticking, with movie flatness that's never real, but this *is,* I thought. This is Rafi now. Real. I raised the camera up to my eye and looking through the viewfinder focused his silhouette. "It only takes one moment to destroy the thing that took a lifetime to create. Right? Wasn't that you who wrote that with the car stereo? 'Let's be careful,' you said, 'I want you with me.' " Click. It sounded very loud with pressure good against my thumb as I pulled the advance lever. "What about Andy, did you tell him? He counted on you."

"I talked to Andy earlier but didn't explain the reasons for Israel. Please stop that camera."

Click. Breathing in sync with my pictures as Rafi turned from the wall and took a step, click, click. "A moment to destroy."

"That's wrong, J.O., I don't believe it anymore. Things don't take a moment because most acts are long time coming."

Click. Why do I keep doing this? I wondered. The pain in my stomach had spread to my hips and down my legs now, sunk right in the bone marrow. My mother told me a story about leg pain once. I shoved the image away. Mr. Saul's fingers were broken. Click, click, I changed the rhythm of Rafi pictures to match throbbing legs instead of breath.

"Stop." He grabbed my arms just below the elbow and forced the camera down. I struggled to get it back to my face again, but Rafi pushed me toward the window where neon had the floor half lit. "I want you with my life. This doesn't have to be get even time, we can maybe come to understanding. I won't be gone forever."

"No." I fought hard to get his hands off, but he was stronger, pinning my arms to my sides. "Let go of me."

"I love you, J.O." Rafi's features were lit greasy cheap by the neon. I watched him start to cry, surprised he didn't look away or loosen his hold because Rafi wasn't designed for crying. A Mag man. He believed tears were meant for women and artists, and I knew by giving that up without a flinch he was giving away his last safety. The dearest thing.

Cramps in my legs twisted up another notch and another till there were fists of light in the corners of my eyes like glowing snowballs. "Get your hands off me." Screaming, couldn't breathe. "Get them off! Get them off!"

Rafi took a step back, his face kind of scrunched by shock and confusion. Pink light hit the chest of his button-down.

"To me you're already gone." I didn't think I could stay standing much longer. "Go to Israel, I don't even know your name." I made a sound, all fucked up.

Raising the camera again I snapped one last picture of Rafi's dark shape that I knew would stay with me the rest of my life. Homeless. Pink in the middle. Already he was a stranger, a foreign man married to nothing.

Chapter 19

People were slowing down their cars to stare at me, or maybe the trashed Gremlin parked on the sidewalk next to where I sat.

The bank was dark. I leaned against its glass doors trying to imagine that strength was oozing from the building into my body. Numbers and purpose. Whenever a car slowed I would duck my head to look at something else, the front of my uniform or cigarette butts piled next to my leg.

I thought about numbers. They felt distant, like kids from elementary school you only remember by both first and last names. Robert Fishbeck, Steven Tate, David Adler, Bruce Bruno. I had told a few boys my father was one of the hostages in Iran, boys I could still see perfectly. Bruce Bruno said he was really sorry my dad was going to die because President Carter had decided to blow it up. And even though I remembered exactly how it felt there with Bruce Bruno's round face and short nose, he was gone. I wouldn't know him if he pulled up right here. The numbers were that way too now, sealed airless in my mind, but still very real. I missed them.

My ass had gone numb from sitting on the ground so long. I lit another cigarette trying to remember small good things, and bring them closer to me, favorite things, but not like that song which was completely fake. "Raindrops on roses and whiskers on kittens," whose favorite things were these?

I closed my eyes. Sitting in the sun with a cold can of Diet Pepsi. The Mag's steely kick in my hand. Someone I love stroking the back of my neck because he loves me too. "Layla," the best song ever. But I couldn't focus on any of them, not even The

Mag, all I felt was cramped legs and stomach. Samantha's bite throbbed.

"Are you needing a ride?" The guy had an accent, middle-aged guy, Ford Bronco, rough, tough, and ready. I knew the sound, he was Israeli. Pulling both knees in close I shook my head and pressed hard as possible against the bank.

"Did you have accident? Come on, come on, I give you ride." Instead of answering I took off my Sun Maiden name tag.

"Why are you sitting out here?"

The plastic snapped easily in half, right between J and O. I dropped it on the ground.

"You want coffee? I take you for coffee, I am Morris, don't be scared."

I ripped my hat and bow into four pieces each, but Morris didn't go away till I started tearing up the calves of my panty hose.

Samantha's sheets were called Huckleberry Sunset, although to me the color looked like a really bad bruise. I took my shoes off and got into her bed. There had been a close call on my way home with the Gremlin because it was impossible to see out the broken back window. Tomorrow I'd have to buy another car. I had eight hundred dollars.

The room was dark except for Samantha's blinking phone machine, and suddenly all I wanted was to hear a voice in my life yet not in my life, so I played her message.

"Hello to you." Mr. Saul sounded like all the energy had been vacuumed right out of him. I wondered if he was in a private room. The message went on for five minutes as he apologized to both of us, said he'd be there a couple of weeks, and would I come visit him soon. He also kept talking about someone named Beamus. "Please explain to Beamus," he said, but I didn't know what that meant.

Samantha's blanket felt good. I missed her, my hand hurt. Just stay here awhile, I told myself, then go to your own bed. Rafi was far away by now, on a plane maybe, or nervously showing his passport to some guy in uniform.

The room was cool. I lay with Samantha's blanket tucked under my chin, and maybe it was because my legs still hurt, but I thought of my mom and the cramps she had.

My mom's favorite saying of all time was a line from *What Ever Happened to Baby Jane?*, a nasty movie. I was glad she only used the line on me once.

In the movie, Blanche—very sweet and horribly abused by Jane—says something like, "Oh, Jane, if only my life were different. If only I wasn't in a wheelchair." And my mom would quote Jane's answer making her voice go snarly like Bette Davis.

We hadn't lived in New Jersey very long when a friend of my mom's opened a bartending school in Nome, Alaska, and we got his rent-controlled apartment. West Village, one bedroom. My mom threw a party to celebrate the incredible luck, but it seemed a little creepy to me. Nome, Alaska, was like Hitler, one of those things people used as an extreme example of cold or bad.

Living in Manhattan again my mom worked driving a horse and carriage around Central Park. I would hang out there in the afternoon trying to act cool with the other drivers, their smell, their slang. "Perfect timing," she would tell me as I ran up and carefully hid schoolbooks under her seat. "I'm head-out on the Five Line." That meant the best spot for customers.

I remembered the day she used her movie quote on me because it was also the first time I ever heard a gun shot. Four o'clock in February, very cold. When I came by after school that day my mom was curled up in the seats of the Little Red, not even hacking. She hated the Little Red, thought it looked cheap.

"Hi." I handed her a cup of coffee sweetened with hot chocolate the way she liked. "Why aren't you hacking?"

"Oh, stop." My mom had on an old ski mask, the kind that covers your whole face, and over it she wore a cap with a picture of Fred Flintstone. "Yabba-dabba-do," the cap said. I decided no one would take a carriage ride with this person in a million years.

My mom sipped the coffee. "This is great, J.O., you will ascend directly to the Kingdom of Heaven for this."

"Why aren't you hacking?" I repeated. We were on the Two

Line, and I glanced over at the other driver, his tux, top hat, and fancy overcoat.

"Carriage ride, folks?" he asked some people walking by. They ignored him.

"See, he's trying," I said.

"Of course he's trying, look at his rig."

The man's black carriage was closed in cozy, I could even see the glow of a heater inside. "So why don't you get one like that?" I began jumping up and down to stay warm.

"He works for Lucky Clover, J.O. The Italians don't have those carriages." The Italians were my mom's stable, that's what they were called, The Italians, and they named their horses after all different operas. I was still jumping, but my feet were numb so when I hit the ground there was an extra second before it registered. The cement seemed hard as ice, though it was dry. I stopped to talk to the horse. "Hi, Carmen, how are you?"

As soon as she heard me, Carmen twisted her head and began chewing at the wooden carriage poles. She was the strongest-colored horse I'd ever seen, almost orange which was why they harnessed her to the Little Red. I thought it looked dumb, like an orange shirt with red pants.

"I'm cold," my mother said. Her voice sounded angry or something, it was hard to know with the ski mask. I wished she'd take it off.

"Beautiful," I told Carmen reaching out to stroke the muscley neck.

"Don't touch her, she's an animal today."

"She's always an animal."

"Yeah, well, today she's crazy, a blemish on the animal kingdom. You know what? I think Mikey double-shifted her again last night, I swear that guy would double-shift his own grandmother if he could find a harness to fit her." She paused. "Sorry, I'm acting like a bitch. It's just cold. I've only had one lousy ride all day, and I didn't put the ski mask on till three."

I got into the carriage and sat across from her moving my face around to fight numbness. "Want to trade coats with me? I'll try for a while."

My mom's coat was thrift-store old with woolly stuff on the

collar, a respectable coat though. I had on the down jacket she owned before. It used to be all white till the dirt got so bad my mom dyed it green, but that didn't cover the holes patched with pieces of duct tape. My mom was saving to buy me a decent coat. I hoped it wouldn't take much longer.

I also hoped she'd trade with me now because I wanted to get us a ride and that was impossible in the leprosy jacket. Being on a ride was the best part. I loved Carmen's skittery trot and my mom cheerful with the tourists: "Denmark? Wow, I've heard it's beautiful. So how long are you in the States?"

Now she said, "I will not have my only child behave like a Dickens character to put bread on our table. Come on, let's go back, it's freezing." As we climbed up to the driver's seat my mom's foot got twisted in the plastic roses stuck all over the front part of the carriage. "Good taste," she kicked the hard red flowers, "cannot be learned or taught. J.O., watch this." Speaking in a completely flat voice and without even touching the reins she said, "Carmen, we're going home."

Before the word *home* was finished Carmen took off into traffic, her mane rippling like fire in the cold wind. Maybe it really is fire, I thought, maybe if I held my hands out the flame mane would keep them warm. Turning onto Fifty-eighth Street someone honked at us. Carmen spooked which tipped the Little Red sideways on two wheels for a second. I grabbed my mom, and she yelled "Easy, easy," to Carmen. "Christ, she's nuts today."

When we reached Fifty-fourth Street it started to snow, not big graceful flakes, but the rainy kind you could only tell was snow by looking at a streetlight. I hated it because whenever the dyed jacket got wet my neck and wrists turned green. It looked like I had caught a weird disease or had been working on some chain gang.

"Mom," I said. "When are you going to buy me a new coat?" I watched her profile as she fought Carmen who didn't want to stop for a red light.

"Soon, I'm working on it."

"Well how long?" It came out nastier than I meant, but the cold was clenching up my skin.

We turned down Ninth Avenue next to a rush-hour bus. I was level with the passengers and could almost smell their closeness, the damp scarves, twice-breathed air. It was getting dark.

"I said soon, J.O., all right?"

Carmen started trotting down Ninth Avenue so fast and forceful it took every bit of my mom's strength with the reins to ease her to a walk again. "Please, honey, I'm tired."

Taking a deep breath because this was risky ground, I said, "Why don't you ask my father for some money? We have the address in California, right?"

My mom shook her head. "I've never taken a penny from him, and I don't intend to start. Not that he's tried." The Little Red went over a pothole that bounced the entire carriage, hard. "I should go work for Lucky Clover, you know? Maybe they'll need someone in spring."

We turned onto Fifty-third. Not much traffic, I could hear the rhythm of Carmen's hoofs, badly shod, flattened and cracked from being on asphalt. "I wish my life were different," I told her. "I wish I didn't have such a loser for a mother." As soon as the words were out I wanted desperately to shove them back wherever they came from. Mean, really mean.

My mom turned away yanking the Fred Flintstone cap down tighter on her head. "But ya' are in a wheelchair, Blanche, but ya' are."

Silence. I tried to think about other things like warm horse bodies and the smell of hay. It was fun at the stable. The Italians had a little donkey who ran around trying to have sex with all the mares, but he was much too small. The mares ignored him except Carmen who always kicked him in the face.

My mom said, "Miles would accuse me of being ungenerous. He believed I faked and said that not faking it, ever, was a kind of generosity."

"Oh." I didn't really know what that meant but wanted to keep her in adult talk. "So, were you?"

"What?"

"Faking?"

"Sometimes." She turned toward me ski mask slightly crooked on her face. "What am I saying, you're thirteen."

"I'm not some kind of baby, Mom. God."

All around us the parked cars had turned watery white, but you could tell this snow wouldn't stick, it was just sleet really. "Just sleet," I said liking the word.

"Miles *was* a baby," she told me suddenly. "Only nineteen when you were born, though that's no excuse. For a few years he'd send checks occasionally, very small ones, with a card that had some message like 'Thinking of you.' Yeah, right. I always tore the checks in half and returned them because I didn't need a late-night guilty thought in the mail, I needed him to try. After a while the checks stopped."

We passed a vacant lot with four men standing around a garbage can fire. "Hey," one of them yelled, "buggy woman." He was a young black guy in an army jacket. "You sure are fine."

I looked at my mother wondering how he could tell with the ski mask. Maybe he knew her. She was looking back at me something almost shocked in her eyes. "Well," she said. "Okay, well."

We were silent for a bit so I watched my foggy breath and pretended to be smoking.

"Listen," she said finally. "I don't want you to end up with the wrong idea about him. There were great times like New Orleans, I mean everything just kind of pulled together the whole year we were there. When we went back to New York and started fighting a lot, in the beginning all one of us had to say was 'Orleans' and we'd make up. We'd remember."

"Orleans," I thought but didn't want it out loud.

"Miles could be so hilarious. Give him any object, a skillet, a piece of string, and he'd do stuff with them so you'd be on the floor laughing for hours."

I tried to imagine fourteen years ago maybe. Miles had taken a photograph of my mom in a New Orleans park that I loved, I kept it in my room. In the picture her arms were spread for balance, eyes tightly closed because she was holding his bicycle on her chin by the kickstand.

"And he cooked," my mom continued. "Miles was a brilliant cook, the type that throws himself around the kitchen like a dancer, no not a dancer, like . . ."

"Mick Jagger?" I asked.

She smiled. "Yeah, perfect."

I smiled back glad to have known this one little thing.

"He had hair to his waist then, thick and dark, and when he cooked he'd wrap it up in my tie-dyed scarf. Besides that, all he wore in the kitchen was gym shorts. Miles had the longest arms and legs I've ever seen, and I used to love watching him in those tiny gym shorts flailing all over the kitchen. It cracked me up."

A truck moved suddenly in front of us, the exhaust going into Carmen's face. She reared. For a second I thought the harness poles were going to break, but then she came down on her feet again.

"Get out of the street," the driver yelled from his window.

"Fuck you." My mother's voice was much too low for him to hear. "Fuck, fuck, fuck," she said. "Easy Carmen, eeaasssy."

"What else?" I asked. "Tell me more."

We pulled up at another red light, my mom folding her slick reins together and popping them the way you do a belt. She popped quietly though. "We'd left New Orleans and were in New York when I got pregnant. Right afterward Miles decided he wanted to move to L.A. That's where he was from."

Part of me was disappointed she'd stopped telling about New Orleans, but still, I had never been too clear on exactly why they broke up. I hoped to get the whole story before we were at the stable and The Italians distracted her. If that happened she'd never pick it up again.

"Anyhow, we fought a lot because I hate California, but finally I agreed to move. As soon as I said 'okay' though, these cramps started in my legs, terrible cramps. It felt as if all the blood had turned to battery acid. They got numb too, especially my feet and the toes would be all twisted under. I thought it was pregnancy maybe, but then even after you were born the cramps started up whenever we talked about moving."

Something from the street had caught in the spokes of one of our back wheels. It made a loud ticking noise that freaked Carmen. "Come on, Crazy Horse," my mom said. "We're almost home."

Carmen flattened her ears.

"I guess you were about ten days old and we were in the living room when Miles told me he was going to L.A. for a month. Trial separation, yeah right. If anyone ever says trial separation to you pick up their favorite fragile thing and hurl it at them because they're not coming back. My legs started then, the worst ever. I couldn't even move from the chair. J.O., it felt like my legs belonged to a dead person while the rest of me was still alive. 'Please,' I said. He came over and I put you in his arms. 'This is your baby,' I told him. 'This is your only child.' You know how infants can't really see? Well, I don't believe that not after the way you met his eyes. But it wasn't enough. It just wasn't enough."

" 'Wasn't enough,' " I repeated watching Carmen who thought she could get away from the ticking noise if she jerked forward.

"He left, and then every once in a while I'd get a thirty-dollar check in the mail. I'm sorry, but I'll lay my body bleeding and broken to die on the street before I'll ask him for a cent."

We were coming up on Eleventh Avenue, two blocks from the stable. Carmen, covered with sweat, pranced frantically toward the intersection and my mom said, "All right, all right," forcing her to a stop. "J.O., hold the reins a sec and I'll fix this back wheel. Hold them tightly, okay?"

Heat and strength seemed to pour right up through the chewed leather. Veins, I thought. Connected to me. My mom had just gotten over to the wheel when Carmen bolted out on Eleventh Avenue against the light.

"Stop, stop," I pulled the reins with all my weight, but it wasn't enough and cars plowed into us. I flew, surrounded by quick-flash accident sounds. Squeal, slam, crunch. People yelling. It took forever, but I landed on my side ripping open the entire sleeve of the green jacket. Down spilled on the street.

Getting up very slowly, hurt arm, not too bad. I could see Carmen lying nearby her body completely stiff and still, but not her head which thrashed in different directions as she screamed.

Lather, white eyes. Pieces of the Little Red were scattered all over, most of it still attached to Carmen, screaming. Cops were there in twenty seconds. My mom pressed me close saying, "Carmen, Carmen, Carmen," as the gun went off. Quiet again, I looked at the back wheel. Whatever had stuck there, ticking, was gone.

Someone was knocking on the door. I opened my eyes, bright light, what time? 9:00 A.M. Where? Oh. Samantha's room. Still in my sweat-dirt uniform, panty hose torn to filthy strips. Nothing left, I thought.

They kept knocking so I put on a pair of sunglasses from the floor trying to seem decadent in case it was Jehovah's Witnesses or some health club.

He was a black guy, young, with a little beard and a polished foxy sort of face, not a comfortable face except for the ears. They were huge and stuck out about a mile from his head. Trustworthy ears.

"Hi, I'm sorry to bother you." With no change of expression he took in all of it, even my hair which was flapping around from Samantha's fans. "Do you know where Jonas Saul is?"

The ears lied, I thought. He's probably someone else Mr. Saul owes money to, and any second he'll smash me against the wall. "Nope," I said. "No idea."

"Well, my name is Ray Beamus from RHP Investments." He handed me a business card. "We had an appointment."

RHP's logo showed a boulder surrounded on three sides by heavy black lines. I wondered what it stood for—Really Hard Part? Rapid Horrible Puking?

"Is that your car out there?" he asked. "Looks like someone had a problem."

Mr. Beamus's tie was covered with tiny flags from all over the world, and I stared through my sunglasses trying to see how many I recognized. "Problem, yeah."

"Are you okay?"

Canada, Italy, Israel, no don't think about Israel. "Mr. Saul's in the hospital," I said. "He had a heart attack."

"Heart attack? How's he doing?"

"I don't know, guess I'll go visit today."

"Well," Mr. Beamus stepped away from the door. "Seems like this is a bad time, maybe I'll call in a month." He turned so I could see the Florida-shaped island of sweat in back of his shirt. From behind, his ears seemed even bigger like cupped hands.

"Mr. Beamus?"

"Ray."

"All right, Ray. You want a can of Diet Pepsi? You look hot."

"I don't need a diet." Ray grinned smacking his almost too flat stomach. "But water would be fine."

In the kitchen he stood in front of Samantha's largest fan with his head tipped back, and his body moving as if in a shower. "I drove all the way from Long Beach with a broken air conditioner. The pool sure will feel good tonight." Looping long arms around in the butterfly stroke, his dark-muscled health filled the room. "What's your name?"

"J.O." I handed him a glass of water.

"Check it out, Jonas and J.O."

"I think of him as Mr. Saul," I said, glad that Ray would probably never see the woodpecker car. It was better this way, no one felt disappointed.

"So where's the invention now?" he asked and got more water. I could hear New York street in his voice, distant but close at the same time like the sound of police helicopters when they circle the neighborhood. "The truth is backyard cars are never worth the trip, you know? I drove down really to see a friend."

Even though I agreed, the words *backyard car* seemed incredibly low budget. But it wasn't, not to Mr. Saul. "Well," I told him, "I'd show you the thing myself, except it's in a shed, and he made this voice-activated lock so we can't get in." Good, I thought, now at least Mr. Saul doesn't look like a total loser.

Ray raised his eyebrows. "Voice activated?"

"Yup."

"You mean it only opens when this guy talks to it?" He took a step toward me.

"Uh-huh."

"He made it himself? Do you know the cost?"

I remembered what Mr. Saul told me the day I saw the lock. "Brains, it cost brains."

Ray's face got even foxier as he balanced his water glass on top of dirty dishes in the sink. It's nothing bad, I realized. Just the expression of someone who's trying hard to get rich. "Well, I wish he were here, cause if it works, and it's relatively cheap, I might be interested."

I'd seen that pointed look on Mr. Saul when he built the car though it wasn't for money. Poor guy, I thought, he had sounded so lonesome last night. Spent. "Wait a minute." I yanked off Samantha's sunglasses, blinking in the glary light. "I have his voice on an answering machine, if we can get it down there."

"Yeah!" Ray slapped his thigh, something I'd never actually seen a person do. "Smart."

Mr. Saul had plenty of extension cord lying around which was lucky because it took over fifty feet to get Samantha's answering machine out her window and across the yard. Easing it carefully toward the shed I could smell my own sweat and cigarettes gone toxic in polyester. I hoped Ray was far enough from me. Just as we held the machine right up to Mr. Saul's lock, Andy came into the yard.

"Hi, J.O., I walked here, three point eight miles."

Amazing, I thought. The night Rafi bought me a stereo he acted like aliens had invaded the planet, but now that I'm in a filthy uniform next to a stranger picking a lock with an answering machine Andy doesn't even blink.

"This is Ray," I said. "Ray, Andy."

"Hi." They shook hands.

Andy looked normal today except for the baby's shoe attached to his ear. "Doesn't that hurt?" I asked pointing.

"Nah, it's good. Keeps me on the ground."

"Okay, let's see if this works." Ray started up the tape, and Mr. Saul's voice said, "Hello to you," but maybe because it was a recording nothing happened. We listened as he apologized about the damage to my car, hoped Samantha was all right, and then, just when he asked me to visit, click.

190

"It's much faster live," I told Ray who looked impressed.

"Yeah? Let's try again."

I shook my head feeling wrong about Mr. Saul's exhausted voice being used behind his back. "I think we should talk to him first. Do you want to see the car? This is his dream, you know."

Ray opened the shed door wide and took in The Car Of The Future. "His dream?"

It didn't seem like a car really, but more like a bunch of clunky pieces that little kids might use for blocks. The curved roof reminded me of a Tupperware bowl he showed me once, but its fat diamond-shaped windows were a mystery.

Squeezing inside the shed, Ray ran his fingers along the bright yellow hood which was facing us, and I saw him notice all four bullet holes. "Why did he design the front end like this?"

I looked at the way the hood came to a point so extreme you could almost prick your finger on it. I shrugged. "Mr. Saul has the only key, so but I can't run the engine for you."

Ray rubbed his beard, a skinny down-the-center-of-the-chin type. "No problem. Really." He had an expression like he wished a friend was there so they could exchange glances. "But that lock is interesting. Listen, is he strong enough for visitors?"

"Can I come?" Andy asked. "I'm hungry anyhow, yummmmm, hospital food! They probably have Jello-O in the cafeteria, and I could do that. Jell-O or pudding."

Ray's Toyota smelled exactly like an Egg McMuffin, and I counted nine McDonald's wrappers crumpled on the floor near my feet. "So, I've been with RHP since college," he was saying. "They're good people."

"Have you bought a lot of inventions?" I asked. A distraction. Even after changing clothes my skin felt used up in the heat, worse because the black sleeveless T-shirt I was wearing had been Rafi's favorite. He used to call me Muscles.

"Inventions," Andy repeated from behind us. His legs were stuck straight out between the bucket seats, one foot tapping restlessly against my knee. Andy had on old orange flip-flops, and

I wondered how he had walked the three point eight miles to my house in them. For that matter how did he know how far it was?

Ray said, "Have you seen that spray stuff you put on bathroom mirrors to keep them from fogging? Steam Away."

Andy said, "Yeah."

"I have too," I told them. Not true, but these kinds of stories were ruined if you said you didn't know what the person meant.

"Well, RHP found that one. It was my contact actually."

"Oh." I stared at the light blue rabbit's foot he had hanging from his rearview. It swung. "So, what does RHP stand for?" I asked unrolling the window.

"Rock and a Hard Place," Ray grinned. "We figure that's where most inventors are when they call us."

Andy maneuvered himself so that his head and shoulders were up front. "Hey, Rafi's gone," he said suddenly with a tiny crooked smile on his face.

Cramps shot through my legs, not as bad as before, but I still felt a high sharp rush like cold water in a cavity. "Why are you smirking? Don't forget he fucked you over too."

"I'm not smirking," Andy said. Then he told Ray, "Rafi's her boyfriend."

"Ex. He's a lying sack of shit, that's what he is." I pictured Rafi's bare back, with the long hook-shaped scar numb to the touch, and the picture made me yell. "Thank you for bringing this to the general public, Andy, in fact why don't you go to Oregon and explain it all to your brother. Rafi's not here because he just doesn't care enough about anyone. Anyone. He ran away to Israel with one hour's notice, isn't that beautiful? Oh, I take it back, you can't go to Oregon since Rafi had the car and the gun. He fucked both of us."

I looked over at Ray who was very quiet, sort of scrunched toward the steering wheel. His expression was carefully blank, eyes straight ahead. This is a scene, I thought. I've actually created a scene and embarrassed people. Even though I knew it was wrong, part of me liked the way they sat there so awkwardly, waiting to see if I'd begin to shriek again. "Do me a favor and don't mention him anymore, okay?"

"Okay, sorry," Andy said touching his baby shoe. "Sorry." He took an RHP pamphlet out of a box in the backseat and started shredding it into tiny pieces.

Silence. We made a right turn onto Hollywood Boulevard, the kind of place where everything looked as if it would be sticky. Even the street names had a gummed-up feel, with stoplights on practically each corner. La Brea, Orange, Las Palmas, Cahuenga.

"Are you from New York?" I asked Ray just to say something.

"Bronx, you?"

"The City. Where'd you go to high school?" New York high schools were a code I understood, not like out here where the only meaning I could get from a name was its sound.

"Bronx Science."

That was public school for smart kids, not quite as good as Stuyvesant, but better than Brooklyn Tech, a party school.

"How about you?" he asked.

I sort of shifted in the seat because whenever anyone from New York heard the name of my high school they either laughed or became politely quiet. "Pinella," I told him.

"Pinella, huh?" Ray laughed, a friendly hooting sound. "I forgot about Pinella, my mother wouldn't let me go there."

His reaction probably should've bothered me, but it felt good to not explain, to be read in shorthand. Pinella was an experimental school which meant you didn't really have to do any work. Most of my senior year I hung around making different types of burglar alarms for dollhouses, no problem. But at least I showed up. My friend Danielle Cruz fell in love with a Norwegian sailor and decided to quit high school, but then their relationship didn't last. She came back to Pinella six weeks later with his hat and a bunch of drinking songs. "An independent project," she said. C plus.

Still on Hollywood Boulevard we were past the movie theaters now and into hard-core discount. No palm trees, no Mexican-styled stuff because these were real Mexicans crowding the sidewalks in a way you don't see on the West Side.

Andy stuck his head and shoulders up front again. "J.O.?" he paused. "Will you come to Oregon with me tomorrow?" The question sounded completely casual, like, Did I want to go to the beach.

Why isn't he embarrassed, I wondered, opening his whole personal life in front of a stranger. "I'm sorry," I said. "I have to get a new roommate, a new car, and probably a new job." It came off sort of friendly and apologetic, though what I wanted to tell him was: Never! No, not for a million bucks. I didn't even have a car, but if I did I was not about to drive it hundreds of miles to be spontaneously combusted by a deranged bald guy. I couldn't even blame Rafi for not going, only for saying he would. "Why don't you just call the cops up there and tell them the problem? You don't have to go yourself."

"I want a photo opportunity," he sang in my ear. "I want a shot at redemption."

Paul Simon, I thought, not in the mood to bounce lyrics back at him. "Well, sorry, can't do it."

"Don't want to end up a cartoon in a cartoon graveyard," Andy continued shaking his head.

I looked at Ray. He was moving his head also, but only to avoid Andy's baby shoe which kept whacking the side of his neck.

"Package," Mr. Saul told us again. "I will only allow a package." He hadn't gotten fake teeth yet to replace the three that were knocked out, and it made his top lip seem a little flappy. He looked taken care of, though. The clean blue hospital gown, bandaged fingers lying neatly on the bed, and medicine smell all around us made me almost glad he was here. Safe.

Ray stood up in frustration but quickly sat down again. "Mr. Saul, Jonas, I'm going to talk straight with you. You're never going to sell that car."

"Why not? It's a good automobile."

Ray rolled his eyes. We had been here forty-five minutes, but Mr. Saul just kept repeating that RHP couldn't have the lock unless they bought The Car Of The Future also. "This lock is only play for children," he said. "Don't you understand that?"

I glanced over at the other patient to distract myself from how stupid Mr. Saul could be. The patient was an older guy, late sixties, with a blurry lightning-bolt tattoo down the side of his arm. He was so drugged up that his whole face had gone loose and smoky. Let go. The guy's bedside table was empty except for a pair of brown driving gloves, the kind with little holes. I wondered who would bring driving gloves to someone in the hospital and if Mr. Saul had been telling him about The Car Of The Future.

"Listen," Ray said. "Cars don't get made in backyards anymore. Ford, Tucker, those guys are ancient history. Do you know how factory cars are built? I don't even think yours is street legal."

"Sort of reddish," the drugged guy said suddenly. His eyes were closed.

"What?" Ray asked.

But the guy didn't answer, and I thought of Samantha's sleeptalk, the omens I never found.

"Young Man," Mr. Saul turned so that his good eye faced Ray. The other one was still bruised shut. "I have respect for you, but you don't understand The Car Of The Future is all I believe in. You see it is my dream to have everyone own it. People deserve my car."

No thanks, I thought. You'd have to have been a serial killer in a past life to deserve that car.

Ray lightly punched the bed near Mr. Saul's leg. "I respect you too, but I don't buy dreams. I buy locks. Want me to say what's wrong with your car? All right, how about that point in front, if you hit anyone with that thing you'll nail them to the wall like shish kebab."

Mr. Saul stared past Ray out the thick window. I felt sorry for him, but also wished I'd had the guts to say this a long time ago.

"How about aerodynamics, huh?" Ray walked to the foot of the bed and leaned toward him, one hand on each of the metal side pieces. "There's a good reason only bugs have your roof and flat windshield. It's got too much resistance. No one wants a car to be fighting the wind."

"But brown also," the drugged guy said, turning over restlessly. "And I swear in my hands it had life of its own."

Ray leaned down even further. No one talked for a moment, and I felt that if you put old-fashioned clothes on us we'd be like a painting. The wrinkly old man in bed with a woman to one side, but the real focus is on the black guy wide armed, strong at his feet. It would be a painting you could read a million different ways, but they all ended up the same. Something wanted, something denied.

Ray began to speak then, listing more reasons why the car couldn't be sold. He was brutal. Mr. Saul continued to stare quietly out the window, but I knew he listened. Finally Ray said, "If that lock works the way J.O. tells me it does I can get you good money for it. Hey, I understand how you feel, my closet's full of stuff I invented. But you got lucky. Use it."

Mr. Saul folded his hands together and placed them over his mouth, thinking. The dark yellow bruise covering his eye looked like makeup, like you could just rub it off.

"It's filled me since the second I met you," the drugged guy said. "No one's seen the world till they've seen your hair, Cassie."

"Of course," Mr. Saul answered.

The absolute recognition in his voice made me feel left out, as if the world really was in Cassie's hair, and both Mr. Saul and this guy knew her. Cassie who? I wondered.

I stood up as Mr. Saul said, "All right, Young Man. Would you mind going outside for a moment while I talk with J.O.?"

"No problem." Ray looked at me. "If your friend with the baby shoe comes back from eating Jell-O, I don't want to be left with him very long."

I nodded.

When he was gone Mr. Saul touched my arm lightly with his bandaged hand. "Is Ray Beamus correct?"

"What do you mean?" Still standing I could see the top of his head was covered with age spots, each one a different shape like fingerprints.

"Don't play these games, it's bad manners. Is Ray Beamus correct about the car?"

"Yeah."

For an instant Mr. Saul's beaten-up face got so sad and stricken

I almost couldn't take it. "I'm sorry," I told him. "I'm really really sorry."

He smiled which was about the last thing I expected. "Young Lady."

"What?"

Mr. Saul rolled up the short sleeve of his hospital gown to where something was attached on the inside of his arm with heavy silver tape. "Here." He stripped it off, and I winced at the sound. "For you."

The flat piece of metal was about the size and shape of a credit card, shiny smooth in my hand. I recognized it immediately since Mr. Saul had once given me a long explanation on the design. "No. What are you doing?"

"Listen to me, J.O., a lock can only be a lock. The future is the prize."

Mr. Saul held my fingers around the warm metal pressing his car key deep into my palm. His hand on top of mine trembled. But not that much.

Chapter 20

Even though I loved it, the painting had to go. It was a very simple watercolor of sun on ocean that Rafi had bought for me at one of those street fairs which mostly have things like paper clip art. I remembered he stood on my bed to hang it. Now, the painting made the whole room seem dirty because I wanted him gone. Every trace. Andy kept me company while I took it down.

"So, J.O., I'll ride the bus, and maybe someone amazing will sit next to me. The Intergalatic Spider Queen. She could ride a bus to Oregon, right? What are you doing?"

"Getting rid of trash." As I jumped off the bed Mr. Saul's car key dug into my thigh. No, not Mr. Saul's, mine. Owning the woodpecker car felt dangerous, it wasn't really an evil car, but still we had never been friends.

I brought the Rafi painting into the kitchen.

"Have you ever been talking with a person," Andy said, "who keeps wiping their nose till you think they're giving you a message. So you wipe your nose too."

I threw the painting into a garbage bag along with a Dodgers coffee mug he'd bought me. "Yeah, I guess."

"Well, it's possible that a totally other person could see you wipe your nose right then, and take it the same way. So, now there's three people doing this. Nose wiping."

"Uh-huh."

Andy followed me back into the bedroom where I dug my jeans jacket from the closet. On its chest was a small silver pin shaped like a revolver with different colored rhinestones covering the grip. It went into the bag also, and I thought, here's our

whole relationship, painting, cup, gun. The only thing I'd given
Rafi was a gold pen that he'd lost almost immediately.

"This is the point, are you listening? I bet you're not listening.
At a party let's say, there could be a entire room full of people
all wiping their noses because they saw someone else do it and
thought that meant their own nose was dirty. You see? I'm telling
you the story of our lives."

"Whatever." Back down the hall again with Andy on one side,
the Hefty bag on the other. I walked out the front door and tried
to avoid looking at our lawn still littered with broken glass and
Gremlin pieces. Andy followed.

"You didn't get it." Standing in front of me he gently took
the garbage bag from my hand. "Can I make a statement? It
won't be festive."

"I don't care."

Andy stared into my eyes with an expression that reminded me
of the gun club, a certain charged blankness people got as they
aimed. When he spoke each word slammed through me even
stronger because there were none of his usual Hee-Hee rhythms,
none of the Andy on parade. Andy said, "I know in your heart
you believe Rafi left because of you. He would've stayed for someone else, you think, but J.O. just wasn't good enough. Wrong.
Rafi didn't want to leave, and his going had absolutely nothing
to do with you. The guy obviously cares a lot. But, J.O., whenever someone wipes *their* nose you always think that means *your*
nose is dirty. See? It's in your mind. I know because I'm the
same way."

I sat down on the mingy lawn and put my face in my hands.
"Maybe you're right, but why didn't he tell me before? I swear
to God, I'll never ever leave people I care about. Friend or boyfriend. If they need me I'll do what it takes. Always." Even in
my own ears I sounded too harsh as if love was some terrible job
you had to stay in forever. But that wasn't it.

The worst part about Rafi, the secret part, covered me like
swamp leeches you have to burn from your skin. To Rafi I was a
piece of L.A. life. The range, The Sun Maiden, J.O. Good memories. And yeah, he cared in a summer-camp romance sort of way,

but it never even came up, never for an instant, that I could go with him. I pictured us in Israel. Packed restaurant, we sat close together with smells I didn't recognize flying around the room. I watched his hands. I listened. "Here is how you hold the bread, J.O. This is where I'm from. Tomorrow we can walk in the old city. This is who I am."

Andy crouched down behind me. "Do you believe in total loyalty?" He began to rub my shoulders. "Being there when you're needed?"

"Yes." My voice was sobby so the word came out in two pieces.

"Well, I need you. I really really need you to come to Oregon." His fingers bored in hard on my muscles. "I don't want to go alone, Carey is more than I can do. If he was someone else's brother, okay, but Carey is the big guy in my life." Andy lit a clove cigarette that crackled sweet as it burned. "You're it, J.O."

Real smart, I told myself, you walked right into this one with your grand statements.

We sat there in silence for a minute and I looked at the broken windows and pieces of my car glinting in the close air around us. Finally I said, "There's no gun." Bad excuse. I knew where to get one, though I very much didn't want to go there.

"So? There's no car either. Gotta move, J.O., gotta make a plan, a game plan for the traveling man. What will you do? Take three umbrella steps."

"Umbrella steps," I repeated, and smiled having forgotten that game for years. "Mother, may I?"

"Yes you may," Andy said.

The square shape of Mr. Saul's present was outlined against my jeans pocket, and I thought of how he created that car, practically gave his life to make it happen. His best. What's my best, I wondered. What's the best I can do? The only strong act I'd committed in my whole life was moving to L.A., but I still wasn't even close to what I came here for. Now I had nothing.

Andy continued to rub my shoulders, and I thought, no, not nothing. I took a deep breath. "Okay, Mr. Saul gave me his car, but I'm not sure it'll make it to Oregon. We can try."

"Thank you." Andy wrapped both arms around my neck.

"What would I have done?" He squeezed tight whispering, "Thank you," again and again in my ear. It was kind of embarrassing.

"Will you help me get the plates off the Gremlin?" I asked. "We need the woodpecker car to look normal as possible."

For the rest of the afternoon I practiced driving. Not easy. The Car Of The Future's clutch felt like trying to push an iron spike into the sidewalk, so hard that whenever I switched gears I had to force my thigh down with my left hand. It took twenty minutes just to get out on the street.

After going around the block twice I decided to avoid looking at the huge dashboard whenever possible. There were dozens of buttons, gauges, and dials many of which were marked underneath with yellow Post-It stickers. MPR, RPM, GASOLINE STATUS, they said in Mr. Saul's shaky handwriting. The biggest gauge of all was dead center and had NUTRITION written in big letters. I didn't know what that meant, but was glad to see the needle stayed on five most of the time.

When I was able to go a block without stalling we drove to the bank. People pointed and stared, which embarrassed me but Andy loved it, yelling, "Nutrition, nutrition," out the diamond-shaped window.

At the bank I emptied my savings. Eight hundred dollars. Even though I knew with all my heart that it was finally the right moment to buy a Mag, the idea of facing Monk alone made me panic. No choice. He was the only way I could get a gun and not have to wait forever for it. I wished Marilyn were here.

"Seven and eight," the teller said handing over the bills. She had a blister on her finger. "Next."

We drove to Andy's house where he called The Sun Maiden to get his shifts covered. Family emergency, he told them. I had pretty much decided to quit there because everything—Danishes, dollar bills, the tiny office—reminded me of Rafi. Now wasn't a good time though since it could make Andy seem suspicious.

We hung around his apartment for a while playing with Fear who didn't even live in a cage anymore. Her tail had grown thicker than my forefinger. "Isn't this great?" Andy showed how she could climb right up his leg. "I want to breed her and name the babies after the seven deadly sins. I want a rat called Gluttony."

"Oh." I wondered how much of your personality was in a name. Rafi told me once that his last name, Oded, meant to be cheered up or lightened. Ha-Ha. "I should leave," I said. "I still have to buy a gun tonight if possible."

"What if you can't?" Andy ran a finger over his crooked teeth.

"Then I'll go to a store, but it'll take over ten days." I picked up my purse. The Mag money inside, all the money I owned, gave the bag a hot wired feeling. Wait till the gun's in here, I thought.

"We don't have that long." Andy stood in front of the door looking at me urgently. "You saw what happened to his cat, and on the phone he sounds worse and worse." He paused. "Get the gun. Okay? Come on, let's do a round of Liar's Poker, it'll make you feel stronger."

I shook my head not wanting to tell him that since Rafi, the numbers weren't alive for me anymore. Two-dimensional, they slept flat on the paper.

"Well, then kiss Fear. It's lucky." He held her out to me squirming in his hands.

"I'm not going to kiss a rat."

"But it's lucky, J.O., I'm serious." As he thrust her toward me again Andy's face suddenly got a pumped-up dazzle, like religion. The tent kind.

Wordless I bent down and kissed the top of Fear's head breathing in the animal smell. Her warm fur felt good against my lips.

Early evening. The sky had a pasty sort of color, and I wished it was any time but now since to me this always seemed like the weakest part of the day. Don't come across too needy, I told myself. Be sure of what you want, stay businesslike, and he won't get to you. Yeah, right. I pulled up in front of Monk's, noticing Rafi's MG was there with a FOR SALE sign in the window. "Look the other way." I said it out loud. "Save your strength, you have to become absolutely focused."

Monk's store had hardly any customers, but felt crowded anyhow from the eight mannequins in fur coats leaning against one wall. They were all kind of spooky and chewed looking, but the coats seemed nice. "Hi." I walked over to Liz who had her back turned, putting another fur on a naked mannequin. She didn't answer.

"Hello?"

"Uh-oh, Plutonium," Liz sang, and snapped her hips quickly back and forth. "Plutonium, Plutonium, uh-oh."

That's when I realized she was wearing a Walkman. "Excuse me." I tapped her shoulder, my finger touching bare skin around her lacy undershirt. It felt very cool. "Do you know where Monk is?"

"What?" She jumped whirling around to face me.

Liz had changed from a month ago, changed more than her clothes or beautiful hair which was two shades lighter now. She had practiced.

"Monk," I said again. "Is he here?"

Opening her mouth slightly Liz put a little-girl naughty expression on her face that to me seemed fake. Dress-up. "Monk's upstairs, who are you?"

"J.O."

She walked over to a small speaker thing on the counter. "Monk, J.O. is here to see you."

Even though I knew the kittenness was attached to her like an artificial limb, it still worked. Liz's tight leather miniskirt and skimpy top made me feel as if I were bundled up in men's tobogganing clothes.

"Surprise, surprise." Monk's voice came crackly weak from the intercom but it didn't matter, he was there in the room obliterating both of us. "Send her up."

"Go to the back exit," Liz said. "There's another big door just to your left, I'll buzz."

Her having forgotten me was an advantage, a small shot of power that would help with Monk, I thought. But Liz started buzzing as soon as I reached the exit, so I had to run outside and still barely made the other door in time. Advantage canceled.

Up a dark flight of stairs where a second door gloomed at me heavily metallic. I knocked.

"It's open," Monk said.

The room I walked into was long and almost triangle shaped with huge filthy windows on one side. It was probably a giant area meant for storage, I thought, before Monk put up these weird angled walls that kept me facing the windows to stay oriented. The whole place reeked. What? Silver polish.

Monk sat at a wood table in the fat part of the triangle. He wore only his Raiders cap and a pair of cutoffs. "Sit down."

I moved slowly toward him, Persian carpet sucking at my feet. No couch here, no easy chair.

In New York I knew a drug dealer who would hang sheets across his tiny apartment so customers never saw where he slept or ate. Like here, a sort of private office. But at the dealer's you could easily make out shadows through his thin sheets, the TV light, his girlfriend sitting there bored. Not Monk's triangle. Solid and clueless it gave away nothing he didn't want to show.

He had both feet up on the chair next to him, so I had to take the only other one which put my back to the windows. In front of me the bare slanted wall somehow erased my sense of direction. Where's The Valley? I thought almost frantic. Where's the ocean?

I leaned my elbows on the heavy wood table wishing he'd turn on a light. We were at the in-between time where you can still see okay, but it's just past comfortable.

Silence. Monk was cleaning thick polish from a silver bowl, his fingers wiping a path of metal bright and bare down its curves. I watched them slip around inside, pointy fingers. "What do you need?" he asked.

"A gun."

Monk smiled. Then he tipped the shiny bowl up toward me, about the size of cupped hands. "Nice, huh?"

My mushy distorted face was reflected in the bottom, so I looked quickly away saying, ".357. Smith & Wesson would be great, but I'll take anything you have." Weak, weak, weak, I thought. Fix it. "Well, not anything, you know what I mean." Even worse.

Monk still held the bowl turned outward from his bare chest. Keep your eyes glued to the wall, I ordered myself. Where's Fairfax from here? I wasn't sure.

"Who are you going to shoot?" Casual question, so casual that if I said I was planning to open fire in a shopping mall it probably wouldn't change whether or not he'd sell me the gun.

"Nobody. I hope."

Monk walked to a door in the thin part of the triangle room. When he opened it light shined through. His shorts were low around bony hips and I could see his entire back which had amazingly healthy, beautiful skin like the pinkish inside of a seashell. There was just enough time to change chairs before he came back.

"Do you miss Rafi?" He held a gun loose at his side.

I stared at it. "Yeah."

"I thought so, you've got that smell. Listen." He took a step toward me, my face level with his stomach. "Rafi's a good guy, smart, but he's like Liz. They don't have real heat."

I glanced out the window. There was the huge needle on the Capitol Records building in the distance. Thunk, the gun hit the table a little too hard. I picked it up, checking first as always to find out if there were bullets. There were.

Rafi's Mag and all the rented ones had been too big for my hands, but not this. A .357 Luger. Holding Monk's gun seemed as if I met a long-lost twin, the way it settled into my fingers with a tailored fit. Its dark wood grip had the words SURE SHOT stamped along the top and was custom-made to feel smaller. A gift, I thought. One of a kind. I stroked the cool barrel and imagined it saying, "What took you so long, J.O.? I waited years."

"How much?"

"A thousand. Shit." Monk sat down and reached deep into his mouth.

How can that be? Does he expect me to bargain? I wondered. A thousand dollars was impossible, but I couldn't leave without my gun.

Monk pulled out one of his back teeth laying it gently on the table. A very white, large tooth, but it must've been fake since he didn't act at all upset. I remembered Mr. Saul losing his teeth, though this seemed much worse. Monk was able to remove parts of himself incredibly easily because he was without a certain kind of stickiness. That made him somehow more powerful than anyone else I'd ever met.

"Do me a favor," he said. "Chew this awhile."

I put the piece of Trident he handed me into my mouth, no hesitation. I really wanted that gun. "About the Mag," I said.

"*Mag*, you sound like Rafi."

I lightly stroked the swirls of its wooden grip thinking crazily for a second of different possible ways to get this gun from the room. "Six hundred is what I have."

Monk took the gun back. "Nope." He cocked the hammer and aimed playfully at the streaked windows. Just having him touch it made my insides clench up with nauseous excitement. "How's that gum doing?"

"Fine."

"Give it here." When the greenish gum was in his open hand Monk broke off a little piece. "I meant to get to the dentist two days ago," he told me molding it around the end of his tooth. "But you know, business first." He stuck the tooth back into his mouth. "I hate gum."

Monk smiled as if that were a joke, but I didn't understand, and his secret grin yanked at me like hair caught in a zipper. I moved my eyes away, down his neck. It was wide and smooth and had islands of shadow all along his collarbone where the late light couldn't reach. I moved my eyes again. No place to look, his hand on the table covered my gun. His gun. Make a plan, I thought. Decide. Act.

In Coney Island there used to be a ride called The Pit which was a big round hole that kept you glued to the walls as it spun so even your cheeks would get sucked backward. I walked to the door, only a gesture. Monk understood centrifugal force. I opened my mouth to offer eight hundred dollars, every penny I owned.

"You can have it for seven. And something else."

Please, I thought, no, please don't.

"Come here."

I went to the table. Monk was standing.

"Explain why I scare you."

"That's it?"

"Yeah."

As I counted out the cash I tried not to let him see the other hundred, but he did anyway.

"Don't worry, J.O., I wouldn't take it all."

Yes you would in a minute, I thought. "Give me my gun, please."

"Explain first." He was very close now with the smell of silver polish and his brown eyes hard on me.

I said, "Because your heat is too much. It's bad." The words felt fuzzy vague in my mouth, and I couldn't remember even if they were true.

Monk's hand snaked around to the back of my neck. "Wrong." He moved his finger there in tiny slow circles traveling butter smooth down my spine. "Heat is what it is, never good or bad."

"Oh," I said, but that was all. His circles were vibrating on the soles of my feet. When Monk pulled me closer the brim of his Raiders cap brushed my head and even his cap had its own slippery life that penetrated every nerve in my body.

"You're scared of the power I could give you. What you'd become."

He's right, I thought. Just close your eyes, lean forward a fraction of an inch, and your whole life will change. So easy.

But then I looked at his chest, no hair, the skin was just like his back, perfect and unbroken. Monk naked would be seamless as a wet stone. I pictured all the thick scars on Rafi's body, a lot of them numb, yeah, but each one had a story, a real consequence. Stuck to him for life. "Give me my gun," I said.

Monk laughed. "If you ever decide to grow up, come see me." He tossed over the Mag.

In my hand now and feeling so good because it truly belonged there bought and paid for. You'll never leave my side, I told it mentally.

"So," Monk said. "J.O. has her very own 'Mag' now, be careful. Guns are not always what they seem."

"This isn't a Mag." I backed toward the door without taking my eyes off him.

"No? What is it?"

"Maggie," I said and locked my fingers around the grip like a secret handshake. Then, not even caring how stupid it looked I opened the door, turned around quickly and began to run.

Outside I drove a few blocks before pulling over to relax. The curled cat weight of Maggie in my lap made me feel stronger. I missed Rafi. If he were here I'd tell what happened as he squinted at me. "Wait," he'd say. "You didn't go with Monk only because he has no body scars? Many people aren't having scars." But he'd know exactly what I meant.

Rafi's gone to Israel, I reminded myself angrily, it's over, don't think about him anymore. Starting up the car again I decided to head toward the gun club. I'd shoot Maggie tonight till my hands couldn't move.

Chapter 21

We left early the next morning with a ton of stuff heaped around us since The Car Of The Future had almost no storage room. Andy sat cross-legged. The space for his feet had been taken up by Fear's cage and a package he wouldn't show me. It was about the size of one of those coffee table books and wrapped in raggedy orange silk. The silk looked really old.

Driving went better than I expected once we hit the freeway, fewer people honked and stared, and also I didn't need the rip-your-guts-out clutch.

Neither of us talked much during the first few hours. Andy sat very still, forehead resting on the window, while I played my Israeli tape from Rafi again and again. The music wasn't too far from rock except its rhythms sounded curvier. Sloped. Rewinding the clearest sections, I tried to bend my tongue around this guy's lyrics as if singing them right would give some secret password. I thought about Rafi. I smoked a lot.

A hundred and fifty miles before San Francisco Andy abruptly turned to me yelling, "I can't take another second of that fucking music, J.O." It was the first thing he'd said in over four hours. "Get rid of it now."

"Fine." I switched off the portable tape player.

Andy rubbed shaky hands over his eyes. "Sorry, sorry."

Silence except for the hum. Whenever The Car Of The Future got up over fifty it made these deep, loud, humming noises like a choir finding its key.

"What are you thinking about?" Andy asked. "Are you imagining Carey? I bet he's skin and bony bones, tell me what you're thinking?"

I unrolled the window so hot wind hit my face. "I was thinking that by now, the last meal I ate when Rafi and I were still together has completely passed through my body. There's no trace of it."

"Oh." Andy held out his arm so Fear could walk onto my shoulder. He had insisted we bring the rat along promising she'd only go to the bathroom in her cage. I was glad actually. All around me were different kinds of warmth: Maggie at my finger-tips, Fear, the cup of hot coffee between my knees.

Outside summer fields stretched endless with checkerboard cows red and black lying in the sun. You're never going to get over him if you don't try, I told myself. Pour energy into other things. "Want to play Ghost?"

"T." Andy picked up our road map and unfolded it huge across the seats.

"S," I said, "and no fair looking at words."

"I wasn't going to be a ghost cheater, I mean it's not—"

Mr. Saul's voice interrupted him, loud and sudden from inside the dash. "You're running out of gasoline," he said. "Ten miles."

We both jumped about a foot. Completely on its own my hand reached for Maggie, finger safe against the trigger before the voice had even stopped. "Yes," her presence told me. "I'm here, I'm yours."

Andy stared as I put the gun back down. "Next exit let's pull over."

We passed a big sign advertising the Zaitztown Broccoli Festival. "That's great," I said. "A whole festival about broccoli." Because I'd only been in L.A. I'd never thought of California as a place where things are grown. Big mistake—we had passed crop after crop. Equipment auctions.

I took the next exit where, as usual, everyone pointed and yelled questions which made me wonder what to do when I got back to L.A. Even though they were into the car, not me, I could still feel their attention, and had started to obsessively straighten clothes or check my face in the mirror whenever we drove by a lot of people. If I didn't learn how to ignore it soon I'd become a fidgeting maniac.

The gas station was pretty large with a mechanic's garage and six vending machines. I walked over to the little room where you paid. A short older woman was right in front of me and she held the door open while saying hello to the two gas station guys inside.

"Hello, Mrs. Voya," they both said at the same time. A burly freckled guy and a shy-looking Mexican.

I squeezed by her and held out the twenty Andy had given me to the burly guy. "Ummm, unleaded." I hoped that was right. Knowing Mr. Saul, the car probably had some secret code where it wouldn't run unless, along with gas, you pumped in a cup of chicken fat from his wife's old receipe.

"Pay afterward," the burly guy said handing back the money. His body reminded me of Rafi's, a friendly kind of burl. So what. Everyone reminds me of Rafi, I thought, sick of myself.

Just as I started out the door past Mrs. Voya again her eyes behind thick thick glasses widened a little. "My, what a lovely car. Is it yours?"

"Yes. Thank you." She was the first person who had actually complimented it, but when I looked at her more carefully I saw why. Mrs. Voya's blue dress was splotched all down the front, though she didn't seem to notice. Her soft round features weren't quite here. Blunted.

I went out toward the car and Mrs. Voya walked with me, leaning close on my arm as if we were friends. "You don't mind, do you? My artificial hip pops in and out like a pop bead necklace," she explained.

"No problem."

At my car she pulled a half-empty shampoo bottle out of her purse, and balanced it carefully on the curved roof. "Look." Instead of shampoo the bottle had grayish water with a few fish swimming around. They were those tiny fish you see in the shallow part of ponds, and I wondered how she got them to go inside a shampoo bottle.

"That's great, Mrs. Voya."

"Yes, I know." She smiled, kind of hazy.

With the nozzle in my hand I walked twice around the car checking for a gas cap. Andy got out to help while Mrs. Voya bent slowly down to read the chrome letters on one side. Mr. Saul had glued them where other cars have their brand names.

"This is a Jonas?"

"I guess so."

"Well, it's lovely. I covet this car." Behind the glasses her eyes seemed to be staring out from a long way away.

I pointed at the hood. "Don't you think it's a little scary with such a sharp front?" I didn't mention bullet holes.

Mrs. Voya shook her head. "No, no, no. The man who made this car is a natural man, and there's nothing in nature that isn't righteous."

"I still see no gas cap," Andy said just as the burly guy came outside. His hair was red, primary red, like the finger paints I remembered from grade school.

"What is that?" he asked.

"A Jonas." I took Mrs. Voya's bottle off the roof and handed it to her hoping the car might look more normal without fish on top. "We can't find where the gas goes." Red-haired men always jarred me a little, I thought, they were unexpected somehow.

"Hey, Hector," the guy yelled. "Come on out and see what they're doing in L.A. You're from L.A., right?"

For the next twenty minutes all of us covered every inch of the car searching for a gas cap. Nothing. I remembered Mr. Saul telling me over and over about The Car Of The Future's pure lines. "A good automobile is smooth, J.O., when you see it your eye must not be disturbed by any interruption," he would say.

"Umm, wait." Hector spoke so quietly we all had to lean toward him. "If it's put up on jacks maybe we can find the tank and fuel line." His shy voice sort of apologized for the idea as if he were positive it was completely stupid.

"That's great," I said. "Thank you so much."

Easing the car onto the hydraulic jack I was very careful not to let anyone see our stuff inside. The gun and rat probably wouldn't have made any difference though since they didn't even blink at Mrs. Voya's fish bottle.

When the car had been lifted the burly guy poked underneath for a long time. "I found it," he yelled finally. "The gas should go in close to this door."

It turned out Mr. Saul had made the driver's side-view mirror into a gas cap which twisted right off, and even had another Post-It sticker inside. NO LEAD HERE, it told us in capital letters.

As I opened the door to leave, Mrs. Voya grabbed my upper arm with a touch that sank in slippery like lotion. "What I possess is this," she said. "Every single moment asks a burning question that you have to answer. Now, here is my answer for you to keep." She wrapped my hand around the shampoo bottle then raised it high in hers so light came through. It made murky sun spots across my chest.

We continued all day. After a while the road narrowed and then we got to redwoods which were impossibly old and gigantic. The most beautiful trees I'd ever seen. The redwoods had a hero feeling around them as if ancient battles had been fought at their trunks where people died to preserve the good. No, that was backward. These trees made people remember what to fight for, they were the actual heroes.

When the sun began setting we pulled over at a small-town diner. Andy went to get food while I stood near the car with Maggie in my purse, the extra weight making its strap dig down hard against my shoulder. It felt good, a constant pressure that stopped just short of pain. I closed my eyes. The long road day was catching up with me, we had left at 7:00 A.M., and though Andy did a couple of hours, I had driven most of it. Carey wasn't so far anymore. I wondered if he knew we were coming.

"Hey, J.O." Andy walked toward me with bags of food. "I saw a park before. Let's go there to eat."

Above us clouds glowed pinkish, a very personal color somehow. Andy took a handful of fries and passed them one by one to Fear through the car window. "You look tired."

"Yeah." From far away church bells started ringing, and the sound made me miss people, Rafi, Samantha, and especially my dad. A different missing. Usually I just felt the cold cave in myself where "father" was supposed to be, but now with these bells I missed the actual person. The California guy who cooked for my mother and acted silly. The long-haired teenager who had given me a name from outer space, not to be an asshole really, but because it meant something to him. "Okay," I said.

Trees blocked my view of the street as soon as we were inside the quiet park. We walked down a grassy hill to some picnic tables, about ten of them grouped naturally like boulders.

Andy said, "I'm going to tell the Carey story, all right? No one knows but me, and this is important. His life choice."

Under my feet the damp ground felt springy, sort of pushing me forward with every step. Easy to walk. "All right."

"Well, here's what happened, though if it wasn't fire it would've been something else. I know that."

My blood kind of perked up the way it did when a secret was about to be told, but then I looked at Andy's expression. He was making funny noises with his cheeks sucked into a fish face, and my excitement went away. This would be a hard secret.

Andy unpacked our food dramatically onto a picnic table, as if neither of us had ever eaten this stuff before. Barbecued chicken, fries, bread, and two Cokes. It felt nice, miniwild, to be here with no one else around.

"In school they had a weekend camping trip for the junior high kids, but I didn't want to go. Carey went, he was fourteen. I was twelve and glad to be away from Hawaii for a whole weekend."

"Hawaii?" I took a bite of chicken which tasted incredibly good. The sky had turned purple blue, it would be completely dark in a half hour.

"Carey was into Hawaiian gods then, volcano gods. He put together a big altar in our room, and used to make up chants we both had to say every night. Older brother, you know." Andy took a long sip from his Coke.

I remembered his mom hanging out with Buddy's bug religion which made me think maybe that kind of belief is passed down like eye color.

"Well, on the trip a terrible thing happened." With one finger he traced over some graffiti carved into the picnic table. *Mike Reece is a jackhammer fuck,* it said.

I wondered if "jackhammer fuck" was meant as a compliment or an insult, but then decided it must've been an insult because the words were gouged so deep and angry into the wood.

"Someone burned," Andy whispered. "In an old sleeping bag. Supposedly a spark from the campfire landed on it, not flame-retardant, whoosh. Danny Rosemen, he was in my sixth-grade class."

Jackhammer fuck, I thought, knowing instantly what had happened. I touched my purse.

"Listen." Andy's voice scared a bird hopping on the next table. "Carey told only one person. Me." Carefully peeling crust off the bread, he wrapped it around his fourth finger like a wedding ring. I sipped Coke which pinched my teeth.

"Carey said everyone was asleep, and he just wanted to see what would burn. He said he didn't mean for it to be Danny, and when the sleeping bag went up Danny screamed and screamed. The material melted to his skin. Carey made me swear. I kept it too, kept it a sleeping secret even with his bad dreams, my one hand over his mouth, the other shaking him. 'Nobody's burning, Carey, it's only a dream.' "

"Why didn't you tell anyone?"

Andy curled both legs up on the bench, forehead resting on his knees. "You don't know my father, J.O." He began to cough then, for a long time, but didn't move or try to stop it. Dry, jerky sounds.

I watched two girls approach the picnic table behind him staying as far away from us as possible. One of them was Oriental with beautiful dark hair hanging almost to her thighs, commitment hair, she must've been growing it all her life. The other one was short with a red baseball cap. In her hands was a shopping bag.

"After that Carey said say-on-ar-a to the Hawaiian gods. He drew pictures instead and then painted."

"Painted what?" I leaned forward to be closer to him, and also so the edge of the picnic table would dig into my ribs. Long day, I needed to focus.

"Well, back then Carey never touched fire, and never painted

215

it," Andy said, busy shredding pieces of chicken. He hadn't seen the girls. "Instead he did these black shadow people, faceless and bodiless, while all the stuff around them looked natural. Sort of. When he started with oil paint mom let him have the garage. She had kicked dad out by then so we were breathing. You know, I'm pretty sure she'd figured out about Danny, but then decided, 'Oh no, not my boy, not this boy.' "

Behind him the Oriental girl was brushing her hair in long intimate strokes. She wrapped it twice around her neck and laid the part leftover like a blindfold across her eyes. The cap girl watched quietly. I wondered how old they were, ten? Eleven? Younger than Danny Rosemen.

"So what about him, Danny I mean?" Neutral voice, don't make it worse. "Did he die?" I tried to imagine waking up on fire.

"No." Andy continued talking with a half-drowsy expression the way people act in a trance, letting words come through them. "For two years Carey painted the same kind of thing, showed it to me, and then used turpentine. Wipe, wipe, good-bye. Silhouettes playing basketball, one of them dribbling with the ball done real. A boy and dog on a winter road, the boy surgically removed so there's only a detailed black cutout. 'Do you see it?' he'd ask me, yelling sometimes. 'Can you see what I mean?' The paintings were tough and scary, and they got better. Haunted. 'Keep this one, it's your best.' I used to grab his sweaty arm, Carey painted with no shirt. 'Tell that to the Pope,' he'd laugh, Hee-Hee, and mush the disappeared people together with a turpentine rag."

I imagined the paintings and felt bad for getting excited. Poor Danny Rosemen. But still, I wanted to see them, wanted to see Carey in high school before his paintings left the world. "But what happened to Danny?" My voice came out lawyer loud.

"Danny's okay. That's a different story."

"Well, what happened?" The scars must be awful, I thought remembering Monk's skin so smooth as if it hadn't been lived in at all.

"Shut up about Daniel, I'm telling you about Carey so just shut up." He punched himself in the leg. "Sorry, sorry."

Silence.

"On his seventeenth birthday Carey changed styles. All of a sudden. Senior year of high school he painted us, me, Mom, and sometimes Dad."

I tried to bring the family paintings clear in my mind not sure why it felt so important to get them exactly right. "Did he still do shadows?"

"No, these looked pretty realistic though a lot were violent. The best ones . . ." Andy tucked his thin straight hair behind his ears which he once told me gave him an extra second to think. His hair was beginning to curl up like a U in front. "Okay, there's a storm and lightning strikes nearby and for an instant you see your room lit that way. Dresser, now. Bed, now. It looks the same, but not the same. With lightning the gloom room you live in becomes strange—pop, crack, then it's over. Well, Carey's best paintings were in that moment of flash though I have no idea how he got it, the light or the color. But there they were, and meanwhile you couldn't talk with him."

Andy started throwing pieces of chicken on the ground, for birds probably. I fought the urge to pick them up. Giving bird meat to birds seemed wrong, the kind of thing that might make them crazy.

Over his shoulder I watched the Oriental girl take a plant mister from their bag, squirt the air a couple of times, and hand it to her friend. Then she got out a pair of scissors. I flinched a little though I'd known it, really, as soon as they sat down.

"There was a name for those paintings," Andy told me. "Carey used to point at them and say, 'The Whole, The Whole, The Whole.' But I'm still not sure if that meant whole or hole." He gestured with his hands. "Anyway, he mentioned it a lot and didn't destroy them till he left for college. All except one, destroying, I mean. Carey let me choose one painting for keeps before leaving. I told you he had a breakdown in college, and then moved to Oregon where dad owns a house."

Extending his arms across the tabletop, Andy grabbed the edge of it on my side. Our faces were close. I had never really looked at his eyes which weren't straight brown like I'd thought. Their color reminded me of grade school art class. A noncolor. You mix together all the paints hoping for an incredible effect, but no matter how it's done, you always end up with the same thing— a sort of greenish violet brown. Andy's eyes. I had completely forgotten about that color till now.

"The Whole, The Whole," he said softly. "Carey only does angels these days, or that's what he tells me. What I see is swirly daggers, I don't see angels in any of that stuff, though I've tried. I really have, J.O." He seemed so sad then as if being able to see the angels would make Carey better instead of the other way around.

I was glad Andy's back was to the girls. The red-cap one cut her friend's hair clean around the neck, and I watched it fall away in one glossy swoop that separated into a mess hitting the ground. Why did she do this, I wondered, but knew whatever the reason it would change her life. Her choice. Getting on hands and knees, the Oriental girl slowly gathered all her hair together and put it in their bag. Carey chose, I thought, and so did this girl, but not me. Not yet. I took Andy's wrist and held it because every single act felt full of huge consequences. The slightest move, the slightest breath.

Andy covered both his eyes with my palm. "Be nice to Carey," he said. "Okay? Please?"

We sat that way for a long time, so Andy never saw the girls leave. The Oriental one walked stiff and silent with her fingers wrapped around her white white neck.

I took my hand off Andy's eyes. My muscles ached and anything I focused on seemed to have a vague shine to it. "Let's find a hotel, we can't be tired for tomorrow."

"Not yet, no." He looked perfectly alert, though I didn't understand how that could be. "I want to make it to Oregon tonight, cross the state line, baby. Can't wait for my date at the fate line."

Andy's face is like no one else's, I thought. Because of its skinniness you didn't expect bushy eyebrows and the large definite mouth, but there they were giving him a face that would stay for generations.

"We've been driving thirteen hours," I said, a little whiny.

"Okay." Andy came around the table to my bench and straddled it facing me. "I'll buy an Itty Bitty Book Light so you can read. Want to read? Or music. You can even listen to the Israeli stuff, turn it up, I don't care." His voice was cracking like a kid's as he swallowed fast between every sentence. "I need to get closer to feel Carey because I don't know what I'm doing. All I feel now is static, and that's not a plan. Sssssssss. No plan there. I need to be in his state." Even in the almost dark I could tell his cheeks were red.

Why did that girl cut off her hair, I thought. How come I can't call my dad? I can't go another inch toward Carey till I get some reasons. He has reasons to put his thumb on, and yeah, they're crazy, but they belong to him.

"What is it?" Andy asked.

"There's too many stories and all of them are missing the same piece, but I don't know what it is." I looked up the hill to where streetlights showed pearly through the trees. "I don't even know what I mean." In my mind Danny Rosemen's sleeping bag went up in flames as he desperately tried to squirm out of it. "What happened to Danny? I mean afterward."

Andy stood. "If I tell you." He walked toward the street so I followed, heavy air lying on my skin like a giant scab.

"Tell me." We moved quickly up the hill because it was getting cold, and I thought how that didn't seem fair in August.

"After Danny got out of the hospital, even with grafts his scars were really bad. For a long time it looked lizardy with these little squares of skin that hadn't settled in yet."

The sidewalk was completely empty. I wished Andy would change his mind about staying here tonight, this town felt safe with its church bells and decent stores that closed before dark.

"Danny was in my class, but I never talked to him. What was I supposed to say? He was like me then. In trouble."

"What do you mean?" Reaching into my bag past Maggie I got out a cigarette. When I lit the match, just lit it without thinking, we both stared at the tiny flame as if I'd done something wrong. Stupid. Fire is like guns, I thought, not good or bad.

"Seventh grade, Danny sat in back of the class and picked at his fingers. Picked and stripped and bit. After a while they got disgusting, the nails all bleedy so people avoided him like he was contagious instead of just horrible looking."

I imagined being him in the seventh grade and the girls and the locker room, and the guidance counselors. I thought I might've killed myself.

"So there he was," Andy continued. We were almost back to the car. "Carey's off like a maniac painting blacked-out people, but here's the real thing eating himself up right there in front of me. Every day. So, I thought, 'What does Danny need?' " Andy smiled then, a tipped-toward-the-past smile big on his face. "Sunflower seeds. I got him two bags, the kind in the shell where you have to work with your fingers to get the seeds out. I taped them to his locker when no one else was around."

Andy opened the passenger door and waited for me to get in.

"It worked, Danny quietly ate seeds the rest of the year, and his hands got better, but that wasn't enough. It turned into a thing. What does Danny need? I'd ask myself. A new binder. Gym socks. He used all the stuff I bought him. Every day I'd see that lizard skin and think, Carey's making art, right? Fuck. What does Danny need? A pocketknife."

I glanced inside the dark car with all our stuff on the seats. We had traveled too much, too far. Didn't even really eat.

"Then the summer before high school he went on a bike trip and came back as Daniel." Talking louder now, Andy ignored the fact that I refused to get in the car.

"Daniel had longish hair. His lizard skin was gone so he looked sort of smooth like the inside of something. Get what I mean?"

I shook my head. Andy pulled out his lower lip, wet and pink. "There, that's how Daniel looked."

"Great." I tried not to sound too sarcastic.

"No, no, it wasn't that bad, or maybe he had changed so it didn't seem as bad. Psyched, you know? Anyway, I bought him these great goggles when he joined the swim team, best goggles around."

Andy reached behind me to scoop Fear off the front seat. The quick way he did it, covering his own embarrassed pride from the goggles was different from the usual Andy.

"I went to all the swim meets." Fear sniffed the air from Andy's shoulder, and I could hear her make little teeth noises. "Daniel was good, not a media event, not even the best on the team, but good. And popular. When he swam all the kids would yell, 'Rosemen, Rosemen.' I bought him a waterproof watch." Andy took a step toward me, his voice more intense than I'd ever heard. "In his bathing suit the scars were really obvious, but Daniel didn't care. Like he was showing them off. We'd go, 'Rosemen, Rosemen,' and every time, right before getting in the pool he'd scan around for his girlfriend. His *girlfriend*, J.O., and she was no loser."

I stared at Andy's face pumped full of the light from his own story, and for a second he reminded me of Samantha. Why? I wondered, they're nothing alike.

"Daniel went to Stanford," he told me as if that were a secret Christmas place where normal people could never go. Movies, I thought. Andy's expression when he talked about Daniel made me see the story and want to ask, "Then what? What happened next?"

Instead I said, "Let's move, we've still got at least three more hours to Oregon." I got in the car.

Andy walked around to the driver's side. "You've probably noticed that I have bad teeth and social skills."

I decided not to say a word.

"But for six years there was one thing I did perfectly every time. I mean every single time. I always got Daniel the right present."

We left the parking lot, Andy going too fast through the nighttime town. "He used all the stuff, and I watched him become . . . I don't know. Something."

I looked out the window. The Car Of The Future's headlights were placed on either side of its pointy front, so they illuminated not only the road, but all the dark trees to our left and right.

Andy suddenly leaned over and began searching through the area near my feet which were propped on Fear's cage. "Where is it?"

"What?" I stared at his hand, way too tense. I wanted a cigarette, but already was smoking one.

He gave me the flat, silk-wrapped package I had noticed before. "This. Here is what I picked when Carey said I could have a painting. It's one of his best, not because it's me though. *Me, me,* who's that great? It's the best because you don't have to be Madame Curie to figure it out."

After five minutes of looking for a light switch, I opened the car door just a tiny bit so the interior light would go on automatically.

"Door is open," Mr. Saul's voice repeated again and again from inside the dash somewhere. Fear sat up blinking. She had fallen asleep in a ball against Andy's leg.

"Door is open, door is open," Mr. Saul practically yelled at us.

I unwrapped the raggedy silk and looked at his portrait. The only thing I really knew about art was to stay away from paintings with clowns in them, but even I could tell Carey was good. Very good. In the painting Andy seemed about sixteen, and Carey had gotten exactly the hunch of his shoulders, the weird way he held his head tipped backward and a little to one side as if trying to hide a birthmark. But more than that.

Andy was cradling something against his neck, something which gave his face an amazing expression. A lover-loose expression so full of undisguised sweetness that I felt embarrassed seeing it with him here next to me. "What are you holding?" I asked. The thing glowed turquoise with a tail of bright blue flame that crossed Andy's chest.

"Faith." He laughed an acid sound. "She was Carey's, not mine."

I peered closer at the colors, recognizing a rat shape now, the whiskers that brushed his ear. "What happened to her?"

Andy pressed hard on the gas, his mouth gone tight. "I don't want to know."

We ended up in a motel right over the Oregon border. Walking with Andy to our room my body felt like it was still in a moving car. The ground vibrated. This place was to keep tabs on us, I thought, seeing our door was very close to the office.

When we had rung the bell at almost midnight a guy, dried leathery, came out in his bathrobe and checked us over. He had a narrow shrewd face, but different than L.A. where the shrewd people I'd seen so far acted as if they weren't. Movie shrewd. They hid it behind menus and talked about leaving "this town, this system." But the hotel guy came from Oregon. No deals, he wore his shrewdness right out there like a bulletproof vest.

After I filled out the registration form he eyed it suspiciously for a long time. On the part for Make and Model I had put A Jonas and The Car Of The Future.

"You have a cat?"

"Yes." That's what I'd written on the pet line of the form because a rat seemed too extreme.

"Extra ten-dollar deposit," he said, face completely expressionless.

Andy put down the money no problem, and I could've kissed him since one "Hee-Hee" is all it might've taken for this guy not to give us a room. "I'll get stuff from the car," Andy said and walked out to where we were parked just at the door. The guy handed me a key.

"It's a double, right? He's my brother."

"Yup." The guy kept his eyes focused behind me probably watching Andy. "Pretty small cage he's got for a cat."

Without thinking I glanced up and slightly to my right as if rearview mirrors were all over the world. "It's a pretty small cat." My nasally voice came out too soft for him to even hear.

Our room was very cold, and everything in it, furniture, carpet, bedspreads, had a reddish brown color that reminded me of brains. Andy laid Mrs. Voya's fish bottle on our night table which was bolted to the floor—I wondered if the shrewd guy actually believed someone might steal it. I stood between the beds, feeling pinched hard by this room. Even the stupid flower drawing on the wall looked like a mouth covered by blood. This is too scary, I thought. Where's Rafi? I don't want to see fire, I want to go home.

Wearing a long flannel shirt I took my jeans off under the covers. Maggie waited an arm's reach away in my purse so I got her out, imagining the good mythy power that could explode with one pull of my finger. Loading, unloading. The gun moved through my hands in perfect logic, the logic of really great machinery. I closed my eyes. I did it by touch, click, spin, click.

"Please be careful about that thing."

I glanced over at Andy lying in the other bed. Shirtless, he had an old paperback called *Fifteen Tests to Find Out What YOU Do Well* on his chest. Strange to be in a motel room with this guy, I thought. "What's that supposed to mean?"

"Don't lose the 'J,' J.O. J no, no J." Andy pulled the blankets up around his neck. I stared at his pointy profile.

"You worry about your brother, I'll worry about Maggie, all right?"

No reaction.

"This gun is a hundred percent dependable." He doesn't understand, I thought, so fuck him and fuck Rafi also because Rafi should be here.

"Forget it," Andy said.

"Yeah, okay." We turned off the lamp. Usually I fell asleep bit by bit, but not tonight. It was like operating rooms when they tell you to count backward, so you say "ninety-nine, ninety-eight," and then just disappear. All at once.

I woke up before dawn. No light really, but the edge was off the darkness. Had there been a noise? I reached quickly to the floor for Maggie.

"J.O.?" Andy's blanket shape was curled up small in bed.

"Yeah."

"I can't do this, I really can't so let's just keep going like today. Festive. I have over four hundred dollars left, you think that car would make it to Canada? Let's try, I've never been anywhere."

His voice sounded the way paper cuts feel, a voice that made me go over and sit on the edge of his bed. "We have to, he's your brother."

"So what. Carey's been almost gone ever since I remember. J.O." He shoved his head under the pillow clamping it there with both hands. "Oh shit."

Andy didn't move as I rubbed his cold back. "It's all right," I told him just for the words. "Okay, okay." Next to the bed there were crinkly noises as Fear shredded newspaper in her too-small cage. "Yes, okay," I said again. Andy grabbed my hand and pulled it to his neck under the pillow.

I said, "Wait," and walked over to our cheap radio tape player sitting on the desk. Classical. Mozart piano music eased bone clean from the speaker and I held my breath astonished to have recognized it.

Back in bed now we faced each other, my hand on his side. Andy's body felt cut off like a totally irrelevant thing you'd pick up in a store, but then put back down again. An automatic pasta dispenser. "How're you doing?" I asked.

"Cold. It's snowing so don't let the dog out he'll freeze, woof-woof, even White Fang. Huskies."

I wrapped myself around him trying to warm, I rubbed the tops of his arms. Andy's eyes were closed. I laid my palms on his chest as he whispered, "I'm so fuckin' thin."

"It's only me," I whispered back.

Without opening his eyes Andy slid both hands up my shirt in one frantic move and gasped when he got there. Shaky breath. "I guess I should tell you now, so I'll just say it. Now. I hope you don't mind." He jerked his hands out.

What? I thought instantly wishing they had never been there. I listed ideas harshly as possible, because that way when he said it I could just nod. He'd say he liked Rafi fine, but being with leftovers disgusted him. No, more. He was gay, though would sleep with women if their tits were big enough, and in a shirt mine looked bigger, but after touching them he realized it was out of the question. Anyway, I smelled bad.

"What?" I glanced over at Maggie winking in the bluish light.

Andy spoke very softly. "I've never done this before."

My muscles went liquid with relief as I tried not to laugh. To believe the world pays that much attention to you, I thought, is a messed-up kind of vanity. "Well, it's really fun," I said. "I think you're going to like it." Kissing his face, his neck.

Andy's shoulder bones were sharp, I could feel their points

close against my lips and for a moment I missed Rafi terribly. His smell and fuzzy bulk. Andy moaned then, almost painful so I looked at his face. It seemed bigger because of the frightened happiness that overflowed from his round eyes and mouth into my own mouth with a flavor smoked sweet.

"Oh," I said something catching in my throat. Andy took off his underwear.

We lay quietly for a long time afterward with sweat drying on our bodies. I didn't want to go to sleep because tomorrow we'd have to decide how to act. Andy rested his leg across my stomach.

"How far is Carey?" I asked to bring up the other thing.

"Close." He paused. "About four hours, maybe five. There's a hospital in Salem, and I figure that's where we'll take him."

I traced swirly shapes on his back, angel shapes. Being scared *with* someone is much easier, I thought. Outside was almost full daylight, and even though we'd both be exhausted I wanted sex with Andy again. The remembering and forgetting. I moved my hand to the inside of his thigh.

"Today." Andy looked at the bright window.

"Yes."

When he kissed me our teeth clicked together like those solid drinking glasses given away with certain items. Large Coke, Super Unleaded, tickets to both shows.

We left the motel that morning on three hours' sleep barely making it before checkout time. Not in sync. Andy held open the door for me at a diner, but I didn't notice at first and bent down to tie my shoe while people kept walking in.

The place was crowded. We sat at the counter for a long time with no waitress, so I stared at all the customers familiar to each other. Above us a handmade sign said, "Johnson baby is a boy! 8lbs, 4oz, Richard James."

Andy and I were quiet. I wondered whether to bring up what happened last night or just pretend it didn't exist.

"Hi." Our waitress was here finally, about eighteen with bleached shaggy hair. "My name is Lola, what can I get you?"

Andy opened his mouth, and I knew like a shot he was going to sing "La-la-la-la Lola" at her. I kicked him hard under the counter.

"Short stack please. And coffee." When she went away he said, "I can't help myself, J.O., it's a fever."

"No it's not, don't make like there's no choice," I told him.

Lola put coffee in front of us. She had a wad of gum in her mouth and blew a bubble that looked way too big and pink for a small white person.

"Did anyone ever sing that Kinks song to you?" Andy asked. "About Lola?"

She sucked the bubble back. "Are you joking? Stupid people have sung that to me since I was like five. I hate it."

"Oh," Andy said.

I took his hand. We ate slowly and by itself the food wouldn't have tasted that great, but since we were traveling it kind of did. Butter seeped everywhere, spotting the paper place mats that had games for kids on them, connect the dots. We overtipped Lola.

After breakfast I called Mr. Saul in the hospital from a pay phone outside. Since no one was at my house to verify the charge I had to use a lot of quarters which left me with eighty-four dollars. Total. Andy said, don't worry, he had three hundred ninety-six dollars, and anyway later he'd play some Liar's Poker with me to help. I reminded him for the millionth time that I didn't play anymore.

"The numbers stopped reaching me," I said. "You'd win." I knew I couldn't explain how Liar's Poker used to feel as if all the serial numbers had a personality that spoke out loud. Doesn't matter, I thought. It was just a trick anyway, like crossing one eye, and since the only person who ever beat me was Rafi, maybe if I could just forget about him the numbers might come back.

On the phone Mr. Saul told me Samantha called him yesterday. "She is going to Belgium because of 'failed love' she says. Everything in storage. If this is failed love then we should all be television actrees." The word was pronounced so it rhymed with fleas.

I glanced at the back of my hand. Samantha's bite was gone,

but I could still picture the circle of teeth marks exactly. I hoped she was all right.

"So, the lease is yours now if you wish to continue living here. Where are you Young Lady?"

I fed six more quarters into the phone, shielding its receiver with my hand to block out noise. Across the parking lot Andy was showing The Car Of The Future to a couple and their little boy, he bounced the hood up and down explaining something. "Oregon," I said. "We can talk more when I get back, but yeah, I'd like to keep living there."

"I'm glad." His voice was long-distance faint, so I stared at the car, a giant yellow bird's head with diamond-shaped eyes. Andy lifted the little boy up to the window.

"How's Ray?" I asked.

"Ray is a wonderful Young Man, we will be working together successfully." Then in a fake careless voice he asked, "How is your automobile?"

The family was walking away and Andy stood by the driver's door waving at the little boy who kept turning around to wave back. "Good," I said. "You made a really good car."

The ocean took both of us completely by surprise since last night had been too dark to see it. All my life I'd heard how beautiful the Oregon coast was, but always listened the way you listen to facts at school: Oregon is beautiful, its capital is Salem, its industry is logging. Yeah, yeah, yeah. But beautiful was too tame a word for the beach spread out on our left with huge rocks jutting from the water like prehistoric animals. Even in bright daylight I felt the haunted magic, the fulfillment of all promises.

I turned left onto the shoulder. We got out of the car and headed down a hill toward the aggressive beach, not like L.A., the giant rocks stood so rough and wild I didn't want to touch them. Windy.

By the ocean Andy put his arm around me. "We're the only ones here."

"Yeah." I was glad to have Maggie in my purse because when

you worked a thing long enough it became more and more power-ful. What did witches call their cats?

"Carey lives up an unmarked dirt road," Andy said. "I hope we find his house before it gets too late."

Familiars, I thought. Maggie is my familiar. "Have you ever fired a gun?" I asked. "We can't shoot here in the day, but do you want to hold it? Maggie's weight has got a good feel."

"No thanks." Andy had an expression like sour lemon. "Mag-gie," he sang at me, "I wish I'd neeever seen your face."

"Very funny."

He said something I missed in the wind.

"What?"

"I know you still want Rafi, I know this isn't us."

"Well, I think about him." I shrugged, hands in front pockets. "Obviously."

"Yeah, but you want him also, don't you?" Without touching me at all Andy leaned close to my ear his voice fierce as the beach around us. "Don't you?"

I closed my eyes. The sun made little nervous patterns behind my lids so I opened them again and began to walk fast, heels sinking in the wet sand.

"It's okay." Andy half jogged along next to me. "Not really okay, but I'll say that. Anyway, I've been thinking I can't just dump Carey in a Salem hospital and believe I'm finished." He deepened his voice making fun. " 'Carey's with trained profession-als now, it's all right.' That's not fair. It won't help to just throw him out there alone to the professionals like last time. I'm think-ing I'll stay up in Salem to be nearby."

The Oregon sand was the color of unbleached cotton. I won-dered how many years it took for all the shells and pieces of rock to be crunched up into beach. "If you would do that," I told him, "then I wish you were my brother."

The wind picked Andy's hair off his forehead, curved high, it was about the same color as this sand. When he hugged me the heavy purse fell off my shoulder unexpected. I almost lost my balance.

"Carey has a gun, I think," Andy whispered. His hands felt sweaty right through my shirt.

I swallowed, breathed, and swallowed again. "Why didn't you tell me that before?"

Laying his face on my shoulder Andy said, " 'Cause maybe there's no gun, you know? Carey might've lied. Look, let's just not say anything for a while, we talk, talk, talk, you and me. Okay? Okay?"

I stared out at the choppy ocean, one hand stroking his sun-warmed hair, the other tightfisted. I dug my nails into my palm. Rafi, I thought. You were supposed to be here, so tell me what to do. Please. Please, I can't anymore, I don't know. I pictured his face the way he used to squint in frustration reaching for a certain word. What was it, I wondered. What was it now?

Chapter 22

We had a hard time finding Carey's place. The house was owned by his and Andy's father who had taken them there as kids, so Andy was depending on old memory to see it. We tried almost every unmarked dirt road branching into the thick woods on either side of us. It got late.

At around seven my nose suddenly started to bleed from nowhere, choking my throat. Andy drove while I hung my head backward over the seat listening to Lou Reed singing muffled on our tape player. Carey used to love Lou Reed so Andy had bought an album for the drive up to Salem. He hoped it would be calming. I didn't quite *get* Lou Reed, never had, and to me the sax on this record sounded like that motorboat noise people will make when you hit them repeatedly on the back. I wished Carey passionately loved another band, even a lousy band, since then I'd be able to find a reference place for him in my mind.

Sniffing, I tried to picture clogged things, pipes filled with sand or water in a saltshaker.

"Maybe he's closer to the next town," Andy said. "What's it called?"

I sort of groped around the seat for our map not wanting to bring my head forward. We didn't have any Kleenex. "Does it matter?" I swallowed iron taste in my mouth.

"No, I guess not."

We drove some more in silence, so I listened to Lou Reed and the car's loud hum. With my head back all I could see was the tops of trees.

"Here," Andy said softly. "This is it, I remember."

Before heading up Carey's skinny road we sat quiet for about a half hour waiting for my nose to stop bleeding. Andy said the air smelled like soap. It was getting dark. Time to move. I bent down and kissed Fear the way I had before going to Monk. Andy kissed her also.

We bumped up the dirt road past houses lit way back in the trees, then after a while no houses. I took Maggie from my purse more by touch than sight, my fingers popping open the cylinder, click, click, too loud. I counted the bullets inside, Winchester hollow point. Andy paused at a fork in the road.

Darker, much darker away from asphalt, and in my head I heard Mrs. Macauly, eighth-grade English, " 'These woods are lovely, dark, and deep.' " What was that? I had been bored. What was that?

Andy turned right then right again up a long steep driveway. Branches scraped against the side of the car, its engine working hard so loud I decided Carey must know he had people coming. I cocked Maggie's hammer, careful, careful, back in my purse again. Hand on the barrel, finger alongside the trigger guard.

Carey's house was tiny, with an old Toyota in front. There were other things in the yard also, dark furniture shapes and small shapes I didn't recognize. Out of the car now, I breathed deeply to get good strong air before going inside, but what I got was scorched material and gas. We walked through the yard past his furniture, two couches, chairs and a rug, all of them pretty burned. How did he do it, I wondered. Most of this stuff is made flame-retardant. Then I almost tripped over a bunch of empty gas cans, the smaller shapes. He must've really poured it on.

Dark house, but not the dark of sleeping people. Something blocked the windows, though when we got close I saw a very faint glow. Standing at his door I felt silly for a second. What were we supposed to say, "Hi, I've come to take you to an institution?" Yeah, right. Then I noticed the gas smell was a little stronger here and didn't feel silly anymore.

Andy knocked. No answer, so he knocked again, hard.

"Maybe he's gone out," I whispered.

"I doubt it." Andy pulled a key from his pocket. "There's no dance at the gym tonight."

I heard the lock turn, heard Maggie rustle against papers in my bag as I gripped her tighter, heard The Car Of The Future's hum still in my head like a catchy song.

My whole body was trembling as we went inside, a caffeine tremble, but much more. The gas smell soaked right into my eyes and mouth, and it seemed as if every other smell I'd ever felt was just preparation for this. I peered around the room, bigger than it looked from outside.

Carey sat at the only piece of furniture, a table pushed against the wall. His face was mostly in darkness because instead of lamps there were a whole bunch of flashlights hanging individually by strings from different spots on the ceiling. So where's the gas? I wondered. Under the house? Splashed on the floor? Then I noticed the wall to my right, the one with windows, had at least twenty of those two-gallon metal gas cans stacked all the way up. The edges of the window frames barely showed on either side.

Carey stood and hit at a few of the dangling flashlights, which made their beams swing fast across the room, across his bald head, Andy, me. He was stare-on-the-street thin, with a pair of red shorts and T-shirt I remembered Andy bought for him a month ago. "Hey it's Smegma, late in the day." Flashlights swung, bright dark, bright dark.

Andy tucked his hair behind his ears. Then he took two steps straight into the middle of the room saying, "My name's Andy."

In the dizzy light I could see that every single bit of space on his walls that wasn't covered by gas cans had been painted. Swirly shapes. Some were huge, floor to ceiling, and some just a few inches, but it was impossible to make out any color. I would've felt the fire even if no one told me, though these shapes were also like grain in wood or thin summer clouds.

You have to stay together, I reminded myself staring at his table. Carey had painted groups of fish on it with long, forked tongues. Everything you do counts, everything you think, everything you say. Concentrate.

233

Carey turned toward me so I got a real look at his face for the first time. His completely shaved head was painted with flames, their centers almost black near the temples, but branching more and more orange up his scalp. Carey was so skinny his head seemed too big for his body which made the flames on it stronger. Vivid. All around us the flashlights still rocked, bright dark, bright dark. "Who are you?"

"J.O." He's beautiful, I thought. Andy never said that.

Carey had the same generous lips and large, far-apart eyes as his mom, but Tina's features had seemed smudgy to me, blurred. Not Carey though. His face crackled like power lines. "J.O.'s not The Whole. What is it?"

Tell the truth, I thought, he's crazy smart. "J.O. Warren is the name I use, I'm weird about my other one."

Carey quickly licked the top of his thumb. "Hey, *Andy*," he said. "She's at twelve o'clock, did you know? Is she twelve o'clock all the time?"

Andy shook his head, and I wondered what he was thinking. "Mostly she's at seven or eight. P.M."

"Are you here to be television spot remover? Out damned spot." He licked his thumb again.

"Not television," Andy said. "But, yeah, we're all twelve o'clock."

They're using some language, I thought, based on the scattered language Andy usually spoke, but this was more extreme. I couldn't follow them.

Carey walked over and leaned against his stack of gas cans. Andy still stood in the middle of the room, speaking toward the fish table though his words went straight to Carey. "The Whole is meant to be caught in glimpses, not head-on. Remember what he told us, 'Here's the message, here's the secret, whoops I forgot it.' See? You'll be removed if I don't remove you."

"Hee-Hee." Carey's laugh reminded me of Andy's fake one except much worse because it had no ground underneath. A screechy noise that must've hurt the throat. He took a handful of wooden matches from his pocket and rained them in a careful circle around his bare feet.

I gripped Maggie tighter.

"That's why they're called fireflies," Carey said. "What are you staring at, four o' clock?"

I had been looking at the pure lines of his face, a face that seemed oversized even without eyebrows and hardly any flesh. "I thought I was twelve o' clock." Fighting with him now? Real smart.

"Don't bullshit the firefly, four is twelve. Haven't you read? Don't bullshit the painter." He paused. "I asked you about reading." He pulled down one of the gas cans and unscrewed its cap.

Don't pick up those matches, I mentally begged him. Stay where you are. I eased a tiny sliver of Maggie's barrel from my purse. "I haven't read too much lately, though the paper gets delivered."

"Carey." Andy moved toward him with both hands held out. "Give me that gas can and come with us. We've got The Car Of The Future, Lou Reed. What else? Ummm, maps, a rat, and your Faith painting from a long time ago. That's better than gas."

Without leaving his circle of matches, or letting go of the gas can, Carey crouched on the floor and reached his free arm behind the rest of the stack. For what? What did he have? "No push," he said. "Go home. I'm so near The Whole, so near it's my respirator and breathing feels like something new. You can't just come here with your four o' clock friend in crusader pajamas. You can't. That's why they're called fireflies." Carey's voice was echoey in the bare room.

"Yes I can," Andy said taking another step closer. "Trust me. Please? This will be for the good." As he bent toward Carey, Andy spread his hands further apart ready to take the gas can or just hug him. The crackliness of Carey's face eased then, a tiny bit, and though I couldn't put my finger on the exact change I knew he was coming around. The flashlights had stopped moving, so it was a little easier to focus. Okay, I thought, now it's only the drive to Salem. Couple of hours. Maybe he'll sleep, he looks like he hasn't for days.

But I was wrong. The moment Andy touched his shoulder Carey yelled, *"Go home."* He lunged upward with the can, splashing gas all over Andy's face and shirt. Knifefight fast. Too fast because by the time I had Maggie out of my purse Carey had splashed me also, barely missing my eyes.

Get it off, get it off, I thought, desperately fighting the urge to rip into my clothes. Andy half crawled backward across the floor, and I was screaming at him, screaming the only words I could think. "Your eyes, Andy, oh, fuck, did he hit your eyes?"

Carey had a gun in his hand, an automatic. They always seemed crueler.

Gas slicked clumps of hair to the side of my face, the smell pumping through my stomach, but not Maggie. She hadn't been touched and was as dry as a warm brick house. "Put the gun down." Shaking in my hand, what did they call people? Soft targets.

"Track and field," Carey told me, "can stop the aging process. She shot him through the heart." He pointed his gun at a gas can in the middle of the stack. Only inches away. "How many do I have inside? One or three? Don't bullshit the magazine."

Breathing gas I couldn't wrap around my thoughts, what do I do? Where's Andy? I wasn't sure, but didn't want to slide my eyes over. Too much sliding.

"One or three?" he asked again. "Bullets. Say it or I'll muzzle flash this gas can and The Whole will be our bouncer. Sometimes it looks like the white patterns on the edge of paper napkins."

That's not fair, I thought, how does anyone know how many bullets he has? All I wanted was to get on my knees and beg him not to kill me and Andy. What do you need, Carey? I'll give you anything. Talk. Distract him the way they do in movies by asking about his reasons. "Why, umm, shit, why an automatic? Do you like them?" I stuttered, my voice all over the place because he had me, had me cold.

Carey whacked his gun against the cans making a sound not hollow. "How many, Cinderella Complex? I read the book and you have a very debilitating disease. One or three?" He repeated the words slowly. "One or three?"

Just guess, I thought, you have a fifty-fifty chance. There were no words though, my mouth filled with gas, I can't, I don't know.

"The Whole flashes so I see what to do," Carey said. "Not some clockpiece. You and *Andy* are both the kind who won't enter, but won't exit neither, so I am E and E for all of us. How many bullets?"

Andy came out from somewhere behind me. "Listen, just listen up a sec."

I looked at Carey's hand thinking shoot it, now, right into the jigsaw bones of his wrist. But I was covered with gas, and didn't know what would happen if I fired.

As if he guessed my idea, Carey moved his whole gun arm behind the cans. "How many? I'll count to ten waiting for your answer at midnight. If you don't answer we'll go up. The Whole. One, two, you have fraction time."

"Wait, let me think, please just—"

But Carey was pushing over my words, "Three, four, five."

"Come on, you don't want to get messed up. Right?" Quiet, J.O., careful, who knows what he wants. And what do you want?

Carey said, "Six."

Moving my feet slightly apart I straightened my shoulders with Maggie beginning to play me so perfect, both hands secure around her. Firing position. Just do it, I thought, fast.

"Seven, eight."

The Indian sacrifices came to my head. Who wants what? Hearts ripped out and held to the sun. Painted shapes twitched in the corner of my eyes, and then something happened. It felt like a blink but more, as if my whole body went dark for a split second and then regular again. The numbers were back much stronger than before. No number. His gun was empty, I knew it the way my tongue knew the inside of my mouth. And it used to be that the numbers appeared like actual people to me, but this was completely different, this was a deep-space feeling far from human terms. My ears hurt. "Go ahead, shoot," I told him easing Maggie down by my side.

Andy turned and looked at me sort of drunkenly with his eyes half closed. "J.O.?" Every hair on his head was soaked by gas.

"You have no bullets," I said.

When Carey began to sob it was so noiseless I only understood from the jerking of his shoulders. By the time Andy got to him he was curled tight against the gas cans. Andy pulled him close.

One moment I was watching them start to rock slowly back and forth, I was up on my feet, okay, and the next moment my muscles just lost it. I lay on the floor. A flashlight was dangling directly above my face, and I closed my eyes feeling it shine like a tiny lucky sun.

Chapter 23

This was the fifth morning I had come to the lake. It was nice with an old pier and trees that blocked every house from sight. I dangled bare feet in the water, my sneakers lying next to me sort of skinned, like vegetable peels.

We were leaving today since Carey's dead Toyota was finally ready. I couldn't have just stuck Andy out here alone while they worked on it. The mechanic had given a wild little laugh as we had rolled it in, filthy, chained behind The Car Of The Future. "I'm not real," he said. "You don't see me." New tires, drums, shoes, fan belt, starter, battery, shocks and radiator hose. Andy's mom and Buddy had Fed-Exed him some cash to help pay for it.

I lay back drowsy against the warm wood. It felt impossible to relax at Carey's house because although we had cleaned and cleaned the gas smell never quite went away. I pictured streams of it hidden inside his walls. And the walls themselves. Filled with Carey's paintings their colors seemed to be squeezing me close no matter where I turned. We slept curled on the floor, and ate in restaurants since the house had no electricity. We took a lot of showers.

Sitting up again I watched an empty wine bottle float around on the water. The cork was still in it. Besides the pier that was the only sign of people, people, I wondered what to do when I got home with about a hundred dollars left to my name. Maggie would have to be sold first thing.

But I didn't want to sell her. The strange part about Maggie was I'd spent days pouring energy into that gun, relied on it as my savior, my only guarantee, yet we'd gotten Carey to the hospital without any shots fired. Maggie wasn't even really a factor that night except in my head.

I stood up, grabbed my sneakers, and began walking back toward the house. Andy would be waiting. He was very nervous about going to live in Salem where he didn't know anyone.

I put my shoes on before starting down the dirt road. The morning air was cooler in the woods with animals rustling the bushes so near I could've seen them if my eyes were trained. Rafi had always talked about us going camping, he loved the woods. I tried to imagine him right now, on a crowded bus maybe, or with friends, but Israel wasn't too clear in my head. I missed him.

When I got to Carey's house Andy was sitting at the table drinking a mug of instant made with hot tap water. "Good walk?"

"Yeah." I picked up Fear who was running around the bare floor. Her paws on my arm looked like little pink hands, I had never noticed how monkeyish they were. "So, when are you leaving?"

"As soon as I finish my disgusting cup of coffee. Why am I drinking this? Forget it, I don't want to anymore. Will you give me a lift to Carey's car?"

"Sure."

Andy rinsed the mug, picked up Fear's cage, and we left. Just like that. It felt strange to walk out of a place not even holding suitcases, but we had been ready with everything in the car for days.

"What will you do when you get back?" Andy asked.

I turned around to see the house one more time. Almost cozy now, its windows were clean and the front yard didn't have scorched furniture in it anymore. "I'll be doing stuff." I paused, but no stuff came in my head, not a single thing, which felt okay, but also too empty. "Stuff," I repeated.

As we got in the car Andy said, "I'll come to L.A. soon to pick up the rest of my clothes. I'll call you." He put Fear in her cage, a birdcage really, and made a big deal out of tying shut the metal door. Hair across his cheek. "Shit, J.O."

When we got to the garage I parked in front while Andy went

inside to pay. They had hosed down Carey's grayish car for us. Even though it looked perfectly normal, I was still superstitious about going near it, the way Hindus won't wear each other's shoes.

"Well," Andy said back at my car. "I guess this is it."

"Guess so." I watched him unload the painting and his small suitcase onto the ground outside. "Want some help?"

"No thanks." He kissed my cheek and left, Fear's cage in one hand, painting and suitcase balanced in the other. Andy had gained weight, I noticed his jeans were a little tighter as he walked toward the car.

"Hey," I opened my door not knowing what or why. "I'll see you in L.A. soon, right?" There should be a diagram, I thought, on how to say good-bye to people.

"Yeah, soon." At Carey's car he put down the suitcase and cage. Then he suddenly walked back to me holding only the painting. "Here, J.O. But don't ever ever sell it, even if he turns into some festive artist and you have to live on popcorn. Okay?"

"Okay." I unwrapped the stained orange silk, and there was Andy at sixteen, the rat on his shoulder. "This is the best present I've ever gotten."

When we hugged both of us just stayed there, breathing, for a really long time.

I sat in my car awhile after he left. The thought of driving hours and hours by myself without even Andy's tape player was depressing. Then I got an idea. Since Carey's night I hadn't handled Maggie much, so it might be nice to fire her at that lake especially if I were selling the gun soon. Also, I hated it when your very last memory of a place was saying good-bye to someone.

I drove past Carey's and further along the dirt road toward the lake. It was a hot morning, though the trees blocked a lot of sun with moody-shaped patterns on the ground.

The lake was still deserted, even in August. I parked at the woods' edge and walked a short rocky stretch to the pier. Maggie was heavy in my hand. At its widest the water seemed about two miles across, safe for shooting since my bullets wouldn't hit the other side.

As I went out on the pier its old wood creaked under my feet. The sound felt louder in the hot sun. Scanning the water I tried to find a target, but there were only trees and lake. Not very exciting. Then I noticed something that glinted brighter than the water's surface, something so far away I almost couldn't see it. Glass? There was a wine bottle here before, I thought, it must've floated all the way out.

I told myself not to be disappointed if I missed because the bottle was just a shine, impossibly remote, but that type of protecting never works. I knew I'd be disappointed anyway. I balanced the bright spot between Maggie's sights, then compensated for distance. The bullet would fall. Hands ready on the grip, I sank myself into the empty moment right before shooting. Concentrate, sqeeze, Bam!

The wine bottle exploded upward like a whole bunch of jumping, silver fish. Unbelievable. I watched sun on glass as all the pieces fell through the air glittering over and over before they hit the water again.

"Straight from The Book," I said laughing, astonished by the cleanness, the accuracy.

There was nothing else to shoot at, so I lay on my stomach and felt the pier which was hot all down the front of my body. I rested the tip of Maggie's barrel on the water curious if she would fire that way.

Prime numbers can only be divided by one and themselves, one, three, five, seven, eleven. I put my whole hand with Maggie underwater which changed her weight. Bouncier, less solid. Moving my arm back and forth I watched white skin against gun against water. Thirteen, seventeen. My fingers opened one at a time. I felt the warm water and Maggie slide through them, and then after a second only the water. Glimpse of her shape. Nineteen, twenty-three. I got up. Twenty-nine. I walked away.

Chapter 24

Driving home was not as bad as I thought. The car's loud hum and the blankness of the road ahead worked like hypnotism, so I said, okay, and sort of tranced along through miles and miles.

At about ten o' clock I stopped at a motel, my muscles tired, but also filled with a windwhipped energy. Road energy, I thought, the energy of distance covered. The motel had movies and VCRs for rent, even a movie Samantha had done called *TAILSPIN! The Crash of Flight 92.* She played one of the passengers, and though *TAILSPIN!* was filmed before I met her, Samantha had told me stories.

Everything in my room looked one way but really was another. The bed shined mean and blue, though when I sat down it softened all around me. Rusty water came from new faucets, and my tiny nightstand drawers held things that seemed much too big for them. A phone book, a woman's shoe. The first pizza place I called said, "Yes, ma'am, we deliver," which made me wonder if I sounded older or if everyone was "ma'am" outside big cities. I hoped I sounded older.

When the pizza arrived I got in bed and began watching *Tailspin!*, an incredibly stupid movie. It felt strange to see Samantha, yet not Samantha—her character was a dippy teenage punk rocker whose punk rocker boyfriend had two broken legs. Flight 92 crashed on a snowy river. I watched a long scene where survivors frantically swam through freezing water screaming the names of their loved ones. Samantha had told me it was really just a four-foot-deep tank with machines nearby blowing out instant mashed potato flakes. She said the scene had taken days to shoot and after a while all the flakes turned to wet, rotten potatoes which stuck in people's hair and clothes. It had smelled awful.

I stared as she flailed around yelling, "Marco, Marco," her head just above water. I pictured Samantha in a Belgian bar, maybe right now. She is whispering things to a good-looking Belgian man across the table, her eyes widened slightly. "I called him The Messiah." The Belgian man is fascinated.

On screen Samantha found Marco dead against a tree branch because he couldn't swim with broken legs. "No, no," she sobbed and clutched his head. Mashed potato flakes were flying all over as Samantha cried, "I love you, I love you." Enough, I thought, and reached out one foot to turn off the TV.

L.A. seemed dirtier than the week before. Pulling up in front of my house I saw the trashed Gremlin still on the driveway. A lot of glass. First thing tomorrow, I thought, this stuff has to go. Mr. Saul was getting out of the hospital in two days, and I didn't want to bring him home to a war zone.

I unloaded the car and went inside heaping my suitcase and the portrait of Andy on the kitchen floor. Samantha had cleaned out everything, even her refrigerator magnets, so it looked as if no one lived here. I could see four rings on the linoleum where table legs had been. "Shit." I walked into the living room also empty except for a clock and one small lamp that belonged to me. I sat on the dusty bare floor.

Out the window I could see Mr. Saul's yard which looked like a vacant lot, knee-high weeds, his shed hanging open. The shed could be a good sign though. Since his voice-activated lock was gone that probably meant Ray Beamus had taken it for the company. I got up and walked around the empty living room. Restless. I wanted food, but wasn't hungry, wanted to drive, but also didn't.

Taking Carey's painting with me I went outside again. Brilliant move. Here I was finally home after two days' straight driving, and what do I do? Go for another drive. On my way past the mangled Gremlin I looked though the place where a door was supposed to be, and noticed my stereo from Rafi was still in there. Amazing. I thought about having it removed before the car was junked. No, better this way. Digging around my purse for keys, I felt something smooth and squarish on the bottom. The Israeli tape.

It was labeled "Rafi's Picks" and I imagined exactly the way he would have bent close to write those words, pen held tight, almost at its tip. I went over to the Gremlin. Without turning power on I stuck the tape in the machine, kerchunk-click, that clean stereo noise. I left its container propped against the emergency brake. Rafi's Picks.

How do they get music onto that shiny brown ribbon? I thought. The kind of thing guys knew. I walked back to The Car Of The Future glad no one had ever explained the process to me. It seemed wonderfully strange. Almost magic.

In the car I headed west on Santa Monica with sun setting in my eyes. Crescent Heights, Sweetzer. What did Rafi say?

My father used to always warn me.

Moving through Beverly Hills now where the big green traffic islands were crowded with people jogging which I thought was very brave and optimistic in all the smog.

It only takes a second to destroy the thing that took a lifetime to build.

Office buildings blocked the sun as I made a left on Century Park East. I remembered him that night at Monk's place.

I don't believe that anymore.

Right turn onto the Little Santa Monica corridor, Fairburne, Westholme. What should I say? How should I be?

Most acts are long time coming.

Okay, here's the plan, I told myself. Go past his house, and if there's a car in the driveway call him from the nearest pay phone, or if there's no car call and leave a message.

But it didn't work that way. As I eased by the house a man was outside, barefoot, trying to stuff a large Hefty bag into a metal trash can. My father.

I parked across the street without looking away from him. The front door was open, and as I watched a big black and white puppy came running outside tripping over its own legs. "You,

you again," my father said, clear on the quiet street. The puppy jumped for the garbage bag, but missed it.

I got out and walked slowly toward him, completely different than what I'd imagined. In my head he had been nineteen like his photograph, or fifty-five. This person was neither. He had thick, dark hair almost to his shoulders and wore jeans with a plain T-shirt. Just a guy, I thought. He's just a thirty-nine-year-old guy.

As I got to the sidewalk the puppy ran at me lightly biting my arm, my sneakers. "Hi dog, who are you?"

My dad smiled. "His name's Larry."

"Larry," I repeated meeting his eye for the first time. It was the weirdest feeling I ever had because I'd recognize this man, this stranger out of a million. The way he stood back on his heels. A certain tight set to his mouth that I knew wasn't meant to be unfriendly since my own face held the same thing. Tell him who you are, I thought, now, now. But instead I glanced over his shoulder to the front yard. "Flowers," I said. The bush I'd taken a month ago was replaced by another yellow one. "Do you garden a lot?" My voice was trembling.

He looked at me sort of puzzled and sympathetic so that I wished I could read minds. "Uh, yeah."

"That's good." Practically in tears, my head yelling: say it, say it.

He put the metal lid on top of the can, and tried to calm Larry who was still leaping around.

"I'm J.O." It's finished, I thought. This is my real father who won't change into a different person depending on how I feel.

"J.O." His expression had a kind of vacantness and that's when it hit, of course. My mother called me J.O., but he would only know the other name. I turned to see The Car Of The Future which was dirty but extremely yellow across the street. I thought of Danny Rosemen in high school, the way he swam. "I'm your daughter Jambalaya Orleans, and that's J.O. because jambalaya isn't a name. It's stew. Why did you name me after stew, even your dog got a normal name."

"Jambalaya? Jambalaya? I can't believe it." His hands kind of clumped against his legs and I thought that if he were holding anything it might've dropped. "Oh my God, look at you." His voice had gone nasal. A genetic trait. "Will you come in?" Lifting his hand, letting it fall again. "No one's home yet, I was going to start dinner. Chicken. Larry, get down. Will you come in?"

"Yeah, okay."

Neither of us moved. I kept swallowing.

"New Orleans," my dad said. "That's where you were conceived, and I don't know, it was so great down there. I wasn't even twenty yet, and we practically lived on jambalaya and rice. It was our favorite thing. I used to call you Jammy while she was pregnant, though I guess naming a kid Jambalaya isn't such a great idea."

"No," I said. "It's not." Then I felt bad because he had been nineteen, a year younger than I was now. And guys mature slower.

We began walking up the brick pathway toward his house. "J.O.'s been all right," I told him. "I like it."

"I like it too."

He went up three stairs and through his open door. I followed, pausing for a second. "Come on in," he said.

And I walked through the door of my father's house.